THE VAMPIRE
OF CURITIBA

THE VAMPIRE OF CURITIBA
and Other Stories

by DALTON TREVISAN

Translated from the Portuguese
by Gregory Rabassa

ALFRED A. KNOPF   *New York*   1972

THIS IS A BORZOI BOOK
PUBLISHED BY ALFRED A. KNOPF, INC.

Originally published in Portuguese as *Novelas Nada
Exemplares, Cemitério de Elefantes, O Vampiro de
Curitiba,* and *A Guerra Conjugal* in 2nd editions, revised,
by Editôra Civilização Brasileira, S.A., Rio de Janeiro.

Library of Congress Cataloging in Publication Data

Trevisan, Dalton.
    The vampire of Curitiba and other stories.

    I. Title.
PZ4.T8148vam   [PQ9697.T76]   869'.3   72.2246
ISBN 0-394-46645-4

Contents

Contents

Contents

Introduction

CURITIBA is one of those several Brazilian cities that are as big as Baltimore and yet almost completely unknown to the rest of the world, often thought to be some jungle outpost visited by errant anthropologists. It is the capital of the state of Paraná, which lies to the south of São Paulo and has replaced the latter as the principal coffee-producing area of Brazil. The identification of Dalton Trevisan with his native city is therefore quite apt, as too few outsiders have ever heard of Brazil's important writers either. Trevisan is Curitiba for that reason (and many, many more, as the cliché goes), an oddly placed writer in an unknown city, off the beaten path that most often leads to nowhere. He is somewhat of a myth in Brazil itself, not because of anything he has done, but because of what he has not done. With fame, instead of going off to Rio de Janeiro to be lionized (and subsequently become the prey of critical safaris), he chose to stay home writing and tending to his family's ceramics factory. This has made him a mysterious person, and those who never went beyond the title of *The Vampire of Curitiba* were doubly in awe.

Like the case of his great and earlier contemporary João Guimarães Rosa, Trevisan's entry into literature was unplanned, even unforeseen. It was accidental, literally. Born (June 14, 1925) and reared in Curitiba, he studied law, a profession he abandoned shortly, and worked in his family's factory. On March 11, 1945, a kiln exploded, fracturing his skull and sending him to the hospital for a month. That was when he saw "for the first time death within [his] eyes and more than by the physical suffering [he] was pained by the

Introduction

revelation that [he] was mortal." This episode and its consequences are similar in many ways to the accident that put Jorge Luis Borges in the hospital and led him to write the story of Pierre Menard, his first piece of fiction.

While still under the pall of that new fear of death, Trevisan wrote a novella in the same year which he dismisses as "youthful nonsense." In 1946 he started a literary magazine called *Joaquim* (a common name in the country) "in honor of all the Joaquims of Brazil." In it appeared contributions from leading Brazilian writers and artists and translations of Joyce, Proust, Kafka, Sartre, Gide, and others, as well as his own stories. During this time he also worked as a police reporter and film critic for Curitiba newspapers. The magazine ceased publication in 1948 and Trevisan took a trip to Europe in 1950. He was married in 1953. For lack of an interested publisher he brought out some of his stories himself in cheap newsprint editions.

Finally, in 1959, the prestigious house of José Olympio published the collection *Novels Not At All Exemplary* and he was quickly famous. Several other collections came after: *The Elephants' Graveyard* (1964); *Death on the Square* (1964); *The Vampire of Curitiba* (1965), which includes *The Magic Ring*; *The Disasters of Love* (1968); and *The Conjugal War* (1969). Some critics have celebrated him as the best in his field, but others, still tied to the rigid norms of the nineteenth century or to inchoate bombast, have been unable or unwilling to fathom the human complexities of his tight little tales, incapable perhaps of following anything not part of the "new obvious," where the depths can only be plumbed with the heavy millstone of the extended metaphor.

Although the tone and perspective of his stories have remained pretty much the same, as Trevisan continues to write, his style seems to have become ever briefer and more concise. The "black" elements of his earlier tales are often present but left unsaid in his later ones. When asked the inevitable question as to when he was going to write "his novel," he replied, perhaps facetiously as befits the question, that his path would lead him to the sonnet and ultimately to haiku. There is really a good deal of sense in what he says, for he does seem to be approaching this more concise brevity, often cloaking with flesh the stereotypes or archetypes we read about in newspapers or hear about in gossip. As he endows his characters with biological life they do indeed become less exemplary, as might be the case if one made a pet of a laboratory mouse, which until then had been a number, a certain phase in a complex experiment. In many ways Trevisan follows Machado de Assis, whom he considers the classic writer of the Portuguese language and who, in the name of *reality*, abhorred *realism*, that good, gray convention we have been taught to think of as real.

There is much talk in Latin America today, too much talk, really, about something called "magic realism." Quite often it merely comes down to a new description of the technique of all great writers, which is nothing more than broadening the vision of their readers, either by outright presentation or by the subtle seduction and capture of the readers' sensibilities. Trevisan, like Cervantes and Machado de Assis, attains this goal by showing life on the bias, as in a painting by Velázquez. With Trevisan, whatever lingering magic might have been left in Cervantes has been squeezed out. This magic is really bookish in *Don Quixote*, only appearing in the actual structure of the novel, since Don Quixote is at once a real person and also a character in a book, the very one we are reading, a circumstance similar to that of the parchments of Melquíades in *One Hundred Years of Solitude*. Therefore, the supposedly haphazard title of Trevisan's first collection, suggested by a friend, might be apt after all. The magic in Trevisan is all interior, more the stuff of magic than magic itself, in line with José Lezama Lima's wise bit of perception in *Paradiso* that Don Quixote is not the successor to Amadis but is Sinbad without the roc. Many of the stories are versions of what we take for reality and subsequently of that older reality called myth. James Joyce, as he reshapes Odysseus, becomes part of the collective Homer, in *Willy Remembers* Irvin Faust reduces Proustian Time, and in a similar way Trevisan puts different flesh on Cervantes' exemplary characters. Borges might catch the ambiguities of "versions" in many of these tales, particularly in "Under the Black Bridge," so reminiscent of Rashomōn or of Machado's narrators, who are never to be trusted. The ambiguity in Trevisan's stories often lies in the act or the thought itself rather than in the words describing it. This can be seen in the loosely connected stories from which this collection takes its title, *The Vampire of Curitiba*, where again we have versions of one character, or, perhaps, one version (symbolized by the name Nelsinho) of many characters. The reader is plagued by these possibilities, but as in the case of *Dom Casmurro* and other works of Machado de Assis he will never know.

This title is also indicative of Trevisan's position and intent. He understands full well that most people (including Brazilians) know precious little about Curitiba, and when the name is coupled with the image of a vampire, all sorts of terrible visions of Borgo Pass will arise. The commonplace becomes mysterious for a moment and the reader's subliminal reaction provides the stories with an added tone or backdrop. Suggestion has done its work with far greater impact than description, and this technique must be looked for in other stories, those of *The Conjugal War*, for example, which Trevisan has mythologically characterized as "the domestic *Iliad*," the most terrible tragedy of all. The small world of Curitiba becomes the great world, but at the same time the great world has been put back where it properly belongs. This is an intent similar to that of Guimarães Rosa, who showed that the incongruities of life in the backlands were the same doubts and pauses that have led men everywhere to ponder the human condition on the grand epic plane.

Progression or development with Dalton Trevisan is more a sense of perfection and dissatisfaction. He says that "the good writer never feels himself fulfilled: the work is always inferior to the dream. When he puts it all together he sees that he has denied the dream, betrayed the work, and changed life uselessly." This dissatisfaction is obvious in the "variorum" quality of his editions. A comparison between two of them brings out a great many changes in individual words and the reversal or elimination of whole paragraphs; sometimes such changes are mysterious and seemingly inexplicable, at other times they give a different slant to the tale or series. Indeed, the translations in this collection most often represent a third version, done from an edited and rearranged copy of the second edition. And there is even a fourth version, for as he looked over the English, Trevisan decided upon a few further changes that did not always concern matters of translation. This shows him to be a dynamic writer (comparable to a jazz soloist) and either the bane or the delight of future scholars. Because he is so forthright in his wish to be left alone and perhaps because of some of his titles, he will no doubt continue to be thought of as a mysterious and obscure person. This is really how it should be, for the situation parallels his work and shows that the more life is laid bare, the more it puzzles and confounds.

GREGORY RABASSA

Translator's Note

THE STORIES included in this collection have been
selected from the following volumes published in Rio de
Janeiro by Civilização Brasileira:

Novelas Nada Exemplares (2nd edn., revised), 1970.

Cemitério de Elefantes (2nd edn., revised and enlarged),
1970 (including *Morte na Praça*, previously published separately).

O Vampiro de Curitiba (2nd edn., revised and enlarged), 1970 (including *Desastres do Amor*, previously published separately).

A Guerra Conjugal (2nd edn., revised), 1970.

In case certain discrepancies should be observed between
these translations and the early original versions, let it be
noted that Dalton Trevisan has always seen fit to make certain revisions between editions of his works. The translation
is based on the second editions listed above with a great
many handwritten changes included. Also, in reading the
translation in manuscript form, the author made further
changes in which the question of translation was not involved.

G. R.

NOVELS
NOT AT ALL
EXEMPLARY

THE CORPSE
IN THE PARLOR

✎ SHE WAS LYING ON HER BACK on the bed, her
eyes open, her hands crossed over her breast, imitating the
corpse out there in the parlor. The afternoon had passed
quickly—the dead man was something quite novel. That
evening there would be no eternal argument between the
dead man and her mother over whose daughter Ivete was. She
heard her mother in the parlor as she looked at the dead man
and scratched herself—the afflicted scrape of nails across a
silk stocking. She remembered the gesture of the visitor who
admired the dead man and then brushed off the cuffs of his
pants. He did not wish to carry home that nauseating smell
of the dead man: every corpse is a flower with a distinctive
odor.

The night wind shook the curtain on the window and
made her bare arms shiver, but she made no move toward
the blanket at the foot of the bed. She could smell the fra-

grance of the wilted flowers and the four candles—when the wicks flickered, shadows would come rushing through the door. And underneath all the smells, the smell of that man. He was there in the coffin, his chin tied with a white handkerchief that was knotted at the top of his head, and he smelled.

She heard her mother dragging her slippers along as the smell which stifled the others for an instant reached her—incense was being burned. It was easier to die than to feel free of the dead man. The burial would not be until the following morning, and until then the stench would spread out furtively through the house, impregnating the curtains and getting under Ivete's fingernails. The visitor had brushed off the cuffs of his pants in vain. He would have to send them to the cleaners.

The dead man refused to leave the house: the remains of an ash from his cigarette in the ashtray, his coat on the chair with the sweat of his body still on it. How could the hat there on the rack be hidden, his hat, with a brim that had been turned down by those hands that were yellow now and crossed on his chest? And through the window, if the girl raised her head, she would see his pajamas drying on the line—his striped pajamas, with stains that no water could wash off. In the mirror—if she were to look there—she would come upon his livid face.

The slippers dragging about in the parlor were no longer her mother's but his, when he would go over to lean against the door to see if he could catch the conversation between Ivete and her boy friend in the hall. Suddenly the rocking chair would begin to move from the slightest breath of his memory—the straw seat sunk in by his weight. No matter how much she swept the house, the girl kept finding innumerable broken toothpicks: he always had a toothpick in his mouth, and after picking his rotting teeth he would take a long time lasciviously scratching his hairy nose with it. He used to roll little balls of bread between his fingers and flip them into the air. Ivete would find them in the folds of her napkin, among the leaves of the ferns, and on the frame of the painting of the Last Supper.

It had been hard for him to die, rocking in his chair for months on end, his chest uncovered because of the heat, his frail chest with hair so long that it had become entangled, grayish, and curly . . .

"That girl has no feelings," he would complain to his wife. "She keeps looking at me as if to say, 'Why doesn't he die?' "

The man who never spent much time at home between his trips as a traveling salesman came back one day to die. He put the striped pajamas on forever and he dragged himself whining from one room to another. His felt slippers would give him away when he went over to lean against the door to listen to Ivete's love-making, and he would stay on guard gnawing his toothpick. The girl would cough to warn him before she came in, and she would find him back in the rocking chair. The shoes provided him with his mean vengeance. Why polish them if he was never going to wear them again? Ivete would leave them like a mirror, but he was never satisfied, and every week the shoes that had not been worn would turn up dirty. There they were now, lined up on top of the wardrobe. If her mother gave them away to the milkman or the bakery boy, the dead man would come back to climb the steps—the girl would recognize the sound.

It had started on the afternoon when Ivete had been dusting the furniture, with her tight slacks rolled up to the knees. She imagined what he was thinking: "That girl's got such skinny legs . . ." He was looking at her furtively from behind his newspaper—the paper was shaking so much that he could not be reading it—until he lowered it, shouting at her to change her clothes, not go around the house naked.

"Cover up those legs! Even if they were pretty!"

She was thirteen years old, and since the salesman's return she had not left the house except to go to school in her
horrid blue uniform. She and her mother were prisoners of
the boarder, with his woolen socks on in spite of the summer, his little balls of bread on the tablecloth, his broken
toothpicks in every corner.

"He's nervous because of his illness," her mother
pleaded with her. "Please be patient."

Ivete would do her homework in the parlor. He would
be dozing or reading his paper and her mother would be
bustling in the kitchen. With her head bent low over her
notebook, she would suddenly feel the fuzz on her arms
stand up: it was his look. He was not asleep—no one sleeps
with his eyelids quivering. He was not reading the news—
how could he read a paper when he was moving contin-
uously?

She was hiding in her room, smoking—the creak of the
rocking chair would not let her study. The man, who could
barely drag himself around hanging onto the furniture,
knocked on her door. He knocked so hard that the girl became frightened and opened the door. He immediately
found the cigarette still burning on the floor. He took the
lighted end and burned Ivete's arm, and his expression was
so horrible that she did not dare call her mother.

"Don't you shout, you little bitch, or I'll kill you!"

She began to wear long sleeves to hide her insane scars.
At mealtime the man would not take his eyes off her, and if
Ivete wanted something she would get up to avoid speaking
to him. The mother, sitting between the two, ate with her
eyes lowered.

When he could bear it no longer (his chair was rocking
with such fury, and why, my God, didn't he fly out the
window?), he would turn the knob and Ivete knew who it
was and would open the door. He would have a cigarette in
his hand, smoking only on such occasions. He would slowly

6

roll up her sleeve and the girl, without shouting, would bite her lips as hard as she could. She would bear up under the cigarette until it crumbled, squashed between the man's gnawed nails.

At night she would be awakened by the argument in the next room. He had been on the road for many years and he was accusing his wife of having thousands of lovers. He roared and demanded to know what Ivete was doing in his house—who her father was. The poor woman swore between sobs that she had been faithful. In the morning Ivete would look at herself in the mirror to see whom she looked like. Strangely, she was a replica of the man: her dark hair, just like his before his illness, his wide mouth.

Her mother begged her to take some tea to the boarder; he did not know that he only had a few days to live. She begged the girl to be kind to a dying man. Why not bring him his tea in his room? Ivete took pity on him and took the tray. She stopped at the door—he was just a poor old man afraid to die.

Before he died he wanted her to forgive him and kiss him on the forehead. He was speaking with his eyes closed, his eyelids quivering. As soon as she lowered her head, he grabbed her suddenly and kissed her furiously on the mouth. It was worse than being burned with the cigarette. She ran to the bathroom, rinsed out her mouth, and brushed her teeth until the gums bled.

He would get out of bed leaning on his wife and drop into the rocking chair—he did not even have the strength to move the chair. From his immobilized body his eyes would follow the girl. She never went into his room again and her mother did not ask her why. When he saw her beyond his reach he began to roar:

"Who was your father? Which one of your mother's lovers was your father? Come here, you little bitch! Tell me his name!"

To get her revenge on him, the girl began to use make-up. Her boy friend would whistle in the hallway and at that signal the rocking chair would fall silent—the salesman would stop his hallucinated flight. There in the dark hallway Ivete would imagine him, his neck stretched out, trying in vain to hear what they were saying. She would laugh aloud so that the spy could hear through the door. Her boy friend would ask her if she was going crazy. When she came back the lipstick would be gone and she would walk slowly through the parlor so that the man, sunk in his chair, would notice the dark circles under her eyes and her wrinkled dress.

Early in the morning the man's shouts would wake Ivete up. He was not sleeping, clutching his chair and complaining of pain. His wife kept him rocking and he would ask her for the names of the other men. With insomnia and pain the dying man was riding his rocking chair. In her room the girl would not go back to sleep, but with the light on, waiting for sleep, she would pray for him to die.

The boy friend had whistled in the hallway and Ivete went out to meet him. The man in the striped pajamas was dying. They stayed there kissing until her mother came out looking for her: she could feel the mustache in all of the kisses. And, lying on her bed, her hands crossed over her breast, playing dead, her heart pounding with joy, she fell asleep. And so the man got up out of his coffin and came into her room.

"What are you doing, you little bitch?"

"Sleeping."

"Don't you have a math test tomorrow?"

"Yes, I do."

"Why aren't you studying?"

"You died, father. I won't have to take the test."

Ivete woke up hearing voices. She opened her eyes: a corner of the mirror was shining in the half-darkness. She could hear her mother's nails as she scratched herself—she had picked off the dead man's lice.

She sat up in bed and through the window she saw the striped pajamas covered with stains rocking in the wind—he was dead. Her mother's slippers were dragging along the hall toward the kitchen.

Standing beside the coffin, Ivete wiped her mouth with the back of her hand—his kiss was biting her tongue. It would be a long wait, it was not easy to get free of the dead man. She lighted a cigarette and looked through the smoke at the old man with the handkerchief tied around his chin— a handkerchief to stop him from drooling. With his eyes barely closed, might he not be spying on her through his long lashes? No, his eyelids were not quivering this time. Ivete sucked in the smoke, wild with pleasure—he was quite dead. Her mother was in the kitchen making coffee for the wake.

The girl leaned over and examined the man's eyelids, his mustache, his mouth. She pulled up his sleeve and, pushing aside the black beads of the rosary, she placed the lighted end of her cigarette on her father's hand, burning it ever so slowly.

GOOD EVENING,
SIR

❧ HE WAS WAITING for me outside the dance. Standing on the corner, he was adjusting the tips of his bow tie and from a distance, thin as he was and of uncertain age, he was smiling at me. He said "Good evening," and I answered "Good evening, sir."

He walked alongside of me, saying that he had seen me dancing with that blonde girl. He thought she was pretty with her painted mouth. I replied that I didn't want to see her anymore. He said that he had gone through a lot of suffering from women—he gave a furious tug on his small blue bow tie. He didn't want anything to do with his own wife, he was married.

He spoke so much and so fast that his voice became sticky with saliva. I lighted a cigarette, and when my hand trembled he asked me if she had excited me, but I didn't answer. He said that he understood quite well, women could drive young men crazy, no pity for them. He was capable of killing a certain blonde girl with treacherous green eyes.

"Look, my eyes aren't green!"

He winked at me, once with each eye. He was no longer talking on about the funny faces on the musicians at the dance. I knew nothing about the world, he said, and his voice grew huskier with every word. He was gently mingling the plane trees, the blonde, the very moon in the sky. Oh, the sound of that voice and the snail-like, slimy saliva on his gold tooth . . . He wasn't talking about the blonde, about me, or about himself; he was talking about someone else—as though I knew who it was. Close to the church we could hear the squeaking of the bats.

He asked what time it was. I didn't have a watch. We stopped at the corner of my street and he brought up the blonde, he said that she had her mouth painted, she was a picture of wild delights, but her look was cold, her blond heart was bitter. He knew about other mouths, his, for example, which was the queen of a thousand pleasures. He wet his lips with the tip of his red tongue: there was the froth of a dying man on his mouth. He had known me for some time, I had never seen him, but he knew all about me, who I was: "A good-looking boy deserves to sit on the throne of the world." I could even ask him for money, he said, he would give me presents that no blonde girl would ever give me. I asked him why he hated her, she was a girl from a good family.

He looked at his wrist watch: three o'clock in the morning. I said: "Good night, sir." He didn't answer, his trembling hands climbed up to the knot of my tie: rats with hot and humid jaws ran underneath my shirt.

"You've got hair on your chest!"

The tips of his fingers were tracing the peaceful gestures of a priest consecrating his chalice.

"Oh, all men do."

His eyes opened up towards the moon and I could swear that they were green.

"My, you're strong!"

That laugh was the squeaking of an old, blind bat. Now he was talking about the weather, it looked like rain, and then there was an expression. An expression of the blonde girl's, the tip of his tongue along his mouth, like a piece of paper underneath a door.

"Aren't you afraid?"

A cat jumped off the wall. When I looked from the cat to the man I saw that the street was empty to the corner: he had knelt down to the moon.

Drops of rain were splattering on the leaves like the steps of people running. I was already saying "Good night, good night, good night." He began to cry, mouth up, biting at the night with his gold tooth. The rain was beating on his face as if all of it were crying, until he hid it behind his hand as his watch glimmered on his wrist.

"Is that my present?"

He looked at the watch:

"It has meaning for me . . . my mother left it to me."

The damp leaves were shining on the sidewalk. All of the trees were dripping. Two doors before my house I stopped.

"You'll have to . . ."

It didn't seem right to call him "sir."

". . . go back now."

As if he wanted to grasp my hand, I kept it in my pocket.

He asked:

"Wait a little bit longer."

All of the trees were dripping. I stood there at the door of my house—the watch in the palm of my hand. He asked me what time it was.

HOTEL ROOM

🐦 IT WAS THE SPARROWS that woke him up in the morning. "Goddamn them," he moaned, burying his head in the pillow as he heard them chirping under the window. The goddamned sparrows were day: another day. If only he could eliminate the mornings of his life, keep only the nights . . . He did not stir, biting the pillow so as not to shout: "I didn't wake up, I'm asleep. They're not sparrows, they're crickets . . ." It would be nice to kill all the sparrows in the city.

His head in his hands, he repeated over and over again: "They're crickets, damn it, they're crickets." To get dressed, instead of opening the windows he turned on the lights.

Where had he found the courage to look in the mirror? He had survived the worst: he was already shaving. He no longer had to look at that face and, scraping his jaw, ask himself: "Why?" The mirror never answered him. He sur-

vived daytime by hating the sparrows. If only they would
not chirp with such joy maybe the sun would stop coming
up.

Lathering his chin, he insulted himself in a low voice:
"Why don't you die?" He felt the coldness of the razor and
his fingers began to tremble. Then he reached for the bottle
and drank from it. Drops of bitterness fell from his eyes
without being tears.

He put the snapshot of his daughter in the corner of the
mirror, the only way to bear his own face. Each time he
finished shaving the temptation would come over him, never
before. He wanted to die clean-shaven, perhaps his wife
would bring Mariinha to see him . . . If only his hand
would not tremble so much—and he laid the useless razor
down on the washstand. It would not hurt: but no matter
how small the cut, blood all over his neck.

Months earlier, he could not tell how many, after an argument with his wife he had hidden himself in that hotel.
She would certainly come the following day to beg him to
come home. She did not come, she sent him his clothing instead. He had been there for months and he still had not
taken his clothes out of the suitcase. He would neither open
the windows nor empty the suitcase. He would leave for
work, from there go to the bars, getting back before dawn.
The last one to leave the office—he was alone, hunched over
his desk, and he would suddenly feel a spider walking across
the back of his neck, which made him shudder: his wife's
look of hate.

During the early days he would look at his watch at
every moment. Until he remembered: he was no longer in
any hurry. The watch stopped and he did not wind it, even
though he would strap it to his wrist each morning—nothing
to do, no home to go to. He would slip along in the shadow
of the trees toward the nearest bar. Everything seemed fine
as long as he did not start asking himself: "What am I

doing here? Where's my home, oh Lord? How's my daughter?" He would cling to friends, they all had their time to go home. All of them had a home to go to.

He could not go back to his hotel room with the sound of the elevator at the bottom of the shaft. He argued with his friends until they changed bars. He did not understand, clinging to one after the other, asking them not to leave him alone. If he were not alone he would not have to think.

He drank, and no matter how much he drank his troubles were just as great. He never went over to the bar to read the newspaper, the world had ceased to interest him. Flies would alight on his hand without bothering him. He would stare at Mariinha's picture, but he was incapable of tears. His eyes would scarcely grow moist after a great deal of effort—not a single drop would fall. He carried a small knitted slipper in his pocket and in moments of greatest despair he would squeeze it with his hand. That was how he saved himself from the days and his self-pity.

He would telephone home and chat with his daughter. Sometimes his wife would answer, no words would be exchanged, each recognizing the silence of the other. The maid would bring his daughter to see him in the square. He would hug Mariinha and frighten her as he wet her hair with his tears. He guessed what his wife would say: "The tears of a drunkard . . ." He had followed her along the street one afternoon—she was even prettier, women who are separated like to fix themselves up—but he was unable to bring himself close to her: touching her would have been like touching a toad. She was already turning Mariinha against him, the ungrateful father who had abandoned his home . . . He felt lost there on the park bench, and when he turned to her he could see that she was worshipping him with her eyes between licks on her lollipop. "It's like a drink, isn't it, Daddy?"— and she would blink at him, she did not know how to wink —"Make-believe, right, Daddy?"

Late at night he would walk by the house, looking up at Mariinha's window like a lover. Once her light was on . . . was his daughter ill? Her mother was stern, she would let her cry at night. She would not allow her to sleep with the light on, the little angel, so frightened of the dark. She was taking out her revenge on him through her own daughter . . . . Even in the photograph where his daughter was smiling she had a sad expression, the one that children have after their father has died and schoolmates ask them "Don't you have any father, kid?" and they make that face to stop from crying.

His route now was from the hotel to work and from there to the first bar and from there to another bar, until all the bars had closed—he was alone. He never got drunk anymore: drinking spared him for a worse fate.

Since he had lost the ability to sleep, he dreaded the time to return to the hotel. No matter how much he drank or how tired he was, as soon as he got back to his room and lay down on his bed, his eyes would reject sleep (sleep would come over him suddenly in a bar and he would doze off sitting down with his head on the table). Then he would begin to hear the elevator, the shuffle of slippers on the way to the bathroom. He recognized the coughing of the fat woman in room 42, the hawking of the old man in 49, the slamming of doors. In the half-light he could make out the suitcase on the chair. The bureau drawers were still empty. When he changed clothes he would open and close the suitcase, still on a trip. If he put his clothes into the bureau it would be the end of any hope.

And if he fell asleep it was worse: he would dream about the elevator. When he got into it he was crushed in among the guests. Each one would give the number of his floor and the cage, instead of rising, would start down. He loosened his collar, feeling a lack of air: there was no ventilator in the elevator. He had been left alone, the others had gotten off without his noticing. He pushed the red alarm button, the cage did not stop, going down into the black depths of the shaft . . .

He would awaken, hearing not his shout but that of Mariinha: "Daddy, Daddy!" He was standing in the middle of the room on the rug with green letters—Lux Hotel. He would beat his head against the wall: it was the hour when he used to get up to cover his daughter or to give her the pacifier that she was feeling for with her little hand, unable to find it. Then he would turn on the lights: if his girl had awakened far away with fear of the dark the lamp would light up the night for her . . .

He did not need to sleep as long as Mariinha could sleep. He would lie down again with his eyes open so as not to dream about the elevator. He said good-by to the little picture, and even though he did not believe in God, he prayed that he would die that night, never hear the sparrows again. He would repeat a random phrase, like wiggling a loose tooth in his gum: "An island is a body of land completely surrounded . . ." If he could only go mad at least— the words would be replaced by others, repeated dozens of times: "Come now, you will say, hearing the stars . . . Come now, you will say, hearing the stars . . ."

When he hobbled through the streets he would drag his feet, he was so tired. When it rained he would not stop his walking or quicken his step. He would return to the hotel, knowing what was waiting for him. As soon as he laid his head on the pillow he would hear the creak of the elevator. Some guest who had come in after him, a traveling salesman most likely . . . It was useless to deceive himself: the elevator was running by itself. What strange guests would it be carrying at night when everybody was asleep? No sooner did he close his eyes than he heard the chirping of the sparrows. He would quickly repeat that they weren't sparrows, they were crickets. They weren't sparrows, they were crickets.

NIGHTS OF LOVE
IN GRANADA

⬛ DURING THE AFTERNOON he saw the women arrive one after the other from the olive groves on top of the hills. Were they coming to a fiesta, with their shoes in their hands? They were dressed in black and the stones hurt their feet, a shoe in each hand. There were so many of them, in such dense mourning, that night descended with them. Then, in the square, they put on their immaculate shoes. Now they are parading past the café and Pedro recognizes them.

The men hide their cigarettes in the palms of their hands and fall to their knees on top of their own spit. Some direct a lover's bit of gallantry to the one who comes all in white in the chill of the evening. Three little doves give love pecks to her wounded white feet. Tremulous hands reach out to touch the hem of her skirt. The roses hit her face without hurting it and mothers kiss their children as she passes. A blind man shouts from the café there: "All hail to the white dove." She bows her head. There is a smile on the wound that is her lips. Pedro, only Pedro, remains seated at his table, not kneeling.

Dinner at the Pensión Don Marcos is at ten in the evening. Wandering through the streets he doesn't feel the sleepiness he had a while back in the café, just hunger. He delayed as long as he could, he knew quite well what was in store for him. It would have been easier to have hidden in his room, thinking about Sunday dinners back home, were it not for the man next door who coughs. Unless he's exhausted he can't sleep because of the coughing in the other room.

Afflicted hands clutch at his feet, but he doesn't stop. If he stops he's lost: bootblacks. Worse than they are the little old women on the sidewalk. It's a narrow sidewalk with only room for one person at a time, and the old women are huddled with their backs to the wall, black shawls on their shoulders. No matter how tired he is, he mustn't step on them—they're blind. He slips past with the step of a thief, but they discover him and without blinking their eyes they turn their heads as he passes. He doesn't give a thing to the thirty-two old women, who, even though he tries to sneak by on tiptoes, hold out their empty hands to him. He has to amuse himself with them until ten o'clock at night when he'll have his lentil soup. Granada would be more beautiful, he thinks, if it weren't for the little old women.

He knows that he's been followed from the café. As soon as it grew late inside there, the other one crossed the threshold like a spy. He's a sad man carrying a cane. Pedro throws away his cigarette and without turning around imagines the spy bending over and cursing seven times: he'd learned to smoke cigarettes down to the last drag.

It's not yet ten o'clock and the young blind girls are circulating in pairs, holding each other's arms. So that the day will not be a total loss, they shout out lottery numbers in happy voices under the deserted balconies. The prettiest one has a scarlet rose in her hair and smiles at the flattery of the characters who lean against the wall, rolling their own cigarettes and spitting. At ten Pedro will sit down to a hot plate of lentils and Granada is where he will sleep.

He goes into the Pensión Don Marcos. At the end of the dark stairs is the dining room. It's almost ten o'clock and everyone is seated at the tables and furtively eating the dark bread in front of the plates.

Pedro's place was occupied by the man next door who coughs. The landlady, coming with the first tureen, tells him that she's taken in some new guests. He'll have to sit at the table with the other man. He's hungry and he doesn't want to argue in front of the boarders, who are peering at him from their chairs. The landlady winks at him with a red eye and nods at the place that used to belong to the cougher: a pair of lovers holding hands over the clothless table. "Love," the fat woman whispers. He nods agreement and sits down across from his neighbor.

The old man is red with fury and from his efforts not to cough. He takes his handkerchief out of his pocket, clutching it in his hand, and raises it to his mouth as he coughs, shaking his shoulders. "Pardon me, sir," he says, his voice hoarse and with tears in his eyes. The fat woman serves the two of them last. "Dirty old woman," he insults her behind her back. "Old whore-mistress!"

He moves in his chair in order to peep at the lovers who had usurped his table. "Love . . . ," he mutters and spits on the floor. "Do you know," he lowers his voice, "that they didn't sleep all night long?" The landlady had filled his plate to the brim with lentils and the old man begins to eat slowly, as if he weren't hungry, even though he finished everything down to the bread crumbs. The soup is steaming but he doesn't blow on his spoon. From time to time he stops to cough.

"It makes me sick when they talk about love . . . ," he says. "As if something like that was love!" He is sitting with his back to the couple and he turns around in his chair. "Look at the rings under the girl's eyes . . ." The old man swallows all of his soup and is waiting to spit into his handkerchief. "I'm an old man and I don't sleep at night, but I like quiet. I pounded on the wall and they stopped their noise. Then, thinking I'd gone to sleep, they started up again . . ."

Pedro imagines the old man with all his clothes on, a beret and a shawl, coughing all through the night. He coughs with his handkerchief at his mouth or buries his head in his pillow, rising up from time to time to spit into the basin. Since he doesn't sleep he needs quiet in order to think, when an attack of coughing doesn't shake the iron bed.

The landlady had asked him for his room. He was old, no friends or family. "This is my home," he affirms. "I don't have any more money to pay the rent, but it's still my home. I want to die in it, in my room, in a bed with white sheets." And he coughs with the wind that has been channeled through the hall. The fat woman had left the windows open so that winter would finish him off. "Love," he repeats, rolling the word around his mouth, "love is so much shit . . ." An attack of coughing strangles him and he leaves the table, tightening the checkered shawl about his neck.

With his last piece of bread Pedro soaks up the last spoonful of soup. None of them will sleep that night: the lovers, the old man, he. There will be no love in Granada for him. In the end he'll manage to huddle in bed, with the light on because of the cold and listening to the old man coughing, thinking about Sunday dinners back home.

THREE O'CLOCK
IN THE MORNING

🌿 THERE SHE IS, embroidering in the light of the
lamp. If she could only finish the work that night . . . Her
eyes close, she's tired and she knows she mustn't sleep. She
feels protected in the hot circle of light—she can hear her
name called by the pictures on the wall. They're pictures of
dead people and their voices resound in a house where everyone is asleep. She had already ironed the clothes, put the rice
out next to the extinguished stove, and filled the filter with
water. And when the voices become quiet she listens to the
dripping in the filter there.

The windows closed, the milk bottle by the door.
Maybe she'll be able to sleep tonight. She puts the needle
and thread into her basket, and with the shadows behind her,
turns out the lights in the living room and hall. Before
putting out the light in her room she lights the lamp on the
bureau, the last light in the world.

Three O'Clock in the Morning

She prays on her knees, her hand to her face, and she lies down on a corner of the enormous double bed. At that hour, on what byways are her husband and sons wandering astray? She lifts her head from time to time from the pillow to look at the illuminated lamp bowl. The light is so weak and if she could cast a shadow in the half-light of the room she wouldn't feel so much alone . . . She glimpses some fingers at the window: a branch of the peach tree, which, with the wind, is touching lightly there. As if the sleepless peach tree wanted to talk to her; it has gaunt fingers and its leaves are falling; it's wintertime.

When she lies down there are footsteps in the street, distant train whistles, and on one cheek she can still feel the heat of the lampshade. She raises her head from the pillow— her eyes keep the lamp lighted. All she has to do is go to sleep (and she knows that she's going to fall asleep, she's so tired) and the flame will go out. The bowl is full of oil and the wick is new, but the flame goes out as soon as she closes her eyes. It could be the wind or her husband, the mouse or death.

She wakes up in the middle of the night—three o'clock is a time for thieves and what thief is stealing her little light? —she was alone in the dark house. No footsteps on the sidewalk, no wind, the peach tree has drawn back its branches. Her sons are sleeping in the next room, but she was alone. They're resting peacefully and since she doesn't hear them, she prays for them not to be dead in their beds. She can't even call them . . . Was the afflicted beating of her heart an illness? She's so frightened that she sits up in bed with her hand to her mouth: "Please, dear Lord, not now, not in the dark!"

Before he lay down perhaps her husband had blown out the lamp. Or the mouse had pushed the wick down in his greed to drink the oil. The same little animal that's gnawing at the silence now: someone else alert in the world. "Gnaw away, little mouse," the woman pleads. "I won't tell the man anything. He'd catch you in a trap and leave me all alone. Gnaw away, little mouse. Please gnaw . . ."

In addition to the mouse, back in the kitchen, the heavy dripping in the filter again. The drops come faster and faster: it's her heart. The animal stops gnawing, its small ear lifted up, and there it is witnessing the woman's death agony.

She knows that the crisis has passed when she hears the mouse again. She can weep, there's no more danger. Let the tears flow freely—she gets up, feeling her way along the wall, and goes over to the bureau. Scratching one match after the other, she lights the lamp.

Her medicine is on the night table, with the spoon and glass of water. After she lights the lamp and takes her drops, she can't do anything except wait for the sparrows, watching the tremulous light of the lamp. She moans involuntarily and her husband mutters:

"Will you ever stop your moaning?"

"I have a pain in my heart . . ."

"You and your pains."

The voice comes from far off, he's talking with his back to her.

"I wanted you to stroke my hair . . ."

Her husband hears ". . . stroke my hair" and snores.

That night she was safe: the light was shining in the lamp. Her husband and sons were asleep. The branch on the peach tree hit the window: "Here I am, wide awake . . ."

She needed one more day to finish the work. It was easy to give away clothes and shoes, but who would want a piece of cloth embroidered down the middle? She was nodding, sitting on the bed, the sated mouse was no longer gnawing at the ceiling, the water wasn't dripping in the filter, and the sparrows were sleeping among the leaves. When winter comes the leaves fall off the peach tree and the sparrows fly off far away. If they fly away, my God, who will awaken her from her death?

JOÃO NICOLAU

◪ João Nicolau BECAME A MAN: he chewed tobacco and spat black. He put on the high-cut boots he had inherited from his father, kissed his mother's white hair, and without any money for a train ticket, decided to walk to the city. Halfway there he asked for a glass of water from a girl on the porch of a house with a wisteria vine. He explained that he was on his way to make his lite. The girl's father, a man named Bortolão, offered him room and board for repairing an old barn.

At night, wearing his boots, he chatted with the dark-haired girl. He nicknamed her Negrinha, maddened by the perfume, which came from her or the wisteria, he could not tell. After the barn had a roof, an aunt of Negrinha's died of a volvulus. During the wake he downed two glasses of cane liquor at the insistence of Bortolão. Feeling drowsy, he retired to sleep. Negrinha went to look for him in the barn, lying with him on the bed of straw. At dawn, while she was still sleeping, he left quite early, not waiting for the burial.

When he heard horses, João Nicolau went off the road. Even though he was thirsty, he did not knock on any door. The boots hurt his feet, the city seemed farther and farther away. He had to take them off and scratch furiously. Negrinha had sprinkled them with cowhage to slow down his flight.

His feet on fire, he dragged himself up to a big old house with a sign over the door that said The Call of Independence, where he asked for lodging. On the following day he forgot about leaving: his blue eyes were red from trailing after the innkeeper's daughter so much. Cristina kept her blond hair in two braids with crimson bows at the ends. Her body, so white at night, was luminous as it trembled under João's callused hands, becoming a phosphorescent fish in dark waters.

She sewed her own wedding gown and João wore his father-in-law's blue suit. With his last bit of strength, his ailing father-in-law asked him to go to the city and get him a bottle of a certain miraculous water. He traveled on a train for the first time, with a brown leather case under his arm.

In the city he was arrested by a detective who was a friend of Bortolão. He spent the night among thieves and drunkards and, since he was thirsty, he drank the whole bottle of miraculous water. On the next day he was taken before the judge, where he found Negrinha and her father. She was three months' pregnant. If he did not put right his evil act he would go to jail for seven years. João Nicolau swore that he loved her and they were married by the judge.

He took leave of his father-in-law and the detective with the promise that he would take good care of the girl. Bortolão gave him a little money to get a start in life and accompanied them to the train: they would go to live in João's mother's house. He went away for a half hour and returned with the case bulging—in addition to the provisions for the trip, he had a rope, a pistol, and a dagger. He got on the train with Negrinha and at nightfall they got off at the deserted station.

On the road he invited his wife to sit on a pine stump and have something to eat. Negrinha was eating some bread and sausage when he attacked her from behind, wounding her in the neck with the dagger. She gave a cry and fell down unconscious. João Nicolau, who was holding the pistol at her breast, watched her fall and, thinking she was dead, put the weapon away. With the rope he hung her head down from the branch of a cherry tree so that all her blood would drain out.

He arrived home all bloody, and in answer to the old woman's questions he said that on the road he had helped a neighbor bleed a pig. But as soon as he had left, Negrinha came to, freed herself from her bonds, and crawled to a nearby house. João Nicolau was arrested the following morning: he was delirious, talking about phosphorescent fish. They escorted him to the jail, where he wept in repentance, hitting his head against the wall. He tried to hang himself with the laces from his boots, but as luck had it, the laces broke. The jailer allowed him to escape in exchange for the famous boots.

Cristina was in mourning for her father, who, on his death bed, had reached out his hands for the water of salvation. João invented a story about an attack on the train by two masked bandits. The other one, Negrinha, had recovered and returned home. While Cristina was asleep, João Nicolau wrote a passionate letter to her at the kitchen table announcing his return and sending the little money he had left for the child's layette. The child was stillborn and Negrinha, poor thing, was too weak to survive the birth. As a farewell she cut off a curl of her hair for him. João Nicolau received it in jail, turned in once more by Bortolão. Cristina was left pregnant, and without means. Then a letter informed him that his mother had died of a bladder tumor.

The judge had sentenced him to eighteen years. Cristina sold everything from The Call of Independence and was now a cook in a boardinghouse near the penitentiary. The hard work and bad treatment brought on a miscarriage. When he learned about it he set fire to his mattress and threw himself into the flames. He was taken to the infirmary with second-degree burns. One of the guards took a liking to Cristina and excited her with the promise of letting her husband escape. She became the guard's mistress but he was transferred to a different prison. She found herself two months' pregnant. In time she gave birth to a daughter who was named Augusta in memory of her grandmother.

João Nicolau had drunk water from a ditch and contracted typhoid fever. In order to support her daughter Cristina went to work in a house of prostitution.

The fever left João Nicolau sad and bald. At night, unable to sleep, he would sometimes think about Negrinha, sometimes about Cristina. He would touch the curls tied together with a grim piece of string. If she had lived, they would have been white with the years that had passed—she was still young in that cluster, black as on the first day. He remembered the water she had given him and how cool it had been, and sometimes, sunk deep in his cell, he would smell the sweetish odor of the wisteria. The other one, Cristina, had given him a wedding picture, and although he always showed up clearly in his blue suit, her face was growing dim. He tore the picture in half, keeping the part with the bride: in the whitish splotch of her head all that he could distinguish was her garland and veil.

In the tenth year he lost all his teeth. Unable to chew, he moaned with stomach aches. His distraction, besides Cristina's visits, was watching the crows, wondering where they took shelter when it rained. There was a palm tree opposite his window: the white buds would appear and from them small, green coconuts, then they were yellow, and the ones that the wind did not blow down became black and shriveled on their stems. No fruit could possibly have been as sweet as those coconuts. No matter how much it rained, one side of the palm tree was always dry.

He was released at the age of forty-four. Cristina was waiting at the gate. She had left the house of fallen women old, ugly, and ill. Her daughter was holding her arm and it was the first time that João had seen the girl.

They went back to the house of João Nicolau's late mother. Big, lazy, any incident amused him: a crow circling in the sky (Where is he flying? Why does he disappear when it rains?) or Augusta's golden curls.

Cristina went out to work as a washerwoman and the daughter took care of João Nicolau's needs. With his ax on his shoulder, instead of splitting wood, he would be surprised at the number of times the spiraling curls bounced on the back of Augusta's neck—her face was an exact fit for the blank space in the picture.

When she arrived home, Cristina found her daughter in João Nicolau's bed. She went to sleep in Augusta's room. At night she heated up the water and brought a washcloth to clean the man's feet. After she had dried them it was his turn to bathe Augusta's chubby feet in the same water. And he would kiss them right there in front of Cristina—the girl would writhe with the tickling.

Cristina served him ground glass in his beans without his suspecting it; he felt such strong cramps that he rolled on the floor, his tongue hanging far out. Now João slept alone in the double bed. One night he looked for Negrinha's curl and could not find it. Cristina had burned it along with the picture of herself in which only the veil and garland showed.

João Nicolau complained of the suffocating smell of wisteria. Every time one of the women would mix ground glass in the plate of beans that they brought to his bed, he would roar with pain and they would cover their ears and flee into the backyard.

One day he died. He was buried by the women and neither one of them wept. With no money for the train they set out for the city on foot. Then Augusta's belly gave a jump— she discovered that she was going to be a mother.

DEAR OLD GIRL

❧ IN THE HEAT of three o'clock in the afternoon the city was asleep beneath the buzzing flies. The boy in a white linen suit turned the corner—"Behold, I see the burning bush"—the asphalt soft and sticky under his feet. All the streets were deserted except that one, jammed with so many people that they overflowed the sidewalks. "It's a funeral procession," he said to himself, "but without a body." The strange cortege extended two or three blocks, and he retraced his steps in a frantic search for the one who had died as groups clustered together in the doorways and then suddenly broke up. "Where's Verônica?" he asked. "She's not singing." A sad and lazy procession, half of it moving back and forth and the other half motionless, while the corpse, with a greasy stench that befouled and moved the flies' hallucinated wings, lay inside one of the houses, although nobody knew which one, for the onlookers searched for it by poking their heads into doors and open windows. Parade or funeral procession, the crowd was following a destiny known to all. He made his way among the others, careful not to step on those who stopped without warning or turned halfway around or suddenly stuck their heads into one of the door-ways. Just their heads—they rarely went in. The doors and windows of the mystical wake were lined with widows wailing for the same dead man and looking gilded with their painted faces. While the men (for it was a parade or funeral procession made up only of men) were decently dressed, the women, crowding in the windows and doors because of the heat burning inside the decrepit houses, wore brassières and panties of striking colors, with red, blue, and yellow predomi-nating, and even when taking their ease they were ladies of great luxury, some of them even having a pair of purple sandals.

All of them, alone at a window or lined up one behind the other on the worn, wavy stone steps that had been eaten away in the middle from the passage up and down of so many feet, all of them, serene or haranging the passers-by in low and whining voices, repeated the same gesture in which, bringing thumb and forefinger together, they made the symbol of lost innocence. Without moving their arms they tirelessly moved their hands, in every door and window, synchronized in such a way that when he looked at them the boy in white linen thought he was at a watchmaker's with swaying pendulums, only these pendulums moved silently. And finally, as if he were behind a clock, he examined each one of them, stopping by the doors and, like the others, poking his head in to look at the ladies or clocks that all showed the same time.

With only a trace of haughtiness, he looked sharply and stared straight ahead, a drunkard trying not to give himself away and making himself lucid (he thinks) to plan his next movement, always forgetting some small detail that betrays him in the end, as, for example, after getting undressed without a mistake under the inquisitorial eyes of his wife, when he finally turns out the light and imagines that he's safe, he hears the honeyed and simple-minded question: "Have you taken to wearing shoes with your pajamas, dear?" With great caution, therefore, so as not to look drunk, the young man was critically analyzing the monstrance of fingers, and, as was his custom when under the influence of alcohol, he permitted himself a silent remark in a slightly sarcastic tone. Resisting the enticing smiles with the gold teeth: "Tell me, love, what are your moral qualities?" He made his way beneath the poignant complaints of the professional mourners, indifferent or insensitive to the pain that made them repeat the monotonous call of: "Come here, sweetie . . . come here, sweetie . . . come here, love . . ." And some of them, indignant at not being heard by him or the others (distinguished gentlemen with umbrellas on their arms, a drunken sailor, barefoot Negroes) after ceaseless beckoning with the idle hand—without speeding up or slowing down the pace of the pendulum on the right—furious at so much useless wailing, maddened by a gesture or a simple look, stepped forward and took them by the hand or arm, drawing them into the stair wells, and the men let themselves be led along or struggled to get loose. Letting go of them, the women calmly went on with the pendular movement in such an automatic way that as they chatted volubly or were absorbed in meditation, they did not interrupt it, and the ones who were busy lighting a cigarette, eating ice cream, or peeling a tangerine did it with the other hand (the left one).

After looking for a long time, at first in the middle of the street, then on the sidewalk, and finally in the doorway, he went up the wooden steps, defending himself from a fat mulatto woman who flung her arms madly about his neck, but since he stood there with his foot in the air looking resolutely ahead, she let him go on, but he did notice the tattoo

of a blue heart on one of her thighs and inside the heart a
name which by coincidence was the same as his. There were
five ladies in the hallway in addition to the mulatto, and
those who were settled on the steps broke ranks up to the
last row, which was sitting on cheap chairs; of these, one—
the last one and the one he had been looking for so eagerly,
so impatiently, almost to the point of despair—was sitting in
an ancient wicker chair, the only one who could give him a
bit of rest after such implacable pursuit. They stared at him
with insinuating smiles, but not she, timid eyes resting on
her tired hands. The boy was wearing a white linen suit and
a silk tie, and while not one of them suspected his black
heart, the old woman—for she was an old woman—kept her
head bowed, and in that defenseless and nostalgic position
even seemed to be weeping for him as he reached the fourth
step, the hallway, and finally her chair. Standing beside her,
he noticed that she seemed to be concentrating on a clipper
that was cutting her thick thumbnail, and he said with a
voice that was not his, it was so husky:

"Do you belong to me, my love?"

While the other ladies on the steps and in the chairs,
swinging their eternal pendulums, turned toward him, startled by the emotion that shook his voice—he was emotional
because he was finally going to have his old woman,—the
old woman (who could have been the mother and grandmother of all of them and could not be confused with the
others because she had her clothes on) got up with difficulty,
leaning on the arms of the chair, and, without interest even
in looking at him, went down the dark hallway saying in a
voice that was tired and annoyed after so many years of sitting forgotten in the yellow wicker chair:

"This way."

Disconsolate or lazy, she went ahead of him, shuffling her
cloth slippers. While he felt no curiosity for the nakedness
of the others, suggested or visible through the panties and

brassières, he trembled as he dreamed of the old woman's intimacies, for he thought of her as *"his* old woman," well-deserved and finally attained after the most frantic old-lady hunt ever in Curitiba. She was wearing—in spite of the heat and the official uniform of two bright-colored items—a simple cotton dress, sleeveless and once scarlet in color. She shuffled in her slippers that covered swollen feet with thick blue veins and behind her, unable to imagine her shape because the red dress was like a shroud, the boy wiped the sweat from his hands in expectation of the mystery of that parade or funeral procession, which, even if he didn't deserve it, she would certainly reveal, thanks to her many decades of life. At the end of the hall, in the shadows that gave off a strong smell of creolin, the old woman opened a door and they both went in.

The room was separated from the hall by a screen that stood a little taller than their heads and was furnished with only a bed and a night table. Looking at the sad bed covered with a greenish quilt laid out carelessly or in a hurry—who knows, it might have been used a short time before—the boy turned to his motionless companion beside the open door:

"The doll? Where's the doll?"

It was true, he felt the absence of a rag doll on a green or gold quilt, but seeing the vague and distracted eyes of the creature, he hastened to correct himself as he realized with fright that eyes do not age—blue eyes, at least—by giving her the first of the gallantries that stumbled across his avid lips:

"It's you, my love. You're the doll."

She smiled with her ancient teeth, the gums had a color that could have been of any shade except that of flesh, and the teeth were drab, as if they had never been used. As he got undressed, behold, he crossed himself. "God be praised, I have my old woman. I, who do not deserve the basest of women, because not a one of them is low enough for me."

35

And with her hand on the doorknob, which made her all the
more desirable, as if she wanted to run away before he could
possess her, she watched him as he got undressed with unex-
pected haste, hanging his jacket on the hook she showed him
behind the door, laying his pants and shirt on the foot of the
bed. He was already taking off his shoes and only then—still
complaining that he did not deserve her—did the old
woman murmur in a soft voice in which he noticed a foreign
accent for the first time:

"I come back, *non?*"

He stopped hearing the slippers as he lay down on the
bed, wearing only his socks, and no matter how great his fear
of bedbugs, he let all his weight down on the grimy quilt
that was marked with occasional stains. He was at peace
with himself; he thought that he was or that he was trying to
pretend that he was, until he discovered two or three openings in the screen through which the all-seeing eye, whether
the eye of God or not, could spy on him, and, putting his
hands behind his head, for the bed had no pillow, he looked
at the bulb over his head that was hanging from a cord spotted with dead flies. After admiring the bulb wrapped in scarlet crepe paper and the wall stained with drops of water, behind the door he saw a colored picture of Ramon Novarro,
from which he quickly withdrew his eyes, because one day—
oh, what nausea came back to him from that day—he had
wanted to be Ramon Novarro, while out in the hallway the
echoes of the mourners came in. Unable to hear them as they
chatted among themselves, he could make out voices only
when they raised them to the loudest pitch of their monotonous litany: "Come here, love . . . , come here, come here,
sweets . . . , come here, sweetie . . . , you there, hey, cross-
eyes, come here . . . , pretty boy, come here . . ."

The room had no window and he suddenly felt distressed.
"It's not a room," he began to repeat, "it's the alcove of my
perdition." He moaned impatiently at the old woman's delay.

If she took too long or didn't come back he was afraid of what might happen. He was already thinking of starting an Our Father or Hail Mary when she came in, disdainful of his nakedness and beauty, which Ramon Novarro himself would have envied.

"Would you pay me, please, sweet?"

She closed the door with just the knob, impassive beside the bed, and, even though it was a request in the ritual of passion, she did not even extend her fingers. Without arguing about the price, he got up and took the largest bill he had from his pants pocket:

"Keep the change, my love."

She smiled for the first time and everything about her became a first time: she held the money and her glasses in her hand while she pulled the dress over her head, mussing the gray hair on her head and around her temples.

"Do you want me to take it off?"

After laying the dress at the foot of the bed, she pointed to the cotton brassière with canvas straps under which the boy could imagine her heavy, wilted breasts, perhaps with hairs on the dark nipples, and he said no, whereupon she folded the money in her hand three times and put it into her brassière. Still standing she opened her flabby white jellyfish arms to him and he caught the first sign of seduction: her shaved armpit, and he thought—"underneath the old woman sleeps the courtesan—" who, with some effort, kneeled on the bed and flung over her shoulder two or three small medals that she wore around her neck. She just put them there, she didn't fling them, because a verb like that implies some kind of quick action and the old woman was clumsy and carried in her movements the lethargy acquired in the wicker chair, and while that was going on, the boy slowly ran his fingers over her smooth back like someone stroking a pet animal, until he finds a lump or wrinkle and then starts to trace slow circles which leave and always return to that hard nodule, and he began to swallow noisily. His hands, sticky with sweat, brutally clutched the neck of the old woman, who had short hair, and drawing her to him, he sensed her reluctance as she still resisted his fierce desire. Turning her head slightly toward the table where there was a roll of paper, she tried to reach out her hand, but the boy stopped her, and, with his eyes closed now, he slowly brought her head close to his amidst useless protests of "*Non* . . ., *non* . . . Not on the mouth, *non* . . .*,*" finally kissing her, and even in the kiss the old woman resisted, keeping her cold and wrinkled lips sealed, her false teeth held tight against the roof of her mouth by the tip of her tongue.

The lady was smoothing out the creases in her shroud when he opened his eyes in agony, for love had not drained his disgust for himself. When he got up from the bed, the quilt ran with the sweat of his back, and, triply filthy, he decided not to wash in order to keep the smell of the old woman's musty flesh on his sticky hands, but she, with all the fever of lust, did not show a single drop of sweat on her face. Neither of them bothered combing, and with the tips of her fingers, one adorned with a false ruby ring, smoothing the disheveled white hair that hung down her neck, she told him:

"Wipe the lipstick off."

The boy would not accept the tissue and wiped his mouth with his handkerchief:

"What a happy souvenir!"

They stood by the door and she faced him for the first time:

"You'll come back, *non?*"

"What's your name?"

"Ask for Sofia."

He was unable to open the door—the yellow tin ball slipped through his fingers.

"I know how to work it, love."

She opened the door and this time the young man went first. At the beginning of the sunny hallway the women were in the same place and the mulatto was sucking on an orange and spitting out the seeds, which could well have been those of envy, and she grunted at the pair: "Me, huh? Me, huh?" As he said good-by to his beloved he kissed her old, frozen hand. He went down the stairs, crossed the street, and, blinking at the sun, he waited on the corner. The house had only one window and he waited for the hand with the false ruby to appear between the green slats of the Venetian blind, and only the hand, for she was ashamed of him or because of him. "Now I can go home," the young man thought, "and embrace my wife and kiss my children. I feel all right now."

He mingled with the people, who, sometimes stopping in front of the doors, sometimes with their heads lifted to the windows, worshiped the images in their niches, indifferent, one might say, to the men's affliction had it not been for the gesture of hope with which all the women swung their right hands, joining the thumb and forefinger together as the symbol of lost innocence, until the boy in white linen left them behind as two botflies buzzed about his head and he said again: "It's all gone now, it wasn't anything. It really wasn't anything. It's all gone now. I feel all right now."

THE FIANCÉ

❧ WHEN SHE PUT OUT THE LIGHTS in the house, the mother left the hall lamp on. She went to bed but didn't go to sleep, waiting. The destiny of a woman is to wait for her husband to return home and, after her husband, her sons. They came in one by one and lay down on their beds. The last was Osvaldo, the one most like his father, fat, almost bald, absent-minded. He had the crumpled look of someone who had slept with his clothes on, his necktie hanging loose from his collar.

"Son," Dona Maria complained, "a person who saw you would think you didn't have a mother!"

Osvaldo smiled without answering. He was missing two front teeth and he covered his mouth with his hand when he smiled.

"You should get those teeth replaced, son. Why don't you wear your new tie?"

It was always the same necktie.

"You've got to talk to Osvaldo." Dona Maria appealed to her husband.

"One of these days I'm going to tell him a thing or two!"

The son baffled him, he wasn't like the others. He never answered back; how could he, they spoke so little to each other. Days later:

"The boy's got no ambition. You talk to him. Osvaldo could make something of himself!"

He sat across from his father at the table. The others conversed; he ate, his head lowered.

He'd come in from the street with his clothes dirty and torn. To Dona Maria's concerned questions he explained that it was nothing, they all knew how nearsighted he was. Later on she found out that he'd been run over by a bicycle and she insisted on calling the doctor to make sure no bones had been broken. His answer was a toothless smile. The mother was convinced that he'd been mixed up in a brawl.

On Sundays the grandchildren filled Dona Maria's home with shouts. The only one who maintained his calm was Osvaldo. He let his nieces and nephews sit on his lap, but he didn't kiss them. Could he have the male sickness? And if his mother were to die, what would become of him? He ate what they put in front of him—had anyone ever found out what his favorite piece of chicken was? His life was a secret from the family.

The old man followed him to the bar. The time he spent there observing his son the latter didn't look at him, and, in the father's opinion, didn't even see him. The waiter brought the bottle, filled Osvaldo's glass, without a word passing between them. He kept his hand in his pocket, sometimes looking at the glass, sometimes at a certain spot on the wall, sometimes simply at the wall. He wasn't aware of the presence of anyone else. Always alone at the back table, he didn't even seem sad.

Dona Maria was waiting to hear her son lift the latch.

The only sound in the house aside from her husband's snoring was that of the birds pecking at their seed. When he came in, Osvaldo would give them hemp and canary-grass seed and change their drinking water.

How many nights had it been that the boy began turning out the lamp in the hall as soon as he opened the door? The mother left it on precisely so that he could find his room. Why did he put it out, then, feeling his way along the dark hallway and knocking the hats off the rack? Perhaps, who knows, he turned out the lamp so as not to see himself in the living-room mirror. But her son, in Dona Maria's opinion, was still a good-looking boy. Could Glorinha have broken off the engagement because he was ugly?

He would finally find his door, fling himself onto the bed with his clothes and shoes on, and smoke one cigarette after another. He would fall asleep, forgetting about the cigarette in his hand . . . He set fire to the sheets and the mattress. With all the cigarette holes in his pajamas, good God in heaven, what his chest must have been like! He hid the hand blackened with burns in his pocket. His mother crossed herself—he could have burned the house down. Osvaldo smoked without opening the window and slept enveloped in the smoke.

In the morning he would cough and sometimes spit blood. Dona Maria brought him coffee in bed, which he gulped down, scorching his tongue, in order to light his first cigarette with a trembling hand.

"My poor son!"

A smile was the answer she got. The old woman preferred not to inquire as to why he put out the hall lamp.

It was on now. Osvaldo hadn't come in. As on every night, the mother was thinking about his engagement. He'd brought the girl around for Dona Maria to meet, she hadn't even known that her son had a girl friend. An ugly girl, a little pale, extremely thin. Osvaldo was a romantic and so the mother liked Glorinha.

The Fiancé

On the following day a truck came to deliver a chest, a table, and four chairs. Osvaldo was buying furniture, the mother was quick to label some shirts and to sew six new pairs of shorts.

Four years later Glorinha and her mother clapped their hands in the hallway. The girl was right at home, she came in without ceremony. It was the other one who clapped her hands, and mother Gracinda was all dressed in black.

"Come in, child. Why don't you have lunch with us on Sunday? Please sit down, Dona Gracinda. How are you feeling?"

Dona Gracinda answered fine, thank you. The matter that brought her to Dona Maria's house had to do with Glorinha's happiness.

"What happened, Dona Gracinda? You've got me all upset!"

According to the other one there was no need for words. Osvaldo hadn't set a date. Glorinha didn't want to die an old maid. Because of him she'd already lost the four best years of her life.

"Mama!" the girl interrupted. "Mama, please!"

Leaving her hat on, the lady raised the black veil from her eyes.

"Osvaldo doesn't talk to me, Dona Maria. He doesn't like me anymore!"

"Your son, Dona Maria, do you know what he is?"

Glorinha begged her mother, for the love of God, to let her explain. During the early days she didn't find Osvaldo's silence strange. She told him her whole life story since childhood, what she did day by day. Osvaldo might be timid; she brought him a cordial which he accepted without a word. Sometimes the girl would leave him in the living room cleaning his nails with a toothpick and go talk to her mother in the kitchen. He didn't argue with Glorinha, he didn't even seem to notice that she'd gone out—he was capable of doing his courting alone in the living room. He would ask Dona

Gracinda, who brought him coffee: "Good evening, ma'am. How are you?" Then he would light his cigarette and the women had to talk to each other.

"My child, the things you're telling me!"

The girl confessed that during the first two years Osvaldo would take off his glasses in the living room, and he was better looking. Glorinha knew that he liked her. By the third year he no longer took them off . . .

"Show more respect, Glorinha!" Dona Gracinda cut her off.

A suspended tear in the girl's red eyes.

"Mama, please!"

Then Glorinha said that her mother wanted to break off the engagement. It was clear that Osvaldo hadn't talked about setting a date.

"My child, what are you telling me? What about him, Glorinha? What does he say?"

"Nothing, Dona Maria. He never misses a single date."

Osvaldo came out of his room at that moment. He ate lunch before his parents did, going to the office at noon. Dona Gracinda asked to speak to him.

"Come here, son. I've just heard something very sad."

He smiled, covering his mouth with his hand. He sat down in the chair beside Glorinha. The mother began to have her doubts about the other women. The boy listened with surprise to the woman speaking—each one spoke in turn—she became upset and averted her eyes.

"My son, don't you want to marry Glorinha?" Dona Maria finally asked.

He said yes, he did. He was Glorinha's fiancé. Of course he did.

"Why don't you set a wedding date?" Dona Gracinda put in. "Why, it's been four years!"

"I've already bought our furniture, Dona Gracinda. You saw the furniture, didn't you?"

The Fiancé

Dona Gracinda lowered the veil over her stern face. She gave her arm to her daughter. Osvaldo tried to speak, the clock struck, and he asked to be excused. It was time to go to work and he had to have lunch. The girl gave him back his ring, which she had carried, not worn on her finger. When she started to speak she burst into tears. Dona Gracinda opened her daughter's purse, took out a small package wrapped in blue crepe paper, and put it on the table:

"Here are your gifts!"

He left them in the company of his mother, ate with his usual appetite, and when he returned to the living room the two were gone.

Glorinha could have been a good girl, his mother thought, looking at the key in the door. Maybe she wasn't the fiancée for Osvaldo. The family noticed no difference in his behavior. Every night he got home later and later . . . still, his father had led the same kind of life.

Then a really strange thing happened: the birds were found dead one morning. Osvaldo had trapped them when he was a child: a finch, a goldfinch, a wild canary, so old that their claws curled around the roost. He fed them himself at dawn, filling the feeder with birdseed and changing the water in the dish. He followed such strange paths that he would bring them a small lettuce leaf . . . They would chirp when the cloth was lifted off their cage, dazzled by the light.

From her room Dona Maria could hear them pecking at their seeds. Once she sat down on the bed with a premonition of disaster. She didn't know what it was. Suddenly she remembered: the birds. Not a sound came from the cages. She found them dead, their small heads in the empty feeders —good Lord, how could her son have forgotten? It was when he began to turn out the light in the hall.

The mother heard the clock strike two, three, four o'clock, and finally Osvaldo's steps in the street. They were

the same steps as his father's. He opened the door, then he
turned out the light. Then, groping in the dark, he knocked
a hat off the rack. Dona Maria only wished he would go to
sleep: the noise of a match, another one, still another . . .
On the finger yellow with nicotine he kept his faithful
fiancé's ring.

The husband was home, the prodigal son had just retired. Dona Maria could sleep. Oh, if she only knew . . .
Turning out the light, Osvaldo didn't come in alone. When
he returned from the last bar—how many nights had it
been?—he ran into Glorinha by the door: dressed as a bride,
a black lace veil over her head.

"I'm going in with you, my love," she said.

Before he could find his key, he saw her slip in *through*
the closed door.

In the lighted hallway the girl had disappeared. Then
he turned out the light: there she was again in his room.

"Don't leave me, Glorinha!"

He lay down with his clothes and shoes on. Sitting at
the foot of the bed, Glorinha told him about all the banal
events of the day. The fiancé was listening, a cigarette in his
mouth and his eyes far off.

Dona Maria doesn't hear the girl's voice there in the
other room and she goes to sleep, because mothers are not
given to understand their children, only to love them.

SOUP

⚕ HE WENT SLOWLY up the stairs, dragging his feet on the steps. He paused to breathe, only once, in the middle of the thirty steps: he was still a man. He went into the kitchen and, without looking at his wife, without washing his hands, he sat down at the table. She filled the plate with soup and placed it in front of her husband.

Eyes red from sleep, the son came out of his room and crossed the kitchen. The man blinked, intoxicated with the heady vapors.

"Where are you going?"

The son turned on the bathroom faucet:

"To shave."

"It's dinner time. Come eat."

The boy took his time, the faucet was turned off. He came out with a towel around his neck, not looking at his father.

"I don't want to eat. I'm not hungry."

The man halted his spoon:

"You may not want to eat, but come to the table."

As on every night, he was famished. He filled his spoon, breathed in the smell of the bean soup, and, pursing his thick lips, swallowed it with pleasure. The son drew on the flower-print tablecloth with his fork. The wife, that one there, was looking at the stove, her hand on her chin.

"I was going out."

The man sucked in the spoonful noisily and with every slurp the son turned his fork in the heart of a daisy.

"You just got out of bed, Your Highness! But me . . . when I lie down in the daytime it'll be to die!"

The son's hand dropped the fork and didn't move.

"You'll be home early, right?"

The mother's tired voice, her back still to the table. Didn't she know that when she defended him she was ruining her son's cause? The man emptied his plate and, laying down his spoon, examined his wrinkled hands.

"These hands," they shook with a slight tremor, "are those of an old man!"

The woman came to get the plate, she filled it to the brim with steaming soup. The husband twirled the damp points of his mustache and started eating again.

"Aren't you eating?"

The son twisted the petals on the cloth with his fork.

"I don't feel like it."

"After dinner you can go back to your room, sir."

He smelled the spoon and sucked in the soup, clicking his tongue. The son got up from the table.

"You stay in your seat until dinner's over, sir. Isn't there any bread in this house?"

The wife brought the bread. He didn't cut it: he took the whole loaf in his hand and bit it several times; then he broke it into pieces, which he lined up in front of his plate, attacking them one by one between spoonfuls.

Soup

"You'll be home early, won't you, son?"

It was the mother again; she'd never learn.

"I'm not going out. I'd rather stay in my room."

The father had the last word:

"It's a disgrace! The head of the house has to have dinner all alone. His son's a lazy bum . . . even when it comes to eating. His wife," he turned around, making the silverware tinkle, "has a weak stomach."

She didn't move, bending over the stove.

"Look at me when I talk to you!"

She turned around, wiping her hands on her skirt.

"After she got old, this one here turns finicky on me. She can't even eat with her own husband anymore, the one who supports her son and gives her money, right?"

"You know why I don't sit down with you."

"No, I don't, Princess. Please tell me."

The son looked at her with astonishment, she'd never gone against her husband's orders. His spoon in the air, the husband asked:

"Did you lose your nerve, then—you're not saying anything?"

The wife turned her back on him again.

"You make me sick to my stomach."

He began to blow on the spoon and he stained the tablecloth with the spray.

"What? What did you say? Repeat that, woman."

The lady opened the stove and while she spoke she stirred the coals, filled it with wood.

"I don't expect anything out of life. But I can't watch you eat. I know it's sad for a wife to get sick to her stomach because of her husband. You suck on the spoon as if it was your last bowl of soup and you eat the bread as if I was going to steal it from you. I don't know what I ever did to God for Him to give me this terrible punishment. I've been a good wife, even though you make me sick. I wash your clothes, I sleep in your bed, I cook your soup. I'll do that until the day I die. You can ask me for whatever you want. But not for me to sit down at that table while you have your black soup."

The son left the kitchen and went down the stairs. The two of them heard the street door slam. The husband faced his wife for the first time. He lowered his eyes, there was still food in his plate—strands of fat floated in the cold soup. Lifting the plate by one side, he finished the rest of the soup and licked the spoon.

PENELOPE

MANY YEARS AGO an old couple lived on that street. The woman would wait on the veranda for her husband, doing needlework in her rocker. When he got to the gate, she was on her feet, the needles crossed in the basket. He would go through the small garden and on the doorstep, before going in, he would kiss her with his eyes closed.

They were always together, working in the garden, he among the cabbages, she in the mallow patch. Through the open kitchen door the neighbors could see the old man drying the dishes for his old lady. On Saturdays they went walking, she, stout, blue-eyed, and he, thin, dressed in black. In summer the woman wore a white dress that was out of style; he, still in black. There was a mystery in their life; it was vaguely known that years before their children had been killed in a disaster. The old people had left their house, graves, and animals and had moved to Curitiba.

Only the two of them, no dog, no cat, no birds. Sometimes, when her husband was out, she would bring some bones out for the stray dogs that sniffed at the gate. She fattened a chicken, then she got softhearted, unable to kill it. Then the man took down the chicken house and planted a fierce cactus in its place. He pulled up the only rose bush that was growing in a corner of the garden. They didn't even dare give the love they had left to a rose.

When it wasn't Saturday, they didn't leave the house, the old man smoking his pipe, the old woman working with her needles. Until the day when, opening the door on the way back from their walk, they found a letter at their feet. No one ever wrote to them, not a relative or a friend in the world. It was a blue envelope without any address. The woman suggested that they burn it without reading it; they'd already suffered too much. He answered that no one in the world could do them any harm.

He didn't burn the letter, he didn't open it, he left it forgotten on the table. They sat down under the lampshade in the parlor, she with her knitting, he with the newspaper. The lady would lower her head, bite a needle, counting the stitches with the other one, and, her eyes far off, she would count the same row again. The man, with the paper folded on his knees, read every sentence twice in order to understand it. His pipe went out, but he didn't light it, listening to the dry click of the needles. Finally he opened the letter. Two words: "Tame cuckold" in letters cut out of a newspaper. Nothing else, no date or signature. He handed the piece of paper to his wife, who, after reading it, looked at him. Neither of them spoke. She stood up with the letter between her fingertips.

"What are you going to do?" the man asked.

"Burn it . . ."

He said no. He put the note back in the envelope and put it in his pocket. He picked up the scarf that had dropped to the floor for his wife and went back to reading the newspaper.

The woman put the yarn and needles in the basket.

"Don't pay any attention to it, old girl. A letter was dropped off at every house."

Do siren voices even reach the hearts of old people? The man forgot about the piece of paper in his pocket; another week passed. On Saturday, before opening the door, he knew that the letter was waiting. The woman stepped on it, pretending that she didn't see it. He picked it up and put it in his pocket.

With her shoulders bent over her work, still counting the same row, she asked:

"Aren't you going to read it?"

He peeped at her over his paper, admiring the beloved head without a white hair, the eyes which, in spite of the years, were as blue as on the first day.

"I know what it says already."

"Why don't you burn it?"

He explained that it was a game and showed her the letter: no address. He opened it and read two words in letters that had been cut out. He blew into the envelope, shook it over the carpet, nothing else. He put it away with the other one and, as he folded the newspaper, he noticed that his lady friend was undoing a mistaken stitch in the scarf.

He woke up in the middle of the night, jumped out of bed, and went to look out the window. He drew back the curtain and in the shadow of the wall he could make out the shape of a man. He remained there, his hand clutching the curtain until the other went away.

On the following Saturday, during the walk, he wondered if he was the only one receiving the letter. It could have been a mistake, there wasn't any address. If only there'd been a name, a date, a place. He pushed open the door, there it was: blue. He put it in his pocket with the others and opened the newspaper. When he turned the pages he caught the face of his lady friend hunched over the needles. A difficult scarf, she'd been working on it for months. He remembered the legend of Penelope, who undid at night by the light of a torch the rows she had finished during the day and in that way gained time from her suitors, waiting for her husband. He stopped in the middle of the story: what if Penelope had been unfaithful to her absent husband? For whom was the shroud she was sewing meant? Had her needles continued to click after the return of Odysseus?

In the bathroom he locked the door and opened the envelope. The two words . . . He thought of a plan: he put the letter away and inside of it a piece of hair from his head. He hung his jacket on the rack, the envelope visible in one of the pockets. While his wife was putting the milk bottle out by the door, he went to bed. In the morning he examined the envelope: it looked intact, in the same place. He examined it carefully, looking for the white hair—he couldn't find it.

From the street he spied on his wife's movements inside the house. She came to meet him at the gate—the reflection of the other man's blue necktie in her eyes. Ah, to lift up the hair from the back of her neck and see if there were any teeth marks . . . In her absence he opened the clothes closet, buried his head among the dresses, and smelled them. Behind the curtain he spied on the men who went past on the sidewalk. He knew the milkman and the bakery man, young fellows with false smiles.

He retraced his wife's actions: whether there was dust on the furniture, whether the dirt in the violet pots was damp or dry . . . He measured time by the scarf. He knew how many rows his wife knitted and when, making a mistake, she had to undo them, even before counting them with the tip of the needle.

He had no proof against her, he never revealed the end

of Penelope's tale to her. While he read he watched the face in the shadow of the lampshade. When he heard steps on the street, standing on tiptoes, he would spy at the window: the curtain became wrinkled at the corner from his wrathful hand.

Finally he bought a weapon. "Why the revolver?" His companion was frightened. He mentioned the number of thieves in the city. He demanded a count of old presents. Could she be making scarves for her lover to sell? In the early evening, the newspaper open on his lap, he spied on his wife—her face, her dress—looking for some sign of the other man: she missed a stitch, had to undo the row.

The wife was waiting for him on the veranda. He didn't come in and he passed in front of the house as if he didn't know her. When he returned, after closing the door, he sniffed the smells in the air, ran his fingers over the furniture, poked the earth around the violets—he knew where his wife was.

Early in the morning he woke up and saw the empty pillow, still warm from the other head. Under the door a light in the living room. She was doing her knitting, still the scarf. Was she Penelope, undoing the work of another day at night?

Lifting her eyes, the woman saw the revolver. The needles struck against each other without any yarn. He never knew why he spared her. As soon as they lay down, he fell into a deep sleep.

There was a cousin in her past . . . The wife swore in vain that the cousin had died of typhoid fever at the age of twelve. In the early evening he took the letters out of his pocket several times—there were a lot of them, one every Saturday—and he read them one by one, mumbling.

He wouldn't stay home on Saturday in order to identify the author. He felt the need of that note. It was the correspondence between the cousin and him, the tame cuckold; a game where he would be the winner in the end. One day the other man would reveal everything, it was necessary not to interrupt it.

At the gate he gave his arm to his companion, they didn't speak to each other during the walk, not stopping at the shop windows. On their return, he picked up the envelope and, before opening it, went into the house with it. He immediately hid a hair in the fold and left it on the table.

He always found the hair, his wife no longer spelled out the two words. Or—he remembered with a new wrinkle on his forehead—had she discovered the art of reading without springing the trap?

One afternoon he opened the door and breathed in the air, as he always did before entering. He slid his fingers over the furniture: dust. He poked the earth in the pots: dry. He went right to the bedroom with closed windows and turned on the light. The old woman was lying there on the bed, the revolver in her hand, her white dress covered with blood. He left her with her eyes open.

He felt no pity, it had been just. The police let him go, he hadn't been home at the time his wife had killed herself. When the funeral procession left, the neighbors commented that his grief must have been very deep because he didn't weep. Holding a handle of the coffin, he helped lower it into the grave; before the gravedigger finished covering it up, he left.

He went into the living room and saw the scarf on the table—the knitted scarf. Penelope had finished her work, it was her own shroud that she had been knitting—her husband had come home.

He lighted the lamp with the green shade. On the easy chair, the needles were crossed in the basket. It was Saturday, he remembered. No person at all could do him any harm from then on. The woman had paid for her crime. He thought then that she might be innocent. The same letter pushed under other doors . . . Or by mistake in his case, with identical houses.

There was a way to find out, he could grow old in peace. If they were meant for him, they wouldn't come with his wife dead, never again. That was the last one—the other man had trembled when he found the house with the doors and windows open. He must have seen the hearse at the gate. Perhaps, who knows, he went to the funeral. He was one of those who jostled him as the coffin was being lowered into the grave—a little water in the bottom.

He left the house as on every Saturday. He walked with his arm bent, a habit from having given it to his lady friend for so many years. In front of the shop window with dresses, some white, he felt the weight of her hand. He smiled with disdain at her vanity, even when dead . . . Yes, that letter had been the last one. No other would ever come.

He went up the two steps to the veranda—"I was just," he repeated, "I was just"—and with a firm hand he turned the key. He opened the door, stepped on the letter, and, sitting in the easy chair, he began to read the newspaper aloud so as to cover up the silence of the house.

⚑ DEATH
ON THE SQUARE

DEATH
ON THE SQUARE

THE TOWN WAS PROUD of its square, with a church, a hospital, a pharmacy, a dry-goods store, a photographer, two taxis, and, in the middle of the rose beds, the bust of the hero. There were old houses with fluted tiles, their street doors opening into dark hallways where at night a bulb flickered under a colored silk shade. Next to the church, brightening a patch of the square, the two illuminated doors of the Santo Expedito pharmacy lingered.

Jonas had prospected for diamonds, had been a professional gambler, and it was known that he had stood trial for a man's death. He had finally returned to our town with that woman. Her gentleman friend had mistreated her and abandoned her. Jonas found her dancing in a cabaret; they got married and had three children. The old druggist died and Jonas bought the pharmacy from his widow.

In the small room in back, with a window on the alley,

he set up his laboratory, where he filled prescriptions, gave injections, and even invented a wax for toothaches. And he would saw rings off the swollen fingers of pregnant women who could not loosen them. Poor people preferred him to the doctor: he got rid of worms in children, conjured away warts, and settlers came to have him put a curse on the vermin in horses and cows. He would mumble his prayers and stroke the sign of the cross on the sick animal with a piece of kindling wood—the worms fell off like the ripe fruit of a jaboticaba tree.

Anita sometimes helped out behind the counter or, with her head bent under the glass chandelier in the parlor, she pedaled furiously on the sewing machine—a piece of adhesive tape covering a varicose ulcer on her leg. When the machine was silent, with the slightest breath of a breeze, Jonas would hear from the counter the murmur of the blue prisms over Anita's head.

He spent his nights at the club, gambling and drinking. He lost his savings at poker and was obliged to sign notes. Jonas noticed that the court clerk would wait until he bought a few chips to allege to have some urgent document to be signed and get up from the table. He remembered that his wife had taken the bandage off her leg. One night he bought a pile of chips, saw Ernesto leave, and with the excuse of having a prescription to fill, he followed him to the pharmacy. He saw the light in the hallway go on and off: the clerk went in. Five minutes later Jonas followed him. He opened the door and found his wife in her bathrobe, wearing lipstick. Ernesto must have heard his footsteps in the hallway and had disappeared.

The following day the woman went to the photographer. Jonas made a hole in the outside wall of the bedroom which he plugged with one of Dr. Ross's Life Pills. In the afternoon he told Anita that he had been called away to cure a sick animal and he said not to expect him back before midnight. He tied his horse to a tree and came back through the alley, hiding in the backyard. He pulled out the Life Pill and peeped into the dark room. After an hour he saw the light in the hallway go on and off. Jonas kept his eye to the hole and the pill in his hand until he swallowed it: the light in the bedroom went on. His wife came in with Ernesto following. The clerk took off his jacket. Jonas ran to get two neighbors to witness the flagrant scene. They came, barefoot and with wraps on, and looked through the hole in the wall, one after the other.

"I'll kill them," Jonas roared in a low voice, a revolver in his hand. "I don't know why I don't kill them." The neighbors communicated with signs so as not to frighten the lovers. Jonas burst into the house roaring, with the witnesses behind. In the confusion, Ernesto fled through the window, leaving his watch on the night table; it was a keepsake, with a lid that opened and the picture of his wife inside. Jonas turned on all the lights in the house. The children came down from upstairs in tears. While his wife packed her bag, he went to the window and fired two shots into the air. Anita left for the state capital on the morning train.

Jonas shut himself up in the house with his children. The youngest, a boy of three, was burning up with fever because he missed his mother. Forgotten on the line in the backyard were two shirts and a piece of woman's clothing. He did not take them in; the sleeves twisted furiously in the wind, dark with dust, until the rain knocked them down and they were dragged under the feet of the chickens.

Gossips whispered that Jonas's plan was to distribute the children among relatives and, with the pharmacy on the brink of failure, disappear into the world. And then, three days later, Anita arrived in town with one of Jonas's aunts. The woman waited in the square, sitting on her suitcase, while the aunt conferred with Jonas, asking him to take her back for the sake of the children. Anita went in and the aunt

left on the afternoon train. For six months the town saw
nothing of the woman.

The curious went to buy aspirin, cotton, combs: only he
behind the counter, the parlor deserted, the house silent, not
even the crying of children. Seeing all the windows closed,
the town wondered how those people breathed.

The oldest daughter did the shopping. The supposition
was that Jonas was slowly poisoning his wife. Black Agenor,
the watchman on the small square, swore that he had seen
her at the upstairs window for a moment. A circus came to
town. Jonas appeared every night with his children and some
people pointed out his love for them. Others noted that they
had their hair combed and were well dressed—Anita's touch.

The clerk changed his route from home to the court,
going around the block to avoid the pharmacy. The town
quivered in anticipation of the day the two of them would
come face to face. "Look," one person said, "there's Ernesto
going down the other street." Or perhaps: "He keeps looking
at the drugstore window." Anita, it was imagined, was cloist-
ered upstairs, never coming down. The pharmacy was a deso-
lation, shelves empty and dusty—of the old stock, only some
São João cough syrup was left.

The Turk in the dry-goods store found two hearts in the
chest of a kid he butchered. Jonas went to get them to put
in a bottle on the drugstore counter. The town saw in the
two hearts, shriveled in fear against the background of the
crimson jar, those of the woman and her lover.

Through the small lighted laboratory window, people
passing in the alley saw Jonas examining a piece of paper in
his trembling hands. One of us with sharp eyes claimed that
it was a blank piece of paper: his farewell note, which he did
not have the courage to write. In the afternoon he would
catch frogs in the marsh and put them in the cistern for
washing clothes. Some hinted that he tortured the creatures,
experimenting with ways to do away with the woman. The

frogs grew silently fat and, according to black Agenor, as soon as they heard Jonas's footsteps in the backyard they would jump into the farthest corner and croak, their jowls quivering with fright.

At night the sea wind would howl, foretelling misfortune; it challenged the spider webs, lifted women's skirts, and bats, coming down from the church steeple, swooped over the square—their squeaks echoed in the hallways and mothers covered their children's throats. Heading toward the corner of the alley went the druggist and the clerk. Jonas opened his walleye wide. Ernesto, slightly lame, was limping more on his left leg, running away from the encounter.

In the summertime the inhabitants would sit in wicker chairs on the sidewalk. The fat women fanned themselves and the old men picked at the eczema on their feet, which had thick blue veins. Such was the calm that the judge's wife, embroidering a handkerchief in her parlor, lifted her head, bothered by the sounds in the house: in the aquarium the little red fish were opening and closing their mouths. Jonas could be seen in front of the pharmacy, his thumbs hooked around his suspenders; he refused to go and bless an infected wart or sell his famous wax, indifferent to the fact that a new pharmacy had taken away his customers. He had not refilled his stock of medicines and yet he would open up every morning. He took the clerk's watch out of his pocket and stood there admiring the picture of Ernesto's wife. At night he no longer turned on the lights in the pharmacy.

On one afternoon that was motionless with heat, he invaded the records office, dagger in hand. Ernesto had fled with his family, abandoning house and canaries. Jonas spilled over the drinking cups in the cages. Days later the birds were found dead: they had flung themselves against the wire and the strands were covered with yellow feathers. His vengeance turned against the town. One night black Agenor found all the rosebushes in the square cut down. Dogs were found dead in the morning, killed by poisoned bits of meat; there was arsenic in it, which made them convulse without a howl. They found a bat with his wings nailed to the church door and a cigarette in his mouth.

If he was capable of such great hatred against the birds and the dogs and the house of God itself, what would he not do to his wife? That was when he showed her off at the carnival dance: dressed in black satin, lipstick on her mouth. Jonas had let his mustache grow and was losing his hair. He passed among us, two drops of sweat on the tip of his long nose, his wife on his arm. They did not join any of the groups of revelers, but danced an occasional number. Anita was drinking raspberry soda, talking to him in a low voice, but Jonas did not answer. They stayed until the end of the dance and, from time to time, as if there were an urgent prescription to fill, Jonas would take the watch out of his pocket, but he was not looking at the time, for the watch had stopped and he never wound it: he would open the lid and make love to the picture. Perverse people insisted at that time that he was poisoning her slowly: "Look how thin she is."

The next morning Jonas was found dead. Whether Anita had poisoned him or whether by mistake he had eaten the food with arsenic meant for her, no one knew. Anita wept, going along in the funeral procession in her black satin dress, and under the veil one could see thick lipstick on her mouth. That night the house, dark for six months, rose up lighting the corner of the square, attracting large beetles, which, when they fell, beat their black wing covers on the stones and lay on their backs waving their legs in the air. And, to the mortification of the town, the light in the hallway began to go off and on again. Didn't Anita know that the clerk had slipped out of town?

The following day she opened the pharmacy as Jonas had always done. No one had the courage to go in, to pick up a pacifier or a toothbrush. She sat behind the counter, her eyes golden in the half-light. Sometimes she would go as far as the door and look at the square: a fat gray rat was crossing the street, running from the church to the hospital. Only a half-breed came in to ask for a glass of water.

On Saturdays people from the interior who came to get supplies would bring their children to see the soldier in front of the dry-goods store: he was made of brass, painted green, fastened to the pole on the corner. The women, colored kerchiefs on their heads, ate bread and raw sausage and gave their breasts to their babies without getting out of their wagons.

Jonas's relatives demanded the children. Anita turned them over without tears, alone in the house at last. The town was mystified as to how she kept alive. Every day there she was, sitting behind the counter. She never tired of looking at the square, smoking one cigarette after another, her eyes almost closed because of the sun or the smoke. Children sent out to buy bread would run past the door.

When the light in the window of the dry-goods store went on the town knew that someone had died: the carpenter was buying cloth, bands, straps, and fasteners (it was the custom in our town that when the coffin was sealed up in the church, the heir would keep the key tied with a purple ribbon). The hammer blows made the old rats who bounded about in the yellow dust stop, curious and with expectant tails.

On the other side of the square was the hospital. The patients went in the front entrance and came out the alley door—the plain board coffins wrapped in black cloth. They were brought in by wagon, dying, white cloths sometimes tied around their heads, sometimes around their necks. The relatives would get out to talk to the doctor and arrange for a room. The children playing in the square would hear the rattle of the dying man and climb onto the wagon, getting dirty from the wheels.

Before funeral processions came out into the square, the

sexton would come running, climb the spiral staircase of the church, and toll the death knell. As the dead man passed, the commercial establishments would close their doors. The men would take turns at the supports of the coffin: the cemetery was close by but the dead were heavy.

Anita left town. She went to the train in her bare feet, a lacquered shoe in each hand so as not to dirty them in the dust. It was said that she was going to look for the clerk. She came back the next day, opened the pharmacy, and went behind the counter. A traveling salesman came in to buy a comb, or drawn by the solitary woman. Even though he spoke to her the only reply was a laugh of blue glass prisms.

The postman would pass with his canvas bag on his arm, one shoulder lower than the other: the train had arrived. People came from far away to see it. It was pretty at twilight, a small train with a thousand lighted windows. At the station the hands of travelers reached out to grab the sugared twists that boys offered for sale in baskets held on their heads. Before he rang the gong the station agent would put his red cap on. The train disappeared in a cloud of sparks that in summer set the fields on fire, and the whistle was so sad that old women by their fires made the sign of the cross.

In late afternoon, lined up on watch on the tops of the pine trees were the small, bald, obscene heads of the vultures. Mothers came to the door to call their young ones who were playing soccer in the field or coming back from the station, silent and absent-eyed because they had seen the train. Anita heard the shouts of love and affliction, and was unable to call her own children.

The silence grew in the back of the alley under the old peach tree, which, with a small cross beside it, was the tree of the little angels—the fetuses buried among its roots. The fatal secret spread over the city and drove black Agenor mad. At night, forgotten by everyone, he would chat with the bronze soldier on the corner until—avoiding the light that went off and on in the hallway of the pharmacy—he would lie down to sleep underneath the hero's bust and, resting his head on the ground, he would listen to the grass grow.

THE WAKE

❧ Doralice lay in the middle of four lighted candles. Lifting the thin cambric handkerchief that hid the dead woman's face, Sinhô showed us the darkened nose and the yellowed teeth under the tightened lip:

"Her lamp went out . . ."

The coffin had been set up in the middle of the parlor, surrounded by chairs set against the walls. At the head, standing, an old woman in black was weeping, the dead one's sister. And in a corner, her chin nestled in her hand, Ivone.

"How are you, sweet?"

She raised her head and I recognized the black, almost glassy eyes.

"Doralice was my friend."

"The friend of all of us," I consoled her, but she drew back from my hand.

"Don't touch me. She's not cold in the coffin and you already want to touch me."

Whispering came from the kitchen, muffled laughter, and the husky voice of Mãezinha, who was asking: "Sinhô, tell us a sad story. Tell us one about her, Sinhô . . ." She pointed to the old woman busy keeping the flies away.

"Mãezinha shouldn't talk so loud."

"The old woman's deaf," Ivone explained.

I went to join the others, each holding a drink, toasting the fat lady who ran No. 111. The legend was that if a young fellow interested her, she would run her hand over her mouth and offer him a gold canine tooth between her thumb and forefinger. When she lifted her glass her bracelets tinkled:

"Damned piano player!"

She wiped away a tear and the mourners celebrated Mãezinha's good heart. She'd taken the girl out of the morgue and dressed her all in white.

Mãezinha went to say good-by to her dead girl, unable to get beyond the rim of the coffin with her melon breasts. Then she kissed the tips of her fingers and, lifting the handkerchief, she touched them to Doralice's forehead.

There in the parlor the old woman was still chasing the flies. Empty bottles were lined up on the kitchen table.

"Men . . . ," Ivone muttered when I returned. "Doing what Zeca did to her."

"What did he do, sweet?"

"You still ask? He threw her out, in the state she was in."

"I wouldn't have done that to my love."

"You're no good either. You think I don't know about your affair with Doralice?"

She began to weep—the sweet tears of alcohol. I rested her head on my shoulder. We were alone in the parlor, the two of us and the old woman, not counting Doralice. The night was endless, we were the living.

The ladies in fur coats and heavy make-up arrived, their skirts so narrow that they could only take steps as long as their shoes. The rancid perfume hung heavy in the parlor, stifling the smell of the dead woman and melted wax. There was a ruffle of emotion among the women—at three o'clock Zeca would be leaving his piano. Sometimes they looked toward the door, sometimes at Doralice. Ivone commented aloud:

"That's the way men are. She killed herself over love for him. He didn't have the courage to look at Doralice in her coffin!"

The women who circulated in the neighborhood came in many times during the night, carrying shoulder bags and smoking ceaselessly, like doctors visiting a patient with a contagious disease. And every time there was a silence, the whimper of the dog scratching at the doorsill could be heard.

"It's Luluzinho," Ivone said. "He already knows."

The old woman went to bring in the clothes from the yard and the little dog slipped into the parlor: small, white, and fuzzy. He began to bark, leaping about the coffin. And before anyone could grab him, he had jumped onto a chair and from there into the coffin, uncovering the face of the dead woman with his paws. They had delayed closing her eyes and they were half-open: I could still see that they were blue. Luluzinho was struggling in Ivone's arms.

"Look how the animal feels."

"He misses the dead woman."

Ivone put him out in the yard and came back to the parlor, blowing the hair off her dress. The old woman, chewing her gums, was smoothing out the dead woman's wrinkled clothing.

A stranger looked into the coffin and then at the door he protested aloud:

"It's not right. This isn't right!"

The indignant ladies moved in their chairs.

"What's not right? He has his nerve! A lack of respect. Shameful!"

"Her feet should be facing the door."

Sinhô and I hurried to move the coffin. When it was picked up quickly it tilted dangerously and Doralice leaned her head over on the crimson cushions.

"She moved . . ."

"They're drunk."

"It's a sacrilege!"

Finally we lined the coffin up to face the door. Sinhô tucked his shirt in his pants and excused himself:

"It's a big coffin."

We commented that it was mass-produced—a lack of consideration not being made to size. There was a parade of musicians, night watchmen, and waiters in bow ties. A crowd of pale people speaking in loud voices as if they knew that the old woman was deaf.

The dead woman and her sister stayed in the parlor. In the kitchen, in the midst of the whispering, a laugh would break out from time to time. After a while the kitchen was evacuated too—the bottles were empty. We were alone, Ivone, Sinhô, and I. He blew his purple snout:

"Good night, sweet prince. There's nothing left to drink."

"Wait for me outside, Sinhô. I'm leaving too."

Ivone opened the extinguished stove and took out a bottle.

"Stay, my love. I saved it for the two of us."

She filled the glasses and came to nestle in my arms.

"No, don't do that. It'll be the end of us. Everything in life's an illusion. Please, love. Don't you have any respect for Doralice? I want to die too. That way they could have just one burial. Oh, my love . . . Please, I'm all goose pimples."

She struggled on my knees and protested in a very low voice. We made no noise and the silence gave us away—the old woman appeared in the doorway. With a shout from Ivone, we separated. The woman looked at us fiercely, following the gestures of Ivone, who opened her purse and, propping her mirror against a glass, began to comb her hair, holding the bobby pins in her mouth. Finally the old woman turned her back on us.

"So she's deaf, eh?"

Then we went back to the parlor. When she looked at the dead woman's silver shoes, Ivone spread her arms:

"The flowers, my God! How come I didn't remember? The poor thing, not a single flower."

She picked up her purse from the chair and in front of the scandalized old woman gave me the money.

"Buy as many flowers as you can, love. Have them make a wreath too. With pretty words." And she smiled lovingly. "You're a poet."

At the first bar I found Sinhô in front of an empty glass, the waiter slouched next to him.

"What happened?"

"He didn't feel well," the waiter said.

Sinhô blindly waved his hand as if chasing flies away from Doralice's face.

The waiter brought the bottle. The flower shop was a long way off and what difference did a wreath make to a dead person?

THE WIDOW

THE OLD FORD bounced over the potholes in the street. I went through the town at dusk, past the flickering doors of the cheap saloons with their drunks at the bar. All by himself, an old man wearing a hat was smoking a long homemade cigarette.

"Can you tell me where Dona Abigail's house is?"

"I don't know."

"She's a widow with two children."

"Ah, Dona Biga. You go straight ahead, then turn left. You'll come to a crossroads. The widow's house is there on the right."

On the side of the road, pairs of glowing eyes lighted up. In the middle of the open countryside I came across someone on a bicycle. He pointed to the distance:

"You're a mile and a half from the crossroads."

That leprous hand in the headlight was a bad omen. At

seven o'clock I came to a crossroads. Furious barking arose from the house nearby. A shape appeared at the door and said that the crossroads was farther ahead.

Another crossroads and finally the silent house. I couldn't make out any light or sound. The widow—it had to be her—appeared on the veranda. She only recognized me when I got to the gate, coming out into the moonlight from the shadows of the orange trees. She disappeared and came back with a candle, cupping it with her hand to protect it from the wind.

"So, you finally got here, Doctor! I wish I'd known . . . I would have killed a chicken."

"Don't bother, Dona Biga. I'll eat whatever there is. What I am now is all tired out from the trip."

"Do you want to rest up a little?"

She led me to the living room, leaving the candle on the table. She pointed to the red leather sofa.

"Take a little rest. I'll be right back."

I dozed off, listening to the hooting of an owl. Suddenly the widow was there in the door.

"I didn't knock. You might have been asleep."

"I didn't sleep, but I had a good rest."

She took me to the bathroom. I held my hands out over the basin and she poured water from a jug. In the bathtub, the remains of foam around the strainer. On a shelf, glasses, three toothbrushes, a rusty razor blade. She'd taken a bath and changed her clothes: print blouse, black skirt, and high-heeled shoes.

I pushed aside the fringed curtain that opened into the dining area where the two boys were already sitting, neatly combed. She offered me the place at the head of the table and apologized for the poor meal.

"If I'd had some warning I would have prepared a better dinner."

"I don't stand on ceremony, Dona Biga."

The Widow

An old woman with a white spot in her eye brought in the plates. With the old woman a tabby cat slipped in, which mewed desperately, rubbing her tail against my leg. One of the children picked her up by the neck and put her back out in the yard, closing the door. A short time later there was the cat, walking around the table.

"She gets in through the broken window."

The old woman took the creature into the pantry. Immediately we heard the racket of a can and the scattering of grain on the floor. The cat was once more expelled from the house. She appeared again, greeted with laughter, and was finally left in peace.

The widow opened the cupboard and held up a jar of preserved peaches.

"Not for me, Dona Biga."

"You'll like them, Doctor. And the children are always asking me for them. They like them so much I had to hide the last jar."

After coffee, the invitation to enjoy myself with the family photographs. In the living room there was a picture of the deceased in an oval silver frame. The children came to the door, barefoot and in short pants—they wanted to see the album too.

"You can't, children. Mama has to look over some papers, isn't that right, Doctor?"

"We don't have much time. I have to leave early tomorrow."

She leafed through the yellowed pictures, almost all from her honeymoon. We went into the kitchen and I had a glass of water—the sausage had been quite salty. The old woman had disappeared along with the cat.

The widow opened one of the doors in the hallway:

"Tito—he's the younger one—doesn't like me to put on make-up. Afonso, the other one, is lazy, but very loving. I'm going to see if they're in bed."

She left me with the stump of a candle. I opened the window; the stars announced good weather. She came back after a little while, closing the door.

"I said I was going to get my glasses . . ." She showed me them in her hand. "We don't have to worry." Then, raising her eyes: "I thought you'd forgotten me."

"Is the door unlocked?"

"We don't have to lock it. It doesn't even have a key."

She went to the night table and put the candle down. She came over to me, wrapping her arms around my neck and kissing me on the mouth. I kept my eyes open—her nostrils quivered like the wings of a butterfly.

"Shall I put out the light?"

"No, love, it's fine like this."

She got out of her dress, her slip was pink.

"Do you know how to tongue-kiss?"

She nodded yes and lowered her eyes.

"Get undressed."

She let the straps fall and the slip rolled down around her waist. She was completely white, the hair under her arms was golden.

Afterward, I lighted a cigarette. She said that she dreamed about me many nights.

"You need somebody."

"I know I do. But I don't want any more old men. A young man who's free is hard to find. All I ever find are widowers loaded down with children."

She began to talk about her husband. At the age of twenty, a little schoolteacher, she'd fallen into the hairy hands of that lustful old man.

"Did I tell you that he had a leg missing?"

He was very jealous, even toward the end of his life, confined to a wheel chair. She would go to buy medicine in town or to see a doctor or a lawyer. When she got back there was that hell of: "Where did you go? Who did you talk to?

I know that the men look at you. And you don't mind at all, you bitch." He would calm down when they went to bed. She only discovered pleasure after the second child.

"I remember when you came into the office. All serious, your eyes lowered, your red astrakhan jacket. You only talked business, a saint made from hollow wood."

"You said it was a pity for a fine lady to be married to a useless old man. Oh, love. He was already in bad shape then."

If she deceived him—it was a husband's curse—he would come at night to tug at her. He changed his mind before dying. He gave her permission to remarry as long as she observed a year's mourning. It was no life living in that godforsaken place with no help in case of illness.

On one occasion Abigail had been operated on and he stayed by her side. She was fat and it took the surgeon a long time to find her appendix. Then the husband felt a slight pain in his left foot. Back home he found a black dot on his toe. Later on they amputated his foot and afterward the leg. He was in the wheel chair for a year and he finally died. Jealous, grouchy, he made love to her night after night. He almost drove her mad with pleasure. The old man wanted to do everything that came into his head because he was going to die. After that she'd never been able to forget what a man was like.

"And now—what's going to become of me now?"

One of the candles went out with a crackling sound. At that instant the cat began to mew under the window, the chirping in the bushes was suspended. It had been a year since she'd known what a man was like.

"Will you come back soon, love?"

"I'll come back, love. I already said I'd come back." I yawned a second time. "I have to leave very early."

She leaped out of bed and with the candle in her hand

picked up the scattered pieces of clothing. She put her hands between the sheets and found the article she was missing.

"I'm going to get the cat." And, closing the door, with the clothes on her arm: "Poor thing, she's just like me."

THE ELEPHANTS'
GRAVEYARD

THE ELEPHANTS'
GRAVEYARD

⁂ THERE IS A DRUNKARDS' GRAVEYARD in my city. Way at the back of the fish market and on the bank of the river there is an old inga tree—the drunkards are happy there. People think of them as sacred animals and provide them with their necessities of cane liquor and fish with manioc mush. For their regular diet they content themselves with leftovers from the market.

When their stomachs growl so much that it disturbs their napping, they leave their shelter and, dragging their heavy feet, fling themselves into the struggle for life. They sink up to their knees in the mangrove swamp hunting for crabs, or, lifting up their red trunks, they watch for a ripe inga to fall.

They know that they are condemned like badly wounded elephants, and they scratch their sores without complaint as they sprawl among the roots that serve as beds

83

and chairs, drinking and nibbling on some piece of fish. Each has his own place, and they politely warn each other:

"Don't use Pedro's root."

"He left, didn't you know?"

"He was here a while back . . ."

"That's right, he felt he was going to snuff out and he took off. I hollered: 'Go ahead, Pedro, and leave the door open.'"

The muddy surface of the swamp has bubbles on it—a lost giant's steps? João puts his fish wrapped in banana leaves onto the coals.

"Did Bellywhopper bring the worms?"

"Didn't you know?"

"Just now he . . ."

"He gave me the can and said: 'Jonas, try to catch some red weakfish.'"

A dying elephant arrives in port from other shores.

"Come join us, friend."

They give him a root of the inga tree, a mug of cane liquor, and a fish tail.

In the silence the buzzing of the mosquitoes shows where each one is posted. Sitting among the roots, they are in awe at the mystery of the night—the lighthouse as it blinks on the top of the bluff.

One of them amuses himself by sinking his finger into his swollen ankle; he gets up, and dragging his pachyderm feet, he goes off among farewells—spoken in a low voice so as not to disturb the dozers. The latter, when they awaken, don't have to ask where the missing person went. And if they asked, intending to bring him a bunch of daisies from the swamp, what could anyone tell them? Each person's path is revealed to him at the hour of death.

The afternoon breeze stirs up the botflies that stick to their deformed feet, and the leaves of the inga tree are flashing like silvery *lambari* fish—with the sound of falling fruit, the nearest drunkards laboriously get up and fight among themselves, rolling in the dust. The winner peels the inga and sucks the sweetish core with a greedy look. Blood never flows in the graveyard—the small knife at the waist is for scaling fish. And in brawls they are incapable of movement—it is sufficient for them to curse at rowdies from a distance.

And those who suffer from delirium, pestilence, the bitterness of gall upon their tongues, the muggy weather, the blood cramps, roar with obtuse hatred at the sparrows active up in the trees, who spit upon their heads before they sleep —the restless chirping is a poison to their drowsiness.

On the shore they watch the fishermen dipping their oars.

"Have you got a few fish, buddy?"

The fisherman throws them the fish he has discarded in the bottom of his boat.

"What makes you drink, Baitsucker?"

"A mother's curse, what the hell."

"Doesn't Chico want some fish?"

"Poor guy, he died of dropsy."

With the haste his swollen feet allow him, he takes leave of his companions dozing along the bank, forgetting to bait their hooks.

Spitting the black inga seeds out into the water, the others ask him no questions: the ivory tusks pointing the way are empty bottles. Chico disappears into the sacred graveyard among the skeletons of grotesque feet that rise up in the moonlight.

HOG-KILLING DAY

✤ AT THE AGE OF SEVENTY Onofre was an old man without morals. He spent almost every day drunk and after drinking he would settle down to beating his wife. Sometimes he would bring women to his place, where he would set himself up with them, disregarding his mate. The children were already married and the poor old woman was obliged to seek shelter in the neighborhood. Eventually she would get a message to come back and take care of him. And when she went back Onofre started drinking again and beat her without mercy.

A week before Sofia had fled to the home of one of her daughters to rest up a little from the beatings and at the same time to wait for him to calm down. The old man decided to butcher a hog and he sent word for her to come and take care of the animal. This time it was their daughter Natália who came.

"Where's your mother?"

"She's back at the house."

"You go tell her to come. If she doesn't come I'm going over there and I'll skin her alive."

When she got the message the lady thought it best to return. She found the door open and empty liquor bottles everywhere. She went to light a fire to render the pork fat.

"Ah, so it's you who've come. That's good, because today's your day. Today I'm going to put an end to your life."

Onofre grabbed the old woman, threw her to the floor, and covered her with kicks and punches.

"Next time learn to stay home and take care of your man."

The woman got one hand free and sank her nails into his face:

"I'll go where I want to and you won't tell me not to."

With great effort, Sofia reached the window, and when the old man stopped, tipping up the bottle to get his strength back, she climbed up on the sill and dropped out, rolling down the pile of kindling wood. Onofre staggered out:

"Did that bitch run away from me?"

Hiding under the wagon she heard him cursing and lashing left and right with his whip.

"You're pretty damned lucky. If you hadn't run off I would have put an end to your life today."

It was she, Sofia understood now, she was the hog the old man planned to butcher. While Onofre went to search in the barn, the woman went into the house and armed herself with the small-caliber shotgun loaded with bird shot.

"Ah, there you are."

"Look at what you've done to me, you bandit."

Onofre looked from a distance, half fearful. The woman was one big wound, all covered with blood.

"You're nothing but a scrap of meat. I don't need you anymore. I'll get me someone younger."

He sat on the bench in front of the house and drank from the bottle with his Adam's apple leaping in his thin neck. He threatened to leave the place after doing away with everybody. He pretended to doze off so that Sofia would get careless, but she held onto the shotgun.

With a great whoop Onofre ran after her, whipping her on the legs and enjoying the afflicted leaps of the old woman, who had teeth marks on her left ear.

"Is it true, old woman, that you had a child before you got married?"

"I'll never tell you. You won't know that until the day you die."

Their daughter Natália finally arrived, drawn by the shouting:

"What's going on, Papa?"

"That old woman stole my shotgun and ran away."

Sofia rose up behind the wall.

"I didn't run away. Here I am."

In spite of being drunk, Onofre was steady, running back and forth and cracking his whip. Then the shotgun went off, raising a flock of birds out of the persimmon tree and the old man fell to the ground. It was a shot meant to frighten from a small-caliber shotgun, but it hit Onofre in the belly because the woman had taken aim, resting the barrel on the wall. He fell over backwards, half sat up, and fell over again.

"Help me, old woman. I'm dying. I've been shot."

His eyes bulging, he stretched out on the ground. He asked for a drink of water. Sofia brought the jug. He was silent, the bottle in one hand and the whip in the other, quite still, so that he heard the chirping of the sparrows as they predicted rain.

DINNER

⚑ CONDEMNED TO DEATH, he was eating his last meal, the gravy smeared on his chin.

"How are things going, son?"

Sucking the pope's nose his eyes twinkled with pleasure.

"Things are all right."

Before him the most precious thing on earth: his son.

"Please pass the pepper, Gaspar."

Then he'll be a man. My son. I'll give him advice: don't drink water without boiling it, don't kiss servant girls on the mouth, don't get married before you're thirty.

"And how are your sweethearts going, Mr. Gaspar?"

The question offended him as much as one of his father's belches. The cold eyes of a stranger: he was nobody's son.

"I don't have any sweetheart."

. . . Don't get married before you're thirty, don't leave

89

any wine in your glass. He drank it down to the last drop.

"What can you tell me about your poetry?"

Thanks to his money, his son has the privilege of dreaming.

"It's going badly."

Every son is a test against his father.

"Come on, Gaspar. Nonsense."

Gaspar's cross-eye was not important to him; neither was the fact that he had six toes on his foot. The son could feel the eye and it bothered him as much as the sixth toe.

"Poetry stinks."

The family had incubated him, making him like an egg that had not matured in the nest: runny eyes in the morning, checkered shorts, the cloth mat on the kitchen wall—"God Bless Our Home."

"Did you go to mass, Gaspar?"

When my father opens his mouth to speak I know the words he's going to say before he does.

"No, sir."

If he knows, why does he ask? He discovered the pleasure of tearing a piece of bloody meat in his teeth.

"I asked you to, didn't I? Why don't you listen to me?"

"I don't believe in God!"

Exiled from my kingdom, fleeing from myself, I met my mother on the road, and then my father, and then the ghost of my grandfather.

Rumbling in the stomach of the father—or the son?

"The anniversary of your mother's death!"

My son, my son, stop fighting me. There's more of me in you than of yourself.

"Your mother never understood me, son."

On Saturdays Gaspar used to listen to the sounds coming from his parents' room.

With no mother and no money in my pocket.

"My poor wife . . ."

Dinner

"Can you lend me something?"

With the pain of angry bites within his heart—a son of Count Ugolino.

The father reached in his pocket, opened his wallet, took out a bank note, smoothed it between his fingers: he felt thirty pieces of silver poorer.

The son looked at the Last Supper on the wall. Judas with the small bag in his hand.

"Wine is the blood of Christ, let's drink it!"

Two strangers.

"Are you going out?"

"Yes."

They both pulled down the brims of their hats, each with the gesture of the other.

THE SPY

✻   ALONE, condemned to be by himself, outside
the world, the spy is spying. It is a big ash-gray house with
square windows, defended by a wall that sparkles with pieces
of broken glass. Even if he does not wish to, he is forced to
learn about the main events in the building with letters on
the façade—the name of a saint, perhaps—he can't make
them out, getting more and more myopic. He caught sight of
the father arriving and leading the girl by the hand. He was
a tall man, a gray mustache, a wool scarf around his neck,
high boots. The girl, about four years old, tiny, pale, and
with such thin legs that it was a miracle she could stand.
The small sweaty hand—the spy could imagine from her
nervous look that the girl, upset because she was leaving her
father, had her hand moist with terror—clutched a package
tied with thick twine where she carried her belongings: a
change of clothing, and, who knows, a handful of sourballs.

Stiff, expressionless, the father talked to the nun wearing glasses. He was explaining—as the spy imagined in his tower—how his wife had put on lipstick and disappeared into the world, leaving him with the daughter. He was putting her into the big house, he couldn't take care of her—he was a traveling man, he dealt in chickens and hogs. The man knelt down, then the girl put her little arms around his neck and refused to let him go: she was very close to her father. A stern type, still resentful of the betrayal, he broke the embrace forcefully and left the daughter weeping in the courtyard.

About eighty girls, most of them between the ages of five and eleven, and among such a large number of children not a laugh was heard. They played quietly with their pieces of cloth, empty spools, and—the most fortunate—rag dolls. During the week they wore striped smocks over their clothes and on Sunday the checkered dresses hanging in the hallway now. There is a number on each hook: on one side the checkered dresses, on the other side the cotton smocks.

From the age of six on they do all the work: they make the beds, polish the wooden floor, sweep the courtyard. In the afternoon, during prayers, they keep busy, some embroidering, others darning, others stitching and doing needlepoint, and before night comes, squinting and bending their little heads, they absent-mindedly hear the muffled voice of the city (the time on the church clock, the creaking of wagon wheels, the train whistle) and, unexpectedly, above the chirping of the swallows and the barking of a dog, the echo of a child's laugh as he plays in the sun.

For each girl under six there is another one aged eleven sleeping in the next bed who washes her face, cuts her nails (if they haven't been chewed down to the roots), and cleans her at the toilet. It is a procession of inseparable pairs, walking hand in hand, going around the courtyard, their little feet cracked from the cold—the younger one with mucus running from her nose, her little hand rolling the hem of her dress. If she whimpered, the other one would scold her: don't be repulsive, don't be a whiner. And a whack lands on the smaller one's soft head. Sometimes the older one, suffering from rickets, is the same size as her companion. As different as they are, the eyes that fill the little faces are all the same—afflicted adult eyes.

Some take good care of the protégées the way a hen does of her chicks. Oh, there is no creature more perverse than a child ill with solitude: that other one there abuses her little friend, punishes her, eats the miraculous—albeit sour—orange that in some way has appeared in the rapacious fingers without giving a piece to her companion, who swallows drily, and if that were not enough, she squeezes a peel into the hungry little eye. And if the young one pees in bed she reports her to the nun on duty who makes her stand in the middle of the courtyard as punishment—the blanket over her head until it dries.

In a corner two older girls are clucking their tongues like two little mothers back from the market:

"This girl is an awful pest."

"Yes. But she'll get over it here."

There is the old women's wing—there are nine or ten of them, wanted by no one, one a paralytic, another a deaf-mute, another retarded because of meningitis, living in isolation. They shout on moonlit nights and sob in their sleep, and they can't look at a man without pulling up their skirts. They call them the loonies, but they do some work: they dig in the garden, split wood, and draw water from the well. The girls watch in frightened silence as the old women pass, swaying their heads along with the buckets they carry in both hands—looniness is catching.

Early in the morning, in pairs, the girls march to church. Before leaving they put on sandals and run merrily, it's the only time they wear sandals, ill-equipped for the treacherous streets. There they go, eyes opened wide under their bangs—all with bangs over pale foreheads, except for the little black girls, even more unfortunate because of that. In the rear, the loonies, shaking their heads wrapped in green crocheted scarves, buried up to their ears, and becoming excited when they pass a priest on the street: for every priest, a pinch for their neighbor.

On Sundays they attend the nine o'clock mass and the girls go in, contrite, their heads bowed, dragging their sandals to keep in step, but not too much so that they won't wear out the soles. During the service, the loonies hide their frightful toothless mouths in their hands and blink merrily at a picture of Our Lady with the Christ child—with his little thing showing. The way back is sad: other children pass by in colored taffeta dresses and with ribbons in their long hair, licking delicious ice-cream cones.

On first-communion days, charitable ladies leave two or three pans of cookies at the entrance, already cut into small pieces. On Sundays the loneliness hurts even more: the arrival of a relative serves to remind the others of visitors who will never come. They walk uselessly around the courtyard, singing rounds in subdued voices, dressing and undressing their rag dolls, pinching each other restlessly, whimpering, and—after the visitors leave—many are punished, made to kneel on kernels of corn. They don't complain, like the people there outside, when it rains on Sunday: it's nice listening to the rain. A flash of lightning illuminates the windows and the thunder muffles the small cries of the most frightened ones; there go the loonies dragging cans along under the eaves. Eluding those on guard, some splash in the puddles, their hair dripping with water. Others amuse themselves by drawing figures on the foggy windows.

They invent their own games: beetle races; powder boxes at opposite ends of a string become a telephone; they watch the ants with loads on their heads; they put fireflies in a bottle to watch them light their little lanterns in a dark corner; and, without fear of getting warts on their fingers, they catch toads and throw them into the air, clapping their hands as they watch them fall, wiggling their legs and smashing on the ground.

Ah, when night comes, the ones sweeping look behind and sweep more rapidly, the ones sewing bend their shoulders and give no respite to the needle between their perforated little fingers, and the ones walking hand in hand in the courtyard get closer to each other—they do everything, everything they can to stop night from coming, a cursed night for those who are afraid. And night comes on the wings of the sparrows who press into the leaves, it comes with the distant barking of a dog, it comes with the bell that rings at the end of the haunted corridor, and, after the cup of tea and a dish of cold cornmeal mush, the last prayer said, they retire to the dormitory, huddling in their beds with only the tips of their noses out. Next to the door, hidden by her cloth screen, the nun on watch puts out the light. They're frightened to death of the dark, and who, oh Lord, can they call to for help? They hear the frogs in the marshes: go to sleep, girl, or the beasty will touch you. The hoot of the owl in the cedar tree, the nails of the bat scratching on the pane—he'll touch you, girl, oh, help, he'll suck at your neck.

The ones who are no longer children think about the fate that awaits them: being sent back to some distant relative who doesn't want them, hired out for all kinds of work in houses where the lady of the house locks the pantry and the prettiest ones are enjoyed by the man of the house and his son. Not one of them has forgotten the words of Alberta, the little Negro girl who fell into a bad life: "I count men for my novena now." The prophecy of the Mother Superior echoes in their tight and anguished little hearts: "They all end up like that. They lose their way because they don't know the world. They all end up as lunatics or degenerates.

The only salvation is prayer, my children." And they pray, pray, until sleep comes.

From the depths of a bed the complaint of a younger girl rises. It sounds more like the whimper of a puppy lost in the night; it might be a toothache or worms or, who knows, the simple fear that one of the loonies will come in the darkness and brush against her and then she'll wake up in the morning with the craw of an old woman. No one goes to her, the sobs become less frequent, and she falls asleep.

The happier ones dream about the little white dove. It was the time that one of the loonies, a paralytic, tamed a little dove from her wheel chair. Wherever she went, the dove went too, and it wouldn't go away except for small flights around the courtyard—then the paralytic would snap her afflicted fingers. She carried a staff in her hand, greasy from so much rubbing: she kept the bird prisoner within a circle of a few feet. It would fly from the tip of the staff to her shoulder and the two would kiss. The girls would stand in a circle, frightened by the cripple and amazed at the pompous little creature, its tail fanning out, showing off its red galoshes, first on one side and then on the other. Then one morning they found the dove dead. The paralytic woman moaned for a whole day and a whole night: the bird was buried in a shoe box and they covered his grave with daisies from the marsh. To calm the loony down they gave her another white dove, which she killed a few days later by sinking her knitting needle into its proud breast.

The big house would be easier to bear if they weren't always famished: when they lie down, before going to sleep or even while sleeping, one can hear the rumble in the empty belly of the next one. In spite of its having no taste, they gobble up the nauseating fare—cornmeal mush. A chunk of meat once a week. Cold mush instead of rice. If some fruit happens to fall into their avid hands—a fig or persimmon, for example—they devour it skin and all, their tongues crusted from punishment. They leave no grass within reach without sucking the sweet liquid from the stems. They eat earth and, some of them, the gold that comes from the nose. Others get attacks of worms and roll on the ground gnashing their teeth.

If hunger were not enough, there is the frightful immersion bath which must be taken with a nightgown on. One of the girls falls ill, is isolated in a small dark room, nothing to do but wait and waste away. The others say their rosary around the dying one; the funeral was in their own chapel, the cemetery was close by.

There was the father coming to visit his daughter or perhaps to take her with him. Waiting in the courtyard, afflicted eyes searching among so many for a very dear little wisp, he did not notice the nun with glasses beside him, who, in a monotonous voice advised him to be strong and have faith: the girl, poor thing, she died. A malignant fever. He'd been traveling far away, there was no way to reach him. His daughter was buried a week ago—they die like flies in vinegar.

On the father's lips the spy could read the words he did not say: If only she had died at home, close to me . . . But, oh, to die all alone in the certainty that he'd abandoned her. The man said nothing, listening to the nun with glasses, and, finally, his head bowed, he began to turn the wedding ring on his finger where the red hairs stood up stiff.

THE RIVERBANK

❧ ONE SATURDAY AFTERNOON Abílio parked his wagon by the riverbank. The raft was on the other side. He jumped down from the seat, where his two youngest sons remained, and, leaning against one of the wheels, he rolled a cigarette. In the distance he recognized his friend Nicolau in his boat:

"How are things, old friend?"

The other man said fine and when he got on land, with a tight face, he asked for the settlement of a bill.

"I've been owing you a lot more before."

And Abílio offered him all the money he had, which the other refused: three days of work were owed.

"I never broke an obligation and I've always been straight."

"But this time you didn't come through."

Taking all the coins from his pocket and stretching out

his hand, Abílio repeated that he was giving him all the money he had. His friend wouldn't accept it, it wasn't enough.

"You're a regular Polack!" the first one shouted, pale with fury.

Nicolau, the stronger of the two, grabbed him by the shirt, pulled him over to the wagon, and was choking him. As his children shrieked, Abílio pulled his knife from his belt and put it into his attacker's chest:

"You're a dead man!"

Nicolau tried to flee, but he couldn't get away, bloody and weak. He ran, stumbling and without direction, pursued by his friend, who caught up with him and stabbed him again, this time in the arm, but he stumbled on and, in front of the raftman's house, caught the next stab. The wife appeared in the window:

"José, a man's getting knifed!"

Hands clutching the wall, Nicolau begged plaintively:

"Abílio, don't kill me just like that."

The fourth stab caught him in the back. Leaning against the wall he dragged himself to the gate. Without the strength to go up the steps to the door, he fell in a pool of blood.

Abílio wiped the knife on a board before putting it away, went to the riverbank, and leaped into the boat. Crossing the river, he stopped rowing for an instant and, cupping his hands, he shouted to the raftman to take his children and his wagon back home.

BARROOMS

⚏ IT WAS A COLD NIGHT and, as every night, the bar was deserted. José sat at a rear table and the fat man came over to him with the bottle. As long as he stayed in the place (and he stayed until closing time), the fat man would leave the open bottle on the counter. José carried a folded newspaper in his pocket and he made damp circles on the table with his glass.

Before he drank, he would read a complete article in the paper. Then, lifting his glass and closing his eyes, he drank it down in one swallow. When he opened them he saw the round shadow of the lamp on the ceiling. The fat man came from behind the bar, filled the glass to the brim, spilling a few drops. José was waiting for the day when, hiding behind the newspaper, he could lick up the drops that had been lost.

With the fourth or fifth shot, he began to drink them in more than one swallow. He stretched his legs out under the table, contemplated the shadow on the ceiling, and read his paper. He didn't look at the fat man with a shiny bald head, a sprig of rue behind his ear. If he took too long in serving him, José would rap the glass on the table.

The place was a dark corridor with three or four tables up against the wall and the bar in the middle, behind which the fat man kept his head lowered among the bottles. On the bar there was a jar of pickles with spots of mold floating in the vinegar.

And no mirror on the wall. José didn't like to look at himself when he was drinking. He discovered that bar and came every night to sit at his table, the newspaper stuffed in his pocket. Always the same paper, torn at the folds. He would read a complete article before gulping the first shot.

The rare intruders who ventured into the bar kept their backs to José. No one likes to be face to face with a stranger in an empty bar. His table was next to the toilet. Every time someone went in there, José could smell the familiar odor of ammonia. He kept his hat on, his face in the shadows, taking his drinks. At closing time, the fat man took the dirty apron off his belly and without looking at his customer began to count the money in the cash drawer.

José would go slowly among the tables, delaying in that way the time to go home. He had a home and a family, but he preferred to stay in the bar, imprinting the damp circles on the table. A cold bar, dark and smelly. He didn't speak to anyone, not even the owner. But he didn't feel alone there. He knew that the open bottle was on the counter and no woman would say: "Please don't have any more to drink . . . In the name of Our Lord and His five wounds, make that the last drink!" He wasn't ashamed to drink in the bar. The fat man was a person of understanding. Besides, there wasn't any mirror.

The fat man was a person of understanding. When José had no money, he would leave the newspaper in his pocket and, after the fifth glass, he was still drinking in one gulp. At closing time, he pushed back his chair and left, and the owner didn't chase after him. José would be back the next night; the watch in the fat man's pocket and the wedding ring on his fat, hairy hand had once been his watch and his wedding ring. Since the other one began to wear it on his little finger, he knew that the owner was married too. Was he subjecting himself to filling the glass of the only customer there out of love for his family?

There was a plate of hard-boiled eggs on the bar beside the pickle jar and no one could have guessed their age, the shells dark with dust. There was no activity in the place and the fat man stayed with his elbows on the bar, the fresh sprig of rue behind his ear. Did he keep the place open out of fear of loneliness, hoping that someone would come in? It was the last bar open on Sunday, although without the cigarette smoke, without the babble of voices, without the blue breath in the mouths of the drinkers.

On that night a stranger appeared unexpectedly in the deserted bar, besides the fat man and José at the back table. Instead of turning his back to José, the stranger sat down at the next table. The owner served him and withdrew. The other one toasted José with his glass and, pale, with a grimace of fear, he poured the poison into his drink.

José was observing the round shadow on the ceiling, the two damp spots on the wall, and, last of all, the stranger, who, after drinking, let his head fall onto the table as his arm hung down to the floor—the glass rolled slowly over to his feet.

The fat man gathered up the money from the drawer and left. José went out slowly and felt his wet socks with every step. Tired as he was, he could have walked all night in the rain. It wasn't time to go home. He'd have to find another bar and start all over again.

THE VAMPIRE
OF CURITIBA

THE VAMPIRE
OF CURITIBA

❧ OH, I FEEL JUST LIKE DYING. Look at her little mouth, the way it's asking to be kissed—a virgin's kiss is the bite of a hairy caterpillar. You shout for twenty-four hours and fall into a happy faint. She's the kind who wet their lips with the tip of their tongue to be more enticing. Why did God make woman a sigh in young men and the whirlpool of the old? It's not fair to a sinner like me. Oh, I'm dying just looking at her, so you can imagine. Stop dreaming, you drunken parrot. It's eleven o'clock in the morning and I won't last till nighttime. If I could only get closer, like someone who doesn't want anything—oh, love, a dry leaf in the wind—and slowly snuggle up to the little bitch. I think I'd die: I close my eyes and I melt away with joy. All I want in the world is two or three just for me. I'm going to put myself in front of her, maybe my mustache will charm her. The devil! She acts as if she didn't see me: there's a butterfly over

my crazy little head. She looks right through me and reads
the movie poster on the wall. Am I a cloud or a dry leaf in
the wind? Damned witch, she ought to be burned alive in a
slow fire. She's got no pity in her black plum of a heart. She
doesn't know what it's like to moan with love. It would be
nice to hang her up head down and let her bleed to death.

If they don't want to, why do they show off what they've
got instead of hiding it? I'd like to suck their carotids, one by
one. Until then I'll sop up my cognac. All because of a bitch
like that one there wiggling all over. I was quiet in my corner, she's the one who started it. No one can say that I'm a
degenerate. Under every son of a good family there's a vampire sleeping—don't let him get the taste of blood. Oh, if I
only could have been a eunuch! Castrated at the age of five.
Bite your tongue, you devil. An angel would say amen! It
makes me suffer so much to look at a pretty girl—and there
are so many of them. Pardon the indiscretion, love, are you
going to drop the stuff of dreams for the ants? Oh, let me,
my flower. Just a little, just a little kiss. One more, just one
more. One more. It won't hurt, if it hurts may I fall down
stiff at your feet. Lord in heaven, I won't hurt you—my *nom
de guerre* is Nelsinho the Frail.

Veiled eyes that beg and flee, why can't I face them? A
fear that they'll catch the flash of crime in my eyes? I
mustn't startle them. Use blandishments and softness. Be
very gentle. I lose out because I'm impatient, how many
have I chased away with a hasty movement? It's not my
fault, they made me what I am—a big chest, a hole in rotten
wood where spiders, snakes, and scorpions breed. They're always making up, painting themselves, worshipping themselves in their pocket mirrors. If it's not in order to get some
poor soul all aroused, what's it for, then? Look at the daughters of this city, the way they grow up: they neither toil nor
spin, and still they're chubby. That one there's one of the
lascivious kind who like to scratch themselves. I can hear her

nails scratching on the silk stocking from here. I wish she'd scratch me all over and draw blood on my chest. Everything in front of me looks red. Here lies Nelsinho, gone to his reward because of a stroke. Tell me, genie of the mirror, is there anyone in Curitiba more miserable than I?

Don't look, you wretch! Don't look and see that you're lost. She's the kind who amuse themselves by seducing adolescents. All in black, with black stockings, whoo-ee. An orphan or a widow? With her husband buried, the wife covers her head with veils so she can hide the pimples that break out on her face overnight—the measles of widowhood in flower. Some go wild, take up with the milkman or the baker. Oh, sad and solitary nights, rolling over in their double beds, fanning themselves, reeking with valerian. Others put on the cook's clothes to go out into the streets hunting for soldiers. She's in black, that nauseating quarantine. But look at her short skirt, she amuses herself by pulling it up above her knees. Ah, the knees . . . Nice and round, with softer curves than a ripe peach. Oh, to be the purple garter that holds up the stocking on that thigh glowing with whiteness. Oh, to be the shoe that pinches her foot. And, being the shoe, to be squeezed by the lady with the small foot and die with a moan. Like a cat!

Look, a car stopped. She's going to get out. Get in position. Oh, don't do that love, I saw everything. Cover up, her husband's coming, damned cuckold. Some of them attract poor boys to go to bed with their wives. All they want to do is watch beside the bed—I think I'd be inhibited. Underneath it all I'm a hero of good will. That guy at the bar swore to me it happened to him. Is that one there one of that kind? Hell, no, not with that fierce look. Some of them even prefer the boy—would I be capable of that? God save me, it's a sin even to think about it. Kissing another man, all the worse if he's got a mustache—you can tell a man a hundred yards away by the cigarette stink. A woman has her own smell—in her armpits she filters out the honey that intoxicates a hummingbird and drives a vampire into a rage.

Young wives out shopping early. Ah, all painted gold, wearing feathers, plumes, and ermine—tear them with your teeth, leave them with their body hair. Oh, smooth and naked plump little arm—if they don't want to, why do they show them off instead of hiding them?—draw an obscene tattoo on it with the point of a needle. Condemn them to hide under black shrouds, bound in chastity belts—throw away the keys. Lord have mercy, there are so many of them and I'm so all alone.

There goes a schoolgirl. Or could she be that other kind of woman in disguise? If I could only find that famous brothel. All dressed in blue and white uniforms—mother of heaven! —parading by with black stockings and purple garters in a hall of mirrors. Don't do that, love, I arrived in a state of levitation: it's the strength of my twenty years. Look at me, I'm hovering three inches off the ground. I would have taken flight already if it weren't for the ballast of my little turtledove down here. Oh, Lord, let me grow old fast. Close your eyes, count one, two, three, and open them, be an old man with a white beard. Don't delude yourself, you drunken parrot. Not even a patriarch can be trusted, least of all with cold showers, Spanish fly, magic rings—I've known heads of families like that!

What if I got run over by a car crossing the street and the police found this collection of pictures in my pocket? I'd be lynched as a sex maniac, the shame of my city. My godfather would never forgive me. Just like the boy who left a trail of bread crumbs in the forest, I can hide a photograph in a magazine in the dentist's office, send another in an envelope to the little widow for the seventh-day mass. Imagine the surprise, the pretended shame, and finally the hours of delirium in the bedroom—the word bedroom tightens a knot in my throat.

The Vampire of Curitiba

Every family has a virgin burning up in her room. She can't fool me, the devil: first a sitz bath, then she says three prayers and goes to the window, her eyes all set to devour the first male to appear on the corner. And she grows old there, her elbows on the sill, the old maid in her vat of formaldehyde.

Why don't I take my hand out of my pocket, love? It's to hide the hairy hand of a werewolf. Don't look now. You ugly face, you're lost. Too late. I already saw the blonde: a cornfield waving under the weight of ripe tassels. She's bleached, her eyebrows are too dark—how can I stop from chewing my nails? For you I'd be greater than the motorcyclist in the Circle of Death. Let it out, you want a good-looking man with a mustache. Well, I've got a mustache. I'm not handsome, but I'm a nice fellow, isn't that worth anything? It's a shame at my age. There I go following her the way I used to follow the band of the Rio Branco Military Academy when I was a child.

With that face of a little hollow wooden angel and all, I know that she gets fun out of looking up dirty words in the dictionary. Arrogant and disdainful, she moves along with a resolute step that brings sparks out of the cobblestones. She's a regular Attila's mare—the grass no longer grows where she steps. It's impossible for her not to feel my eyes running up her arm like the slime of a snail. If there's some transfer of thought, she must be feeling the seven kisses of passion on the back of her neck.

She's far off now. I didn't give her the rose with the ashes of a swallow's heart to breathe. The blonde gets dizzy, she feels strange and lets herself go at the same time. A select bestiary of bat, swallow, and fly! Mother of heaven, I even used flies as instruments of pleasure—how many did I pull the wings off? A glow lights up in my eyes, I die without getting her. It's not fair. I roar to heaven: how do you get to have a face without pimples?

I despise you, cruel virgins. I could enjoy every one of them—and not a single one has cast her mad eye of lust on me. Oh, if I were only the devil and could bewitch them, be a dark and filthy goat. They'd crawl on their knees to kiss my hairy tail.

Oh, so good that afterwards there's nothing left to do but die. Calm down, boy: admiring the marching pyramids of Cheops, Chephren, and Mycerinus, who cares about the blood of slaves? Help me, oh Lord. Spare me the shame, oh Lord, of an onset of tears in the middle of the street. I'm a poor boy in the damnation of his twentieth year. Should I carry a jar of bloodsuckers and at the moment of danger apply them to the back of the neck?

A blind man doesn't smoke because he can't see the smoke, so, Lord, sink your needles of fire in my eyes. No more being a mangy dog tormented by fleas and turning around to bite his own tail. As a farewell—oh curves, oh delights—grant me the grace of that little woman passing there. In exchange for the lowest female I'd walk on hot coals—and I wouldn't burn my feet. Oh, I feel just like dying. Look at her little mouth, the way it's asking to be kissed—a virgin's kiss is the bite of a hairy caterpillar. You shout for twenty-four hours and fall into a happy faint.

INCIDENT
IN A STORE

◢ NELSINHO PUNCHED THE CARD in the clock and went down on the elevator with the bookkeeper. He asked the other man to cover for him with the manager in case he was late: he was going to have lunch with an uncle who was back from a trip.

"Why don't you talk to the man yourself?"

The hero bit the corner of his nail and sucked in a drop of blood from time to time.

"The oaf gets me all upset."

At the bar on the corner he gulped down his first aperitif in one swallow.

"Watch out, boy. You're drinking too fast."

By getting involved in someone else's life, the bookkeeper wouldn't complain of the day he got flung down the elevator shaft. Nelsinho downed two more drinks and went out into the sun-drenched street. He looked at his wristwatch, but with no hurry or direction, following the ladies from a distance: oh, he'd forgotten the dark glasses he could have used to admire their endowments without giving himself away. He couldn't resist the attraction of an ice-cold glass of beer and he wiped his mustache.

He blessed God for woman, so well made for caressing—white mice, Angora cats, guinea pigs. Some he would have liked to fondle on his lap. Others he would ask, rolling his eyes, to burn the hair on his chest with the tip of a cigarette. Wherever he turned his head, there they were, naked arms, the golden down quivering in the light breeze. They went forward with firm steps, their pink cheeks trembling, indifferent, and so distracted that they looked at him as if they were looking *through* him: a cloud, a piece of paper, an empty suit of clothes. Turning in irritation he followed the bounce of hair on their necks and the swing of their skirts to the enticing turn of hips.

A panting dog, the tongue of sun panting on the back of his neck. He took his jacket off and threw it over his shoulder like a toreador with his cape of glory. He was ready for love, except for the humiliation of his empty wallet—even the lowest of women has her price. If he put another IOU in the cash box the bookkeeper would report him to the manager: the end for that spy was the elevator shaft. He felt drowsy, flooded with drink; the benches in the square invited him for the rest reserved for heads of a family. He resisted bravely and turned down a side street. At that moment he spotted the girl on the opposite sidewalk—"That's her." Unctuously and with false modesty—"Thank you, Lord. I'm not worthy."

Without losing sight of her he prepared for the boarding operation. The posters on the wall suggested that perhaps she was on her way to the movies. He put his jacket on in order to make a good impression and crossed the street. He caught up with her after a few steps and pretended to be reading the advertisements. His sinister figure of a cheap gallant arose in the window: since when does the image of the Nosferatu cast a reflection? He rubbed his handkerchief on his nose where a pimple was throbbing—too late to squeeze it. Then Nelsinho's heart exploded: a friend of the family was coming in his direction. Thank God he still hadn't seen him when he ducked behind the column of an entranceway —he'll see that I'm following the girl.

She was admiring the dazzling posters of Ava Gardner and she hadn't noticed Nelsinho. Before she could look through him—sheet of paper, cloud, empty suit of clothing —he greeted her with a smile and was careful not to show his black tooth. The ingenuous girl returned his smile. He waited behind the column for a while. If only the family friend hadn't appeared. Upset, he fell into a quick march and caught up with the girl, who was opening the shop next to the movie theater.

"Are you going in now, love?"

She almost gave a cry, raising her hand to the low neck of her yellow blouse:

"Ooh, you frightened me!"

With his half-smile he looked discreetly to see if he was followed.

"So this is where you work."

" . . . "

"Who do you work with? Oh, by yourself, eh? That's important, eh?"

" . . . "

"What about your boss?"

"He's got a cold."

"What kind of a store is it?"

It was a run-down building with double doors. The girl opened one of the doors and put the key into her purse with a bamboo handle. Nelsinho glanced inside. He couldn't see anything.

"Mattresses, cushions, pillows."

"What time do you quit?"

"I stay until six."

"How about my meeting you after work?"

Don't chew your fingernail, you poor bastard, you'll bungle it.

"How about it? Can I?"

She smiled and there was a small drop of sweat on her upper lip: yes.

"Oh, what's your name?"

Oh Lord, show me no mercy; he'd committed the first blunder, turning his bad ear to the girl. He'd missed her name and he didn't dare repeat the question. At his feet the cloud of fire was trembling on the pavement and how could he resist the seduction of the cool shadows?

"Can I come in for a while?"

He went in ahead of her as she still protested:

"There's nothing to see."

He couldn't see very well in the shadows and he squinted: piles of mattresses rose up in the corners. The girl leaned over to release the catch on the second half of the door. The hero encountered her callipygian face—who would have thought it on a skinny girl like that!—and he got tremendously excited. I'm tired, Lord, there are so many women and I'm so all alone. She couldn't get the bolt out and she stood up, blowing on her finger:

"See if you can do something. Pull the bolt up."

Having stopped drinking, he felt what he was again: a leprous dog. In the shadows, a few steps away from the girl, he could make out the mustiness of the damp and run-down store. The girl moved to the other door and Nelsinho, shaking off his torpor, saw the wavy floor with rotting boards under his feet, and as he passed her he made a furtive caress to smooth her auburn hair as it fell down over her thin, freckled shoulders.

"No. Don't touch me."

Nelsinho bent over to release the bolt, bringing back her languid and perverse accent—"No. Don't touch me."—in a rejection which, by being so indolent, was more of an invitation. He changed ideas and gave the door a kick, making it close slowly. All at once, slipping away from the door, he caught a glimpse outside of a fat taxi driver in shirt sleeves sitting by his cab and yawning from the heat, who turned his head toward the store. It was too late because the door hid him.

To Nelsinho's surprise he was not left in the dark: two luminous rectangles were projected on the floor by the transom. The girl, still not understanding—good Lord, will I be forced into a carnage?—began to pull up the bolt on the second door. He took the few steps that separated them. Coming from behind, cupping his hands, he grasped her breasts. His long search was rewarded and under the webbing and stays at last he found the soft peace of her two small breasts. Startled, still holding onto the bolt, unaware of what was going on, she muttered:

"Damn you . . . You make me sick!"

In the hero's good ear it was a lover's complaint, with a certain aftertaste of fury. The girl let go of the door bolt and sank her nails into his hands. As she sank her nails in, Nelsinho squeezed her breasts with all his strength. Crushing the deceptive texture of the brassière between his fingers, he found the firm, sweet flesh of the real and nascent breasts. As he clenched his hands he was glad that he bit his nails, because he didn't hurt any more than was necessary until the girl stopped resisting and moaned, her head tilting back. Then he let her turn around. Releasing her breasts, he took her face in both hands. She whirled and hit him on the right leg with her purse.

He kissed her hard on the mouth. She resisted, unable to draw her face back. The hero opened his lips to catch his breath. The girl stared at him with surprise through her two cat lenses. Then he kissed her again. She continued to resist, but not very much: she let her arms drop and the purse was lowered. Nelsinho drew his head back for an instant to breathe. And the girl responded the third time, her mouth still closed—he hefted one of her breasts in the palm of his hand. It was precious and fragile, like a warm egg in a nest.

He stopped kissing and looked around: the light from the transom was reflected on the scarlet calico of two or three down quilts and some blue cushions. With his hands on her face, he pulled her to the pile of mattresses. The girl fell with a moan, her dress rose and revealed a white slip trimmed with lace. On his knees, he tried to kiss her again, his fingers clutching at her breasts. The beauty withdrew her face and since he also wore glasses, he was forced to take his off. As they rolled off the improvised bed he almost cried out in fear that he had broken them. He held her face still and managed to reach her lips, and, while he was kissing her, he began to raise her dress, from the soft curve of her round knees to the expanse of her white thighs. Her panties were mesh, he tore them.

He was fascinated by the girl's overcast glasses—were her eyes open or not? She was motionless, panting out of fear or pleasure. Nelsinho buried his nose in her dry auburn hair: cheap perfume. The girl was quite still, her eyes closed—oh Lord, which one of us is the victim?

Before leaving he looked around: in the back of the shop, a table with a typewriter. He felt around on the dusty floor until he found his glasses, and, a bat condemned to hunt in the shadows, he looked at the infantile mouth that had been aggressive with lipstick before and was now defenseless with its thin half-opened lips. He got up and at his feet, on the square that was reflected there on the floor under the tremulous strip of luminous dust projected by the transom, he saw the pink mesh item.

Incident in a Store

A well-mannered boy, he turned around to button himself up and tuck in the medals that tinkled in the air. For her part, the beauty adjusted her slip and the pleats in her skirt, smoothing it several times with her hand.

He returned to his timidity and felt like weeping. How should he act in the presence of women? He didn't want to be late for the office. He even thought of asking what time it was.

She too must have been late in getting the store opened. She went to the second door, picking up her purse on the way, and pulled the bolt up. As a gallant gesture, Nelsinho opened the other door. He opened one of the sides wide and bent over to pull the bolt, which came out easily. With a start he remembered the fat taxi driver who had heard or seen him kick the door. He looked outside and squinted: the car wasn't there. The girl went over to the typewriter. Oh Lord, you gave me the voice but not the words. Should he apologize, make a date for when she got off, or ask what time it was? Before she turned around he left without saying good-by.

He pushed down the lever and looked at the card. He was back on time: the incident in the store had taken only a few minutes. He sat down at his desk, put a piece of paper in the machine. Then he discovered his raw hands, stained with blood. He went to the bathroom to wash them, afraid of infection. When he looked for his handkerchief he realized that he had left it in the store—it had his name embroidered in the corner.

Suddenly he saw himself in the mirror, pale with fright. He wet his hair and slowly combed it: Nelsinho's fabulous hair. He smiled, half surprised and satisfied with himself. He bowed his head and murmured: "Thank you, Lord."

A MEETING
WITH ELISA

❦ IN ORDER TO GET OUT of the rain, the hero went into a bar and drank two cognacs, admiring himself in the mirror out of the corner of his eye. Following the waiter's instructions, he pushed back the grimy fringed curtain, went through the kitchen and into the yard: the first door on the right.

On the way back, as he slipped along under the eaves, at the door he ran into the woman with a child in her lap. He was going to pass when she spoke:

"You make believe you don't know me, eh?"

Her face in the shadows, her back to the light, who could it be?

"Hey, Elisa! What are you doing here? You've put on weight."

And he thought: I wonder how many months' worth.

"I say hello and you don't even look at me, is that the way it is?"

"I'm sorry. I didn't hear you. How long have you been here? What are you doing?"

She'd been working in the bar for a few months. Crazy to get back home, but where's the money for a ticket? Dying because she missed the little boy she left with her mother.

"A man asked me to live with him in Curitiba. I don't know whether or not to go."

"You give your son to your mother to take care of and you end up looking after someone else's."

The child understood and began to cry.

"Wait till I put him to bed."

Elisa covered the child and ran across the yard toward a shack. When she got to the door a girl of about nine came out, walking unhurriedly in the rain. She passed by Nelsinho with her head down and went into the kitchen.

Like a beast who, even though domesticated, licks his master's hand and feels the compulsive enjoyment of blood, Elisa came toward him though he was already looking at her harshly and without pity.

"How are you set for boy friends?"

"Nobody wants me."

He pulled her by the arm and kissed her. Elisa had a broken tooth, where the tip of his tongue came to lodge. With his hand he grasped the panting girl's breast.

"Just because I said nobody wants me?"

He stood looking at her without speaking. He no longer had any voice. Elisa went to see if anyone was in the kitchen.

Nelsinho came out of his shelter, and, beside the house he saw several tables and benches in the open; crates of empty bottles were piled up there. In one corner a table was hidden by a screen. And his crazy head was working: where's it going to be? He took off his glasses, wiped them on his shirt. He heard the girl's sandals on her way to the room—I bet she went to see if the child's asleep.

As soon as the beauty came back through the drizzle he grabbed her.

"Let's sit down, love."

"Can't you see that the bench is wet?"

"Then find a better place."

Cold beams of light trickled through the cracks in two windows and lighted up the puddles. Elisa found a burlap bag under the eaves: it was dry. She rubbed the bench vigorously, they sat down behind the screen. With trembling hands he unbuttoned her blouse and exposed the two breasts. The drizzle dampened the back of his neck and the girl ruffled his hair with her chubby fingers.

"I haven't got much time. They might miss me."

"What time do you leave, sweetie?"

"I live here, dopey."

The hero chewed his nails in despair.

"The child's asleep. Couldn't it be there in the room?"

"That's a funny one. What about my daughter?"

"What daughter?"

"Come on, the girl that went by here."

"I don't know. She's your daughter?"

"Yes. I think she's suspicious. I've got to go in, but I'll be back."

"When?"

"In about twenty minutes."

The boy bit her on the ear lobe.

"Be patient, love. It can't be now."

Elisa closed her blouse, but she didn't get up. She told of how her husband had made her unhappy and then had taken off. She missed her son, obliged to turn him over to her mother because he cried a lot and she lost her job. If she could only find someone who would take her to Curitiba. He didn't even have to take her, just pay the fare for her and her daughter . . .

"Look over there."

Nelsinho turned his head, she ran off. He was alone, where could she be? Among the piles of crates there was room for two people standing up—in spite of the mud, at least it was under the eaves.

The light of a candle in the courtyard startled him. Someone coming to get a bottle of something? He huddled behind the boxes. The girl—it was the girl—passed by, cupping her hand to protect the candle from the wind. She felt around the tables, went over to the outside doorway and came back—without any bottle. Nelsinho turned as she approached or went away.

He bit off the shouts that came from his heart because of a scare like that. He couldn't open the outside door: trapped. Between the wall and the house there were two menacing points. He was going to see what they were when he spotted the light of the candle again.

This time the girl was holding the hand of a woman, who must have been the owner's wife. In panic, the hero thought of sinking into the mud. Whoever saw him would only notice a cockroach huddled under the foot that would squash him. He crept over to the wall, invisible because of the miracle of his delirium.

He stayed the way he was, his right leg bent, his foot against the wall, not turning his head. One way or another, I'll get out of this. She'll see that I'm well dressed, a boy from a good family. Motionless in the drizzle, hemmed in in his corner, he followed their movements obliquely as the two came, and went looking through the piles of bottles. The candle lighted up the whole area, they couldn't help seeing him —unless the hand of the Lord Himself had blinded their eyes. Concentrating in front, he was able to perceive in the candlelight that the two lances pointing at his chest were the handles of a wheelbarrow facing the wall.

No reflection flickered on his glasses. He squatted in the dark corner and began to weep softly—oh, he hadn't counted on that. By the good Lord in heaven it was the last time: the drops of bitterness ran down his chin onto his fine polka-dot tie.

He heard the sandals and quickly wiped his eyes. The beauty didn't discover him in his hiding place until he stood up.

"What are you doing there?"

"Wow, a whole bunch of people came out."

"Who came? Did someone see you?"

"Your daughter and a damned old woman. I think she was your boss."

"But did she see you or not?"

"She might have."

She came over and hugged him:

"Poor boy. Your heart's pounding . . . Come in from out of the rain, love."

All of a sudden he was looking for another place. Embracing, they stumbled through the yard, their feet sinking into the puddles. Under the eaves she fit exactly between the handles of the wheelless wheelbarrow. The point of the tongue rolled over the roof of the other mouth, coming to rest in the imperfection of the tooth.

After combing his hair, Nelsinho adjusted the wave in it.

"How do I get out?"

They were walking. He in front, she behind.

"It's locked."

"Let me, I know how to open it."

The hero was already on the outside. Elisa shouted in a troubled voice:

"Where will I see you?"

He answered without turning:

"In Curitiba."

FINAL WARNING

❦ NELSINHO SAW THE LADY get off the bus. She exchanged glances with an individual who was leaning on the corner. The woman went into the movies (it was the two-o'clock show), and he noticed that Múcio—the man in question—went in after her.

With the lights out, Múcio sat down beside the lady in one of the back rows and the two began to chat softly. Nelsinho couldn't hear them from his seat, two rows away. He was sure that they weren't paying much attention to the picture. In the middle of it Múcio got up and left the theater.

The hero excused himself, sat down beside the lady, and whispered that he had to speak to her very urgently.

"Are you crazy? You know very well that I'm married."

The boy explained that that didn't make any difference as far as he was concerned.

"Watch out. I'll call the usher."

"Come on, you devil you, you think I didn't see?"

"My life is no concern of yours."

"Not mine, but your husband's maybe."

"If you say anything, I'll tell him you've been following me."

"That's an old story," he retorted. "I've found out things about you that are really juicy tales."

Odete got up indignantly and went up to sit in the balcony. Moments later the boy came to settle down next to her.

"What's the matter? Can't I talk to you? Did you know that your husband has a mistress? Did you know that they meet at night? You still don't know, right? I've seen the two of them together in lots of places. I know he doesn't spend much time at home. He shouts at you when you ask him for money. He's been seduced by that woman. It pains my heart to see you discarded. You're the only one I ever liked in my life. Unmask the chippy. She's married too. A mother with children, who can tell, maybe some by your husband . . . Her husband travels a lot on business. When he's away she shows what she really is: a big flirt. There could be tragedy if someone told her husband when he got home. It's foolish to fight with him. You know what men are like. They're weak —they can't resist a pretty face at all. Be careful of that adventuress who gives in to him with her eyes closed. You want a piece of advice, Odete? Look, you do the discarding. Do the same thing he's doing to you."

Without answering, the beauty went down to sit in the orchestra, still followed by Nelsinho. She threatened to tell her husband as soon as she got home. Well, if she said anything, he'd reveal that he'd caught her with another man. Odete went out in a fury, she even forgot her parasol. At home she described the incident to her old mother:

"You can't go to the movies alone anymore."

She was advised by the old woman not to tell her husband anything. He was very nervous, something unpleasant could happen. Odete, oppressed and sleepy eyed, insisted that the boy was crazy. Wanting to get her in trouble with her husband could only be the revenge of a lovesick person.

At that moment our hero was calling up the husband.

"Good evening, Seu Artur. How was your trip? It's nice to travel—when your wife stays home."

"What's this all about? Who is this? I don't understand."

"This is a friend. The name doesn't matter. It's a delicate question. I don't know what to say. Where to begin. While you're away your wife has a love affair. No man deserves being cheated like that. I'm going to tell you what I know. Your wife . . . She has a lover!"

"You swine! I ought to shoot you down. Have you got any proof, you coward? Speak up, then. Who's been seeing my wife?"

"A certain Dr. Múcio."

In the sudden silence, before the curse exploded, Nelsinho hung up. Then he took a sheet of very white paper and smoothed out the wrinkles. The smile lasted until he finished the letter that he was composing by printing with his left hand:

Dr. Múcio

Great son of a bitch
I warn you to watch out! Watch out!
From today on I will pursue you
I haven't done anything foolish yet because I don't want to dirty my name
Starting today I'll make my plans
I've already considered your wife and children
But since you're a coward you only deserve a bullet in the head

And I warn you to think carefully about your wife and children

And other innocents suffering in the world because of you

Shameless impudent coward

Think about the future of your home because your life will be short

If you keep on taking away the honor of married women

You're married too and you go around putting horns on husbands

Not just me there are a lot of others

Don't think I'm a coward like you

I've got the courage to blow your brains out

Maybe you won't see the new year in

I'm going to clean up Curitiba

I only want revenge

I'll spill your cursed blood on the street

Watch out for your hide

This is your final warning

A VISIT
TO THE TEACHER

🔲 TWIRLING THE PACKAGE on the loop of blue twine, Nelsinho stopped in front of the decrepit building with an ash-gray front. He checked the address written on the wrapping—God bless the mothers of Curitiba, most holy ladies!—and, feeling his way along the sinister corridor, he caught the stench of garbage turning sour in the corners. He had been careful to make sure that Dona Alice would not be home—it was four in the afternoon, he'd chosen that time for a reason—and, his duty done to her family, he would leave a message with the janitor: he had a date with a gilded lady at the sailors' bar.

Bumping along, the elevator dragged him up to the third floor. If he hadn't been a hero of character, he would have left the package there by the door and good-by Dona Alice. He sighed softly—after all, a person's first teacher, she'd taught him how to read, to write his name, the four mathematical operations—and he rang the bell. No sound from the other side. He remembered that she was an old teacher, she still thinks you're a boy in short pants. It would be impossible to give her the package and leave: she'd receive it like an apple on the first day of school. She wouldn't let him go until he had a cup of coffee and listened to her old-maid complaints. I'll ring again and if she doesn't answer I'll take off. He felt the object—it was wool, maybe a muffler—and he decided to leave it by the door. It was too late: tired slippers softly shuffling along. Two turns of the lock—an old maid guarded by seven keys.

"Hello, Dona Alice. Do you remember me?"

Above her thin body the absurdly puffy face trampled by sleep, unhealthy rings under the eyes. Through the crack in the door she said that his face was familiar but that she couldn't remember his name.

"It's Nelsinho, from Curitiba. I was your pupil at the Tiradentes School."

She opened the door and gave a small-toothed smile:

"Goodness, child, how you've grown! Good heavens, how long has it been . . ."

She was a sliver of an old woman—the louse offering herself to the student's ax. He was surprised that she was shorter than he. He remembered her well, a rainbow with bare arms with the blackboard in back, a bouquet of blue wisteria perfuming the room—oh, how beautiful she had been to childhood's myopic eyes. She came up to his shoulder in her cloth slippers—the same small, spaced teeth, the shadow of down on her unmade-up face.

"On Saturdays I rest after lunch. The doorbell woke me up."

Dwarfed, she smoothed her hair, dark with gray strands peeping through.

"I came to deliver this package. Dona Eponina sent it."

"Mama always takes advantage of other people." She

squeezed the package in her slightly trembling hands. "Wool socks. It was awfully nice of you, Nelsinho. Mama never heard that they've invented the mails."

She examined him with frightened eyes:

"So this is Nelsinho! You turned out to be quite handsome. Don't be embarrassed. My pupils are the children I never had."

He was silent: old teachers always talk too much.

"Are you still so quiet? Won't you come in?"

"I'm sorry, ma'am, I'm in a hurry."

"Don't stand on ceremony. Please come in. Let's talk a little. I want to hear all about you. How are your classmates?"

Nelsinho went into the living room and through the open bedroom door he saw the wide double bed. She closed the door:

"You've got to excuse the mess. I just got up."

He sat down on the edge of the sofa and was answering —damn it, he'd left the hatchet in his other coat!—her questions about school, studies, classmates. One married and the mother of two children—Virgin of heaven, how time flies! Another one killed in a plane crash—the curly-headed one, Sérgio, her favorite.

"Were you angry with me, Nelsinho? More than once I put you out of class for punishment. Making you kneel on kernels of corn, how awful! I was a horrible old witch, wasn't I?"

The most beloved of horrible witches—intact in his memory, a black skirt and a blouse, with embroidery, that was immaculately white.

"Will you ever forgive me, Nelsinho?"

"Come, now, Dona Alice, I deserved it."

"Tell me, what are your plans? Would you like to be a doctor?"

"I don't know, Dona Alice. I'm all mixed up."

"Don't be silly, child. A fine big lad like you. How old are you?"

"Twenty-one." He exaggerated by one year, and the big flushed face of an afflicted young man was once more that of the schoolboy with a sinful hand in his pocket. Covering up his embarrassment, he dramatically revealed his desire to break away from his family. Be himself. Turn his back on his home town, like being born a second time.

"You've got your whole life in front of you, Nelsinho."

Pensive, she crossed her legs—oh, how many pencils had the boy dropped in order to take a peek at her chubby knees. For years all he had to do was close his eyes and he'd see two delightful curves rise up and light up the darkness. He'd caught a glimpse of her garters once: they were black, not purple as he'd imagined. Ah, they still wore garters in those days . . . Come on, she wasn't so far gone, ten years older than he, twenty at most.

"Maybe I never should have left home."

"Do you have regrets, ma'am?"

"Please, child, don't call me ma'am. I feel so old next to you. Look, let's make a pact. We're two old classmates reminiscing about our schooldays."

Unable to distract himself with a pencil, sitting uncomfortably on the edge of the sofa, the hero listened to her for more than an hour as she recalled times gone by: she didn't offer him a drink, not even a cup of coffee.

Her sad life consisted of leaving home for work and coming home from work. If the word home could be applied to that apartment without air, sun, or light. She didn't get along with her fellow workers at the office—she still had moral principles, she came from a Catholic family. She couldn't bear the atmosphere, the vulgar, easy women, the terrible promiscuity. A girl who lives alone has to keep her self-respect. Mother of heaven, how hard it was! Besieged at all hours, everywhere: every man is a great swine. As soon as he finds out that a girl lives alone, he takes on the airs of a conqueror. Some come to pound on her door—more than once she threatened to call the radio patrol. She didn't sleep well, frightened by dreams of burglars under her bed.

She had no gentlemen friends. She'd been engaged two years ago, the fellow didn't make much, no means to get married. Five months ago he was transferred to São Paulo and the separation left her all the more upset. Disillusioned with life, at the point of not knowing what was to become of her. She wanted to visit him in São Paulo, where he lived with his mother, who, for her part, didn't care for Alice— without even saying why. Neurotic old woman, possessive of her only son, she wanted to keep him for herself. Alberto didn't have the courage to leave her and she wouldn't dream of living with her future daughter-in-law.

She would rather have stayed in Curitiba, but how could she? After the scandal with the principal of the school, a married man, in which she was innocently involved—I don't know if you knew about it, Nelsinho. Sad, depressed, she fell ill then, had a bad cough: shut up for a year in the sanatorium. The doctor recommended she get far away from the cold of Curitiba.

"Oh, Nelsinho, if you only knew . . ."

It was getting dark, the streetcars were quieting down. It was Saturday, and, filled with emotion, she squeezed his hand:

"It's wonderful to see someone from Curitiba."

Nelsinho pretended to be interested in the pictures on the wall—pine trees at sunset—without interrupting the monologue of that wilted and empty heart, that useless shell of a vanished cicada. In August, for the last time, she'd spent a few days at home for her parents' golden wedding anniversary. She couldn't go back at the end of the year—all vacations canceled at work. She spent Christmas by herself, the worst time to be alone. All alone in her apartment, she thought about the happiness in all the homes. Dressed the way she was, with a new blouse and gloves, she dropped onto the bed, her eyes glued to the ceiling. She finally dozed off early in the morning, listening to the streetcars, the drunken arguments, the neighbors celebrating around the table—oh, he didn't know how people on the fringe of life felt.

"What finally happened with that fiancé of yours? If he loved you so much, why did he leave you?"

Because of his mother, who had heart trouble. A terrible fraud, she threatened to die if her son left her. The next morning the beauty opened her eyes in despair and wept for three days, without the courage to look at herself in the mirror, go to work, or go out onto the street. Not washing the make-up off her face, not cooking, eating milk and hard crackers. Night and day thinking about herself at home with her family. Her only joy was visiting Curitiba. For a whole month she was the guest of honor, everybody making special efforts to please her. It was February—a sob cut off her words and Nelsinho kept his eyes on the pine trees. He was able to lower his eyelids but he still saw them glowing in the darkness—and she was only able to get back in December.

"You don't know how lucky you are, child. You're going back there now."

Huddled in her corner, she made herself even smaller and hid the face turned towards him with her hand.

"When are you leaving?"

"Next week."

The hero tightened his stomach to lessen the gurgling of his famished insides. In the silence, between phrases, the loud series of rumblings could be heard.

"Sometimes I feel like giving everything up and going on a lark. I know that they talk about me in Curitiba. They say I came to Rio to have a good time. Poor me, living the life of a nun. If my fiancé doesn't make up his mind soon, I'll lose all hope."

A Visit to the Teacher

She was discriminated against at the office. The others got raises but she didn't because she fought off the boss's dirty hands—all bosses are pigs. She dreamed of going back to Curitiba, doubtful whether her father would take her back into the house.

"If my fiancé doesn't make up his mind soon, I'll lose all hope. I might even do something crazy, do what the girls I work with do. Instead of playing the boob, waiting for a letter from young 'massa' while he hangs onto his mother's skirts."

It could have been out of pity or simply from hunger, but Nelsinho quickly put in:

"Do you have anything on tonight, Dona Alice? If not, would you like to have dinner with me?"

He bit his tongue in regret: he didn't have much money and he couldn't spend it on the teacher. He'd come to Rio to have a time with the gilded ladies.

"I'll be ready in five minutes. Make yourself at home. Do you want some music? I'll put on a record."

He took a few steps in the dark living room. A dark, tight cubicle: the kitchen. On the table a glass of milk covered by a saucer and an empty plate: not a single crumb. Dona Alice appeared at the bedroom door.

"I'll go on one condition: that I pay half."

"You're my guest, ma'am."

"What's wrong with that? It's the custom here."

"Maybe here, but not where I come from."

"A real Paraná man, eh?"

During the third record she came back:

"I'm all set."

Dressed in blue, gloves folded in her hand, wearing high heels now. She'd put a ribbon in her hair but she wore no make-up. No earrings, bracelet, or ring—didn't she want to put on make-up, didn't she even have an engagement ring?

"Do you want to wash your hands?"

A good Paraná man, even though he felt like going to the bathroom, he declined. Before opening the door Alice excused herself, went back into the bedroom, and came right out again without her gloves.

"Is there a restaurant near here?"

"Restaurants are what there're plenty of."

In the elevator they rode down with a person who kept his hand in his pocket and looked her up and down.

"Did you notice the way that fellow looked at me? This building is a little suspicious."

On the sixth floor there was a girl who worked with her and gave wild parties. She mentioned a restaurant where she'd been with her fiancé a couple of times.

"Do you want to go there?"

"Is it far?"

"No. I like to walk."

The automobiles were speeding by and as they crossed the street she took his arm. Feeling the calm touch of her hand, Nelsinho examined her out of the corner of his eye. She was tranquil—it was a natural gesture of defense. When they got to the sidewalk, Alice withdrew her hand.

"I'm ashamed of the poor shape I'm in. Do you know that our conversation did me good? But that's enough about me. Tell me something about yourself. What about girl friends?"

For the first time she had brought up a subject that interested him. Nelsinho described the catastrophe of his last passion. He didn't intend to fall in love with another woman until he turned thirty.

It was Saturday, eight o'clock on a hot February night: couples in the shadow of the trees, hiding in doorways, and in the distance lying on the beach.

"Be careful, son. There are a lot of cheats around here."

She was looking down and Nelsinho was unable to tell whether she was serious or was teasing him. He caught the looks of other couples, who seemed to be whispering behind their backs. They seemed scandalized at the age difference between Nelsinho and his companion, thinking they were a pair of lovers.

Along the way a fat man came over to talk to Alice.

"This boy's from my home town. Look how healthy he is. He isn't one of these ghosts from around here."

Touching her on the arm, the man insisted in a low voice:

"Look, love. Don't do it, sweetheart."

The beauty laughed—the suspect sparkle of a gold tooth. She was like a different person, not the desperate girl in the apartment, leaning on the shoulder of the fat man, who hugged her very intimately.

"Have some respect for the boy, Moreira. Remember, he's from Paraná. He'll think I'm scandalous."

The hero bit his lip with rage. In the presence of that guy she took on protective airs, the bitch.

"Be patient, Moreira. Not today. Call me tomorrow, all right?"

A red light went on in Nelsinho's head, flickered, and went out.

"Let's go, sweetie."

She'd called him—sweetie. Oh, if she only knew: the only woman who had called him "sweetie" when he was eight, and he'd never forgotten.

In the restaurant Alice nibbled on a piece of white meat of chicken. She didn't have any appetite, she'd eaten late, the big-city life.

"Ma'am . . ."

"Don't call me ma'am. Treat me like a friend."

"Have another piece. You're so thin."

Be quiet, mouth! It was too late: Alice lifted her terror-filled eyes towards him.

"So I'm thin, eh? You think I'm thin too, eh? I haven't been well. A bad cold."

"I'm going to have another cognac. Aren't you drinking anything?"

"Orange juice. To keep you company."

The beauty recalled her fiancé. Nelsinho sipped another round. Alice finally accepted a beer. She talked about soccer. Alberto was a great fan. She'd learned all about it so she could talk to him. A poor consolation for his absence was listening to the games from São Paulo on Sunday.

"I don't smoke, thanks. It's not good for me," and she coughed into the handkerchief she held crushed in her fingers.

Be quiet again, mouth. She had delicate feelings, delicate health: a whole year in the sanatorium. Nelsinho imagined the patients' orgies, it seems that the fever excites them. A marked woman in her home town: a girl weak in the chest. Once cured she came to Rio to have a good time —she was talked about too much to get married. Trying to play the virgin: the so-called fiancé must have been a lover, maybe a pimp. Oh-oh, I'm getting high.

"Shall we go?"

His plan was to go straight to the sailors' bar. The waiter brought the check.

"Let's split it."

"What's that, Alice? Please. Otherwise I'll be offended."

They set out again, he a little in front, hurrying. Breathing hard, Alice spoke less.

I'll leave her at the elevator and she'll never see me again. He pushed open the door, quite agitated.

"I wonder what time it is."

She looked at her wrist watch:

"Eleven-thirty. It's early. Come in for a while. It was quite a walk."

The fire in his head lighted up and didn't go out: all the lights on now.

It frightened him to see her so down-hearted: the puffy face was strange on that dried-out body.

"I'll make some coffee. Then you'll be rid of me."

She opened the door and took off her shoes.

"Women are crazy, wearing such tight shoes."

She went to the bedroom to put on her slippers and on the way she put a record on the phonograph.

"Come in here, you can hear better."

The beauty went to the bathroom. He sat down on the edge of the bed. He picked up some records from underneath the phonograph: "For dear Alice, with love from . . . To dear Alice, from her loving . . . Alice, always beloved, with the love of . . ." On each inscription on the jackets there was the name of a different man, and he put them quickly back on the rack.

She came back from the bathroom without her jacket, in a black silk blouse now. Nelsinho noticed that she'd put on lipstick: they were fleshy lips, meant to be bitten, not kissed. Before him he had a worn-out and tired woman who could have been the little teacher's mother—mixing up the daughter with the mother would be a betrayal of his sweetest childhood memory.

Perplexed, Alice turned her face when she met his look and shuffling in her slippers, she opened the curtain and leaned on the window sill.

"Come see."

A group of young people practicing a carnival march.

"My days as a teacher were the happiest in my life."

It was a narrow window and when she pointed at one of the little black boys she leaned against him, rubbing his arms with her breasts, which were opulent in spite of her stunted chest.

"My, it's cold! I've got goose pimples all over."

"How can you sleep with all that noise?"

With her hand over her mouth she had a coughing attack. In Curitiba the word was that she hadn't been cured, that she'd been deceived. During dinner he'd seen her cough more than once keeping the handkerchief in her hand. Her eyes grew wide with terror when he said she was thin. Wiping away the tears, she replied that the noise in the street was nothing. The streetcars were hell. For the first few months she used to toss in bed until morning. In time you get used to it. Sometimes she took a sedative, she didn't want to become addicted—she was very nervous.

"Look at all my goose pimples . . ."

She went into the bedroom to change the record. Nelsinho spat into the street from the window. Since she hadn't started making the coffee:

"I have to get back to the hotel."

Busy with the phonograph, she didn't even raise her eyes:

"Is someone expecting you? If not, stay here."

Without answering, Nelsinho went to the bathroom— I'm lost. What now? Two turns on the key and he urinated, careful not to make any noise. How could he jump out the window, even from the third floor, if there wasn't any window? He looked at himself in the mirror, good-looking, even if he was bashful, and he gave a little belch: wow, I'm drunk. Curious, he opened the cabinet and behind the jar of cream he found a box of condoms. His mouth tasted bitter, he'd smoked too much: he squeezed a little toothpaste on his finger and rubbed his teeth. He smiled at himself: he didn't know what to do. He rehearsed a few farewell phrases until he decided on one of them. I'll open the door, wave from a distance—Good-by, beauty!, and I'll run for the stairs.

He opened the door and halted, his hand in the air: the lights were out. The room was in the red glow of the dial on the phonograph where a record was playing softly. He imagined that Alice had gone back to the window. Or that maybe she was in the kitchen making coffee. Then he heard her moving on the bed.

A Visit to the Teacher

He took a few steps and stopped, hesitant in the middle of the bedroom. She turned over in bed again. He owed her something for having taught him how to read—he went forward dragging his feet, fearful of tripping on the rug: there was no rug. He stepped on a soft object that must have been the package with the socks, still unopened. He made out the bed in the shadows, the two pillows, and, lying there, the lady, completely naked.

Nelsinho bumped into the mattress with his leg. When she saw him beyond her reach, she stretched out her arms, begging, fingers clutching at empty space. Undecided, the boy rested his knee on the bed. A squeak of triumph in her chest, Alice put her hands around the back of his neck: her face blood red in the dim light, she searched for him with the open mouth of an emaciated and lascivious vampire— and, unable to wait, the tip of her tongue darted out from between her teeth. He let himself be kissed—oh, bitter beery hiccup—and he said good-by to childhood forever. The needle came to the last groove and began to scratch the record, but neither of them turned it off.

ON THE EAR LOBE

NELSINHO OPENED the outside door, swayed on the brick sidewalk, and in front of the door he came across Pasha nestling in the burlap bag used for the wiping of feet. The dog discovered who it was too late and rolled down the three steps with the kick. Old and sick, he didn't even growl, just whimpered with pain, trembling, dragging his leg, disappearing into the back of the yard. The boy knocked on the door and, without waiting, opened it and went into the deserted kitchen. He heard voices on the radio in the small living room and tiptoed in that direction.

From the hall he spotted the old woman in the rocking chair, the bowl held at chest level, avidly swallowing spoonfuls of bean soup. Motionless by the door, he hadn't fooled her: the old woman was noisily slurping the soup as she followed the radio serial, her ear glued to the speaker, and, although there was nothing to show her attention had been caught—not even blinking her eyelids or quivering her nose as she opened her mouth wide while the spoon was still sunk in the bowl—she had been aware of his presence ever since he had stepped off the bus on the corner. Above the actors' impassioned voices she perceived the crunch of his shoes on the sand, the soft touch of his fingers on the door, and she never turned her back on him—it was not like her, old matador-woman, to be careless with the bull. The hero waited in vain for the day he'd catch her in the attic on the edge of the stairs . . .

"Good evening, Dona Gabriela. Did Neusa get in yet?"

"She's in the bathroom changing." And, according to the rules of the game: "What a fright you gave me, son!" And the spoon scraped the bottom of the bowl. "Poor Pasha, so old he hasn't got the strength to bark."

It was a warning not to underestimate old matador-women: she knew about the kick given her pet mongrel. She put the bowl on the table beside her and with a trembling hand reached for the half-full glass of beer.

"Having your little beer, Dona Gabriela?"

With an obscene expression of pleasure, she drank with her eyes closed.

"I got it from Noca."

"Is it the first one?"

"Yes, it is."

"Have you finished the bottle of rum already?"

A mustache of foam on her wrinkled mouth.

"Speak low, Neusa might hear."

In an enticing way she showed the last yellow canine tooth among her rotted roots.

"There was only a little left."

"How about another one?"

"You're my ruination, boy. Just a loan, eh? I want to pay for it."

"Zèzinho didn't lighten his wallet for you?"

"You really don't want me to tell you, do you?"

A sigh in the depths of the old woman as she gulped down what was in the glass. The boy hastened to serve her.

"It's good I hid it," and she gave a belch. "This cough . . . I'd like to see him find it."

"Do you have a lot of money?"

For the first time the old woman turned her face all the way around. She faced him without blinking—don't avert your eyes, Count Nelsinho, or you're lost.

"Oh, poor me. If I had money do you think I'd be moaning and suffering in this chair? There are people who think I have, right?"

The bubbles of foam were hardening on the fuzz on the old woman's upper lip.

"Do you want another bottle or not?"

With a finger swollen with knots she plucked threads from her skirt.

"Don't tell anyone, son. If you do, they'll hide it. They don't give me a drop."

"Don't worry. It'll be our secret."

"Careful, watch out for Neusa."

He turned around and couldn't hide a grimace of displeasure.

"What is it, sweet?"

"That dress."

It was even comical, worn, but well preserved, with black and blue checks.

"What's wrong with it?"

"You know the horror I have."

Virgins, you've got to make them crawl. They'll wash my feet and I'll dry them on their perfumed hair.

"Do you want me to change it?"

Someday she'd stand up to him, not today:

"I'm silly, do you want me to change?"

"Don't be foolish. Wear what you want."

144

Neusa stood on tiptoes to kiss him and went to change. He turned his face and, wrinkling his brow, he could see the mummy there, her neck twisted to get the last drop of beer. The empty bottle left the old woman bitter. As soon as he was settled in the chair:

"Oh, my son. You mustn't ask what sickness is. God save you from suffering like me. An old person can die and no one cares."

Make a cross on your mouth, you ominous she-devil.

"You're quite right, Dona Gabriela. Where is everybody?"

"Lígia went to the movies with Artur."

"What about Zèzinho?"

"He went too. Do you think I'd let the two of them go alone?"

This harpy deserves to be drowned in a barrel of rum—she and Zèzinho the blackmailer.

"Aren't you afraid to be alone?"

She leaned back in the chair and as she smoothed her skirt over her bony knees she brought her dull feet with swollen ankles into view—a labyrinth of thick, purple varicose veins.

"An old person is always alone. You mustn't ask what it's like to live like this. I wouldn't wish what I go through on anyone. I'm the one who knows that this isn't any life. God forgive me, sometimes I think He doesn't exist. If He existed He wouldn't let me suffer like this. I never hurt anyone. I swear to you, Nelsinho, I never killed a fly."

A Pharaoh sitting in a sarcophagus, she tightened her transparent hands with blue spots on the back, where two or three flies were perched, on the pointed knee.

"It's right for everyone to pay for their sins. Not for me. I never wished evil on anyone. I killed myself washing clothes in the cistern. I wore my fingers to the bone polishing the top of the stove. I ruined my eyes with so much

sewing at night. If anyone should have suffered it wasn't me
—it was Carlito. This should have happened to Carlito."

"Didn't Carlito die?"

"Yes, he died, but he lived a happy life. And he didn't
suffer when he died. He spent his days drinking and spending money on tramps. I wore myself out working. I was condemned to end my days in this chair. He got everything out
of life and he died fast, in the strength of his manhood."

"What did he die of?"

"Head cancer. He died with no one around. Asking for
me to forgive him. They came to get me so I could see him
when he died. I said they could send me the body for the
wake, I wasn't going to forgive him."

His hands deep in his pockets, Nelsinho tramped about
the room, hemmed in. Pretending to admire the Last Supper
on the wall, he made fearsome faces at the plague-ridden old
parrot. He aimed at her with an imaginary shotgun at his
shoulder. Even though she didn't chase the flies, she lifted
her hand and scratched her neck, right on the bull's-eye.

"Are you listening, son? Don't let happen to you what
happened to me. I was young like you once. God save you
from suffering like me."

There she was, ready to put a curse on him, the mad
queen. What had happened to her had been well done, the
punishment of heaven.

Still talking, she went to the stairs and opened the
pantry door. She stepped into the darkness, bent over, and
without turning on the light pushed aside the cans of sugar,
beans, rice, and pulled out another bottle.

"Pray for me, my son. Don't ask what my life has been
like. I don't know what it's like to sleep anymore. Sitting on
the bed I keep listening . . . The racket of the bats. A black
cricket in the kale patch. Pasha's teeth grinding out there on
the steps. If it wasn't for my little beer, I don't know what
would become of me."

"Why don't you see a doctor?"

"My only hope is for a miracle."

The miracle happened: Neusa appeared at the door. With a leap, the boy grasped her hand, pulling her through the hall into the next room. Before leaving, Nelsinho stuck out his tongue at the old woman, who was busy pouring her drink without making any foam.

He took off his jacket and lay down on the sofa with a moan. Neusa went to close the window (Zèzinho, at the age of eight, was the witch's eyes), and as she raised her arm the white blouse rose up and revealed a portion of flesh: I know I really shouldn't, I'm so thin, with an ugly cough—if I don't take care of myself hair will start growing in the palm of my hand. The beauty sat down on the edge of the sofa and he stretched out his legs, crossing his feet on the coffee table.

"Please, Neusa. Don't ever leave me alone with her. Look, in order to tolerate your grandmother, a person has to be a saint. Why don't you put some ground glass in her bean soup?"

"Talk lower. She's listening."

"The radio's on."

"She can hear what the neighbors are saying through the walls."

"I suspected that. She heard me kick Pasha."

"Grandma's a witch."

"You people should move her up to the attic. Maybe she'd fall down the stairs."

"Don't be silly, love. Stop talking about that horrid old woman."

"What did you do today?"

He stretched his arms out along the back of the couch. Neusa leaned her head on his shoulder.

"Worked."

"When did you get home?"

"A little while before you got here."

"Does your boss pay overtime?"

"Not a cent. He's an exploiter."

"Did he ever try anything with you? Did he try anything funny?"

"Don't be silly, love. He's a married man."

"So?"

"He knows I've got a special boy friend."

"How does he know?"

"Haven't you ever come to pick me up?"

"What did he say?"

"He thinks you're very nice. He even asked me when the date was."

Ah, the date. The only date you're going to have is with Pasha. She snuggled against his chest and, lifting her head, kissed him on the ear lobe.

"Are you going to make me wait a long time, love? I can't stand it with that she-devil anymore."

"Don't do that. It gives me goose pimples."

The girl took his head in her hands, gave him a frantic kiss: the tongue was offered in the half-opened lips.

"You're always sucking on a peppermint ball."

"Do you want me to spit it out?"

"What a mania!"

It's the chance to save myself: make a scene and good-by beauty!

"Don't get angry, sweet."

With her eyes she looked for a place: the vase of violets? The window, closed. She stared at him with tears in her eyes.

"Do you want me to swallow it?"

"If you like me, you'll swallow it."

She swallowed the ball whole with difficulty. It hurt and a tear came out of each eye. This one won't get away from me—she's all mine.

"I was only fooling."

"I do everything you want me to."

"Everything, Neusa? Really everything?"

She offered him, yes, her mouth swollen with kisses. The boy's hands tightened on the back of the couch—I know I shouldn't, it's crazy. The old woman's in the other room and there's nothing we can do about it. He caressed the girl's smooth arm lightly. Oh, oh, do you know the delirium of flesh in flower? The hand slid along—I'm weak, Lord, I'm not worthy, I took an oath that I never would again, I . . .—until it rested on the peeled pear of her breast. Do you know what it's like to hold that little breast like a goldfinch in a trap? In ecstasy Nelsinho opened his eyes: the beak of the goldfinch was pecking its owner's hand.

Crushed in his embrace the girl freed one hand with effort and put it under his shirt—were they five fingers or the five damp little legs of a fly that made him shiver from head to toe? Melting with pleasure and also so as not to pass out, he closed his eyes a second time—now it was a tickling on the roof of his mouth and he felt like howling.

The springs of the sofa exploded. Good Lord, what if the old woman should come in suddenly? He sat up with difficulty supporting the weight of the girl, clutching like a frightened child at its mother's skirt. Panting, he breathed through his mouth and with trembling fingers opened her blouse. He held her away from the sofa to get the blouse off her arms. Then the brassière slipped off the girl's throat. The discovery of the small breasts was always new, just like two equal halves of a lemon—and he hastened to kiss them. Every time the baring of the little white dove breast was a revelation and the pains of the world lost their meaning.

He barely had time to conjure away the old woman—a drowned man going down for the third time—and he rolled and they both rolled on the sofa, too small to hold them. They couldn't lie down. He held her by the waist and they stood up.

He held her off for an instant in order to take off his

shirt with a tug. He sheltered the fainting beauty, both of them starting to kiss again with the fury of famished young animals stealing food from each other's mouths. As he ran his frantic hands along her delightful virtues, he found the clasp of her skirt and undid the single button. The black skirt slid down and revealed a strip of panty-pink. He took a step back and the skirt slipped down to the girl's feet: Neusa, oh; oh, Neusa! All afflicted, she moaned softly— Please, please! Desperate—would the old woman think it was Pasha?—he lifted her with both hands until she was his height. She understood, rose up onto her tiptoes, and it was a perfect fit.

The hero hovered two inches off the floor. Fluttering on the wings of madness, he began to repeat: Think fast. What's your name? How old are you? Answer quickly: what's your name? Fast—and before he could answer Dona Gabriela came into the room.

The two separated, each one staggering to one side with no sound. Nelsinho's heart was going a mile a minute and one vein he never suspected he had was beating in his forehead as if it would burst: help me, mother of heaven.

"What's the matter . . . what do you want, Grandma?"

The sound burst forth from Neusa's throat—and it wasn't her voice. The old woman drew back her outstretched arm and shook her head, examining them in silence, her eyes wide open. In the dark texture of wrinkles a blue glimmer of mistrust.

"Why are you so quiet?"

The hero became stupefied opposite the old woman who faced them without blinking.

"Why are you standing, girl?"

"I . . . I'm going to change the bulb."

"Did it burn out?"

"Just now."

"Were you behaving yourselves? I know that Nelsinho can be trusted. What are you waiting for, girl? Go get a bulb in the pantry."

Neusa stepped on the pile of clothes on the floor. She had to pass within reach of the hag beside the door. Now she puts out her hand, grabs the girl—I have to make a killing. Nelsinho spoke quickly so that she would look at him:

"Do you want me . . ." his voice cracked and he went on without breath, "to get you another beer?"

"That's kind of you, son. In a while . . . If you only knew. I felt so alone there in the other room. A small pain in my heart. I thought it was all over."

The girl came back quietly, hiding her breasts with her hand:

"I've got the bulb, Grandma."

She took off her shoes and climbed on the table:

"There."

She went to sit down beside the boy who was wiping the cold sweat from his forehead. Still watching the old woman, almost without seeing her, his glasses became fogged. With a sigh the old woman sank into the easy chair and pulled the black shawl, powdered with dandruff, over her shoulders.

"Oh, my daughter, if you only knew . . . I was telling Nelsinho," and outside the felt slipper the shriveled foot was suddenly shaken by tremors like those of a dray horse chasing off blowflies. "I'm paying for someone else's sins. Oh, my children, I hope you never know what suffering like mine is," and she belched.

The old witch is tight.

"Another bottle, Dona Gabriela?"

A thousand bottles wouldn't make her shut her mouth.

"I like you Nelsinho. Like a son. God save you from having to suffer from my illness. Pray for me, my son."

He was defeated, he knew it well: he lowered his head and fastened three buttons on his shirt.

"You don't want to end up like me. Only I can say. This isn't life."

Watching her blind grandmother and agreeing with her, "Yes, Grandma. That's right, Grandma. Sure, Grandma," Neusa undid one, two, three buttons and kissed him again on the ear lobe.

ETERNAL LONGING

❧ NELSINHO TURNED THE KEY in the door and faced the girl, who was standing in the center of the living room:

"There's no one here. The family's away."

Laura teetered slightly. Letting her purse slide down her arm, she raised her hand to her eyes.

"The room's spinning."

He left the purse lying on the rug.

"Hold onto me, sweet."

Without taking a step he held out his hand and the beauty came over to nestle against his chest. He lifted her chin, looked at her pale face and closed eyes—he bit her lips with a hungry kiss. When he felt the vacillating weight he led her to the sofa, where she collapsed. She rolled her head on the back of the sofa and among some unconnected phrases she babbled a name that wasn't Nelsinho's.

"You don't like me." The honeyed voice of a whiny girl. "You never treated me well."

"I'm crazy about you, flower."

The hero had his jacket off.

"You devil! You only like to humiliate me."

"Come on, that's silly."

He managed to get her jacket off with difficulty.

"I wasn't to blame for what happened."

"I know that."

"No. You didn't forgive me."

Why, oh Lord, does it take two people to make love?

"Let's go inside."

She didn't get up and he didn't lower her skirt.

"Tell me you love me."

"Can't you tell? Do you want to go to my room? Or my parents' room? There's a double bed there."

"Will anybody come?"

Lost in the mist of drink, she adjusted her eyes:

"Here? In your parents' room?"

"What's wrong? Is it some kind of sacrilege?"

An enormous all-blue Christ covered the wall for the width of the bed. They sat on the crocheted spread.

"What a beautiful spread!"

"Beautiful's the word for your breasts, love!"

When she kissed him desperately, she moaned as if in pain. Nelsinho felt his tongue sucked in by the famished mouth.

"You wouldn't look at me."

"The guy was my friend."

"Nadir was my love," and she whimpered on his shoulder.

"He's dead. Now take your clothes off."

She unbuttoned the black and shiny silk blouse.

"Turn out the light."

"Why?"

"Just because."

In the darkness he opened the door slightly—the glow from the hall invaded the room. The hero pulled off his shirt. In her slip, her legs crossed, Laura was nodding with her hand on her chin, disconsolate.

"Take those clothes off right now."

His pants were already rolled on the carpet. She stood up, unfastened her skirt. Impatient, Nelsinho grabbed it and flung it carelessly in the direction of the dressing table.

"Don't throw my clothes on the floor!"

Laura jumped from the bed, picked up the silk skirt and folded it over the stool. She took off her slip. She took off her brassière.

"Take it all off."

She took off her panties. She halted indecisively in the middle of the room. She retreated a few steps and stood in the shaft of light—naked, twice naked! Before the hero could take flight, she closed the door and lay down beside him. He reached out his hand, softly stroking her shoulder. He ran his titillating fingers over her breasts: two pears, which, because they were so ripe, quivered under the weight of his pecking.

"Oh, sweetie, you're wicked."

"Lie still."

Amidst moans she babbled a thousand complaints.

"No."

He stopped his movement.

"Slowly, sweet."

He went back to slobbering over her hair, her neck, her shoulder, slowly, ever so slowly.

"Make believe I'm Nadir."

Underneath him the girl's body trembled.

"Oh, don't talk. For the love of God. Don't talk about Nadir."

In order to distract himself, Nelsinho ground his teeth

and remembered the immortal lines of Casimiro de Abreu: "I remember! I remember! / I was small . . ." With the third repetition, when he reached the line "How harsh the orchestra! How insane the furor!" she gave a cry.

"You're tearing me!"

Trampling over the verse, he lost consciousness. He came to with a light hand stroking his neck.

"You're in fine shape and I ache all over."

His eyes were heavy under the soft tickle of the nails and he raised his eyes to the blue painting on the wall:

"Oh, if Nadir could only see us . . ."

The blade of the guillotine fell and the hero's head flew far off, still talking in astonishment:

"What kind of madness is that?"

He felt his wounded neck, lighted the lamp on the night table:

"Are you crazy, girl?"

"No." And with eyes closed, nibbling on his chin. "I'm thirsty."

With the assassin's blow of the nails on his neck, he took three leaps on the carpet, hiding his parts with one hand. He opened the dresser drawer, took out a set of his father's pajamas, and put on the pants; they were too long and he had to roll up the legs. He went to the kitchen and came back with a bottle of gin, a pitcher of water, and some ice cubes. Laura put on the pajama top, all buttoned up. With both hands she tied the tails together, lying at ease on the sacrosanct family bed.

"Do you think I'm pretty?"

Oh, what an urge to roar and throw her out: little bitch!

"Do you tint your hair?"

"Ever since he died."

Under the pajama top, nude and like an offering, one of her legs folded.

"Oh, fake blondes have been my ruination. Peroxide hair and dark eyebrows!"

Nelsinho poured them both generous drinks, she lighted two cigarettes. They stretched out on the dozens of crocheted squares, a whole year's work by his mother's diligent hands.

"How was Nadir? Was he better than me?"

"Don't you have any respect for the dead?" And showing her breasts through the open top, "What do you think of me?"

Mother of heaven: two round little cupcakes decorated with a cherry on the tip.

"There's not another like you!"

The beauty's head lay heavily on his arm.

"Was he better than me?"

"You're a colossus," and she bit him hard on the pap.

"Jesus, Laura. Don't bite, it hurts."

Enlightenment in the drooling thread of a voice:

"No one would give anything for you . . . Skinny as you are!"

She grabbed the glass, drank it to the last drop, and with a hoarse voice:

"He was my first love!"

With dreamy eyes she recalled her lost beloved. She would never be the same; proclaiming that she was someone else even to the point of dyeing her hair. She only wore a black silk blouse—a widow's shroud.

"It's too late to cry now."

"I'm all raw."

"Don't exaggerate, sweet."

She was trying to play the virgin—which she'd never been. She curled up on the corner of the bed, wrapped in the spread.

"What's wrong?"

"I hurt."

"Don't play the saint. How many did you have after him?"

"Since he died I haven't been the same. It was different with Nadir. With him it was for love . . ."

"I know all about that. He was a colossus—isn't that the word you use?"

All offended, she sat up on the bed, put out her leg, and pulled her stocking up onto the thigh that glowed from being so white. He grabbed her. Laura defended herself furiously, wasn't she an unconsolable widow, mourning in eternal longing?

"No, please. I don't want to. Please. Not now."

Later on he let her get dressed in peace. He turned on the lights and looked around. Proud of himself, he felt like a hero all painted gold: the bedroom was a battlefield, there on the bed the corpse was bleeding from its wounds without staining the sheets.

"By God, I'm more of a man than my father."

THE LOST HERO

❧ THAT CREATURE won't take her eyes off me. The nerve of the dame, with someone next to her! It's true that some guys don't catch on. When it isn't a case of pushing them into someone else's arms—that seems to excite them. I finished my affair with Lili, I don't know whether you knew. I want to rest a little. Don't look now. She's eating me up with her eyes. Yes, that one, the one at the back table.

I'm not telling you anything. Man, Lili was an experience for me. When I met her I didn't know who she was. We were introduced at a party. As soon as I shook her hand I guessed everything: warm and damp. That look—a wren with a broken wing—restless and misunderstood. In the middle of the sentence she breaks into a sob . . . Mistrustful look, with her secret. She poses as if she's not giving herself away. It's there in the touch of her hand, the flutter of her eyelids, the sway of her hips. Some start the game themselves: I adore strong types, the kind who crush you in bed, who slap your face—it's true, they like to be mistreated. Others are delicate: pauses in their speech, gentle gestures, the ring on the small finger pointing at this or that. They make sure they're accompanied by lewd old women, mother or aunt, whose arched hand you kiss. Or by an ugly girl friend, with the hope that you'll say: Look at Lili, she's got a heart of gold.

Her eyes are like pernicious anemia. They don't seem to blink, they grow and grow and want to devour you. Lili is one of the difficult kind, or pretends to be. She invited me to her apartment the next day. Come in, sit here. Closer, I won't bite you. Oh, you know, man, I'm a lost hero. I'm not telling you anything (he coughs). I have to get some cough medicine. Then I explained: I'm not that kind, Lili. I know, I'm a sharp girl—and she wet her two fingers with her lips to fix a curl on her head. Oh, love is such fun. Is it fun? Yes, it is. It's wonderful. It was a formal visit. There wasn't anything between us. At the door she wrapped herself around my neck—naked under her silk kimono. She tried to kiss me, then I lighted another cigarette. I hate tongue kisses, I have to spit—not in front of her, of course, the little devil's not to blame—to get the taste out of my mouth. I found out that you had an affair with so-and-so. Don't try to deny it, Lili. It's one of that low-life's lies. I'm not what you think I am— if my man found out he'd kill me. Aren't you afraid of him? Just imagine if someone told him. Oh, he'd kill me. Oh, Nelsinho, you're so strong—I don't look it, do I? She offered me a marijuana cigarette, I have the feeling she's an addict. She goes crazy, she wants to nibble, she likes to bite—look at the results (puffy face, a pimple on the chin). I've been like that ever since I was little. I'd see passion in my cousins' eyes. The tragedy of having been too good looking (come on, now, you still are, Nelsinho, you still are). There are more than enough kisses in my lips for all the blondes in Curitiba.

You can see from this picture. It's me at the age of five, in a sailor suit. Lili almost drove me crazy over that picture. She'd drink and then she'd roll on the floor to get me to put on a uniform. What uniform? Well, a sailor suit that she'd improvised herself. Just imagine—a grown boy this size!—with short pants and a cap with a ribbon and silver letters. And she'd dream all night, talking in her sleep, I couldn't sleep. In the dream she was the one dressed as a sailor. I'm not kidding you. Rocked in the cradle by maestro Carlos Gomes in person. The maestro in full dress and high shoes with velvet spats, you know who he was? A satyr disguised as a musician, who undressed her with leather gloves, because he had erysipelas on his old-man's twisted fingers. Don't ask me the meaning of it. She refused to tell me—it would have shocked me.

She's looking at me as if I were naked, the bitch. I don't know what they see in me (a slow examination in the wall mirror). I seem to be the type they like. Lili was gnawed inside with jealousy over the success I had among her girl friends. We'd go to the movies and she'd keep an eye on me instead of paying attention to the picture—look at the screen, girl, afterward you'll complain that you didn't understand it. Don't turn around, for God's sake. The guy with her just noticed. The one with gray hair, distinguished looking. A lot of girls prefer a family man, I think it's insecurity. Lili confessed to me about her first experience. A poor fat man, I don't know how many children. He chased her so much he almost drove her crazy. In order to get rid of him the poor thing finally gave in. His wife found out and went looking for satisfaction. You can choose, then, the wife said, her or me. I've already chosen, the family man announced. Right then and there he left her and the four children. Later on Lili left him—an old man of fifty! He threatened her: If you don't love me there's nothing left for me but to die. The little bitch answered: Die, then. Two days later the guy committed suicide: cutting his wrists, taking poison, and turning on the gas. When she found out, she commented: So he died, fine! I'm quite happy with my little sailor boy.

I was the one who settled accounts with her because of the old man—you shouldn't treat creatures like that well even if you want to. Look at the devil provoking me over there. She's crazy to do it in front of the guy. When one of them gets a hold on you she won't leave you alone for the rest of your life. They're all the same, crazy jealous: You don't love me. It's not the same anymore. Where did you go? You looked at someone else. If I took too long on the street she'd be waiting for me at the door. She liked to drink out of the same glass, at the place my mouth had been. She couldn't stand tomatoes but she tried hard to eat them just because I like them. In order to arouse me she'd get dressed in front of the window—in the building across the way all the peeping toms in Curitiba ran for their binoculars.

At night it was egg yolks with white wine. In the morning, baked apple served in bed—why don't you stop drinking, love? Don't be a bore, Lili, you give up smoking. Oh, you only want me for one thing, I'm not only that. She showed me the scar on her wrist with several cuts. If you leave me I swear I'll kill myself. First I'll write a letter to the newspapers—and she'd come out of the bathroom naked, dancing a rhumba with a towel around her waist.

In hopes of reviving the lost love, she asked him to hit her. Abuse me, love. They all like to be punished . . . Not a little tap but a full slap with five fingers. Let the creature be sorry, with her swollen face, that she can't earn a living for you. Let them be the way they are, never apologize. If she loses her respect for you, man, you're through as a pimp.

UNDER
THE BLACK BRIDGE

❦ ON THE NIGHT of June twenty-third, Ritinha da Luz, sixteen years old, unmarried, with her housemaid ways, left work and headed for the house of her sister Julieta, who lives behind the Black Bridge. She was crossing the railroad tracks when she was attacked by four or five individuals, who were joined by two more people. Then she was raped by each one and left in the bushes. Her weeping attracted a policeman, who took her to the station house.

The girl had never seen the men and didn't know what to attribute the attack to. She gave information that she hadn't been a virgin for more than a month. And she didn't know which one of them was first, because when she was grabbed and thrown down they covered her face with a jacket. Dragged along the ground, she felt strong pains in her breasts and other parts. Besides that she was brutally beaten so that she wouldn't call for help. She appeared in a black silk skirt and red knit blouse that were dirty with mud. On her body, besides many wounds, there were dry leaves, grass, and dirt. The time was around ten or eleven.

Miguel So-and-So, forty years old, married, railroad fireman, left work at half-past ten and when he crossed the tracks noticed three soldiers and a woman in a suspicious position. He felt a tremendous desire to practice the act with the unknown woman. He went over to the group and, aided by the soldiers, grabbed the woman, taking off her clothes and having relations with her, although by force. He pulled her down and in order to muffle her cries he covered her face with his fireman's jacket. Sated, he helped the soldiers, each of whom in turn used the girl, watched by some onlookers in the distance, until two of them left the group and also took advantage of the Negro girl.

Miguel is completely regretful of his bad deed and as a proof he offered to marry the girl, whose name he didn't know and only at the station house did he discover it was Ritinha, that is, as soon as he could get his separation papers because he's married at the moment.

Nelsinho So-and-So, minor, thirteen years old, student, on the night of the twenty-third found himself talking under the Black Bridge with his cousin Sílvio and two other boys when they spotted three soldiers and a civilian attacking a woman, who was pulled to the ground and immediately taken advantage of by the civilian, and because of her shouts she had a jacket over her head. He went there, half mistrustful. After the civilian it was the turn of the three soldiers, and finally Nelsinho, who was followed by Antônio.

When the fun was over they were on their way home, satisfied, when they were arrested and taken to the police station. Nelsinho doesn't know the Negro girl and is bothered by what he did, attributing his attitude to his young age. He promises that it won't happen again, because things like what he did can only serve to ruin a young man's future.

Under the Black Bridge

Alfredo So-and-So, twenty years old, single, soldier, found himself at night under the Black Bridge in the company of his comrades Pereira and Durval. After some time Durval accosted a girl, with whom he went into some nearby bushes beside the railroad tracks. Then Alfredo and Pereira followed their comrade and, one after the other, they took advantage of the wench. When they were about to leave, an individual appeared who presented himself as a crossing guard and in exchange for silence he demanded that they hold the girl while he had relations with her. Then they dragged her to another place farther off and better hidden where no one would hear her shouts. Two more boys arrived, one of them about thirteen, and, helped by everyone, they also took advantage of the Negro girl. Since it was late, Alfredo went back to the barracks with his comrades. Only on the following morning did he find out about the mess he was involved in from the order he received to report to the police station.

Durval So-and-So, nineteen, single, soldier, found himself with two friends near the Black Bridge where he was waiting for some woman to spend the night with. A woman appeared, with whom, after some conversation, he went into the bushes because the girl liked his blond hair and blue eyes. His two comrades went over and each in turn took advantage of the girl.

Suddenly a surly civilian appeared, who, passing himself off as a railroad watchman, showed great interest in joining the party, to the displeasure of the girl, who didn't like his flat nose, stringy mustache, and rotten teeth. Then they dragged the Negro girl to a more distant spot where her shouts wouldn't be heard. Then two fairly young boys arrived, who, helped by the others, took advantage of the girl. Satisfied, Durval and his comrades returned to their barracks.

Pereira, eighteen, single, soldier, found himself at ten at

night on the Black Bridge with his comrades Alfredo and Durval when the girl passed by and Alfredo exclaimed: "There's a pretty little dark one." She stopped and asked what he'd said. They began to talk and Alfredo suggested they sleep together. She answered: "This blond has got his nerve" and that she wasn't going to sleep with anyone, but that he could go along with her. Alfredo left with her, followed at a distance by the others. At the end of the wall along the railroad tracks they stopped. When the deal was made, they went into the bushes. She wanted money, but they couldn't pay since their pockets were empty. They were coming out of the underbrush when the crossing guard appeared: "Since you went with the soldiers you have to go with me too." The girl said: "Look at the bum" and "Beat it, you stink."

The guard, who was a big, grimy dark man, insisted on taking advantage of the girl, having been rejected. That was when he threw her to the grass. The fellow smothered her while she cried and tore her hair.

Sílvio So-and-So, minor, fifteen, was with his cousin Nelsinho under the Black Bridge and they got a good look when the girl went by. The soldiers made some remarks. One of them invited her to go to a room. She answered it was better in the bushes. They all went into the brush. Then a civilian appeared and insisted on abusing the girl.

On the way from the roundhouse, along the tracks, Miguel came upon three soldiers and a tramp, who was having relations with them. He felt a great desire to join in the fun and he proposed a deal to the woman. She insulted his manhood by calling him: "Pimp, stool pigeon, cuckold." Indignant at such insults, he decided to prove that he was a man. He grabbed her, with the help of the soldiers, but he couldn't bring the act to an end because he didn't have the energy in his nervous state. It was the soldiers who held her mouth to muffle her shouts.

The first one to have the girl was Durval, the second

was Alfredo, the third was Pereira, the minor Nelsinho was the fourth, and he, Miguel, the fifth. Ritinha submitted willingly and spontaneously to the desires of the others, but when Miguel's turn came she tried to refuse and they had to hold her down so that he wouldn't be demoralized as a man and in the eyes of his family.

Ritinha was weeping under the Black Bridge. She didn't know who had done her mischief since one of the soldiers had put his tunic over her head. They were identified by the boy José, who saw everything from a distance. Two weeks previously Ritinha's father had died in the hospital of a stomach tumor. She'd been deflowered a month ago by a blond soldier named Euzébio.

The house where she works is a wooden house painted yellow. The mistress is a fat lady, short and dark. Ritinha cleans the house, washes the clothes, and runs errands. The mistress's husband is named Artur. She has to take care of the couple's little girl. When the child cries, she holds it head down by the legs, then the little nuisance loses her breath and is quiet. The mistress gave her a pair of old shoes as a present and sold her two secondhand dresses which she took out of her pay.

She didn't ask for money from the three soldiers because she found one of them very nice, with very blond hair. It was when the watchman arrived and told her to climb over the wall because one wasn't allowed to go through railroad property. Ritinha jumped over the wall and behind her went the four men who later on were six or seven. The girl began to cry, attracting José, who remained spying in the distance.

The sullen-looking guard roared: "You have to know a man or else I'll kill you. First it was Durval, then Alfredo, followed by Pereira, now it's my turn, hey, hey!" Ritinha began to shout and tried to run away, but she was grabbed by the arms and legs.

The subjects threw her down on the other side of the

wall. They did whatever they wanted to with her and she was flung aside there, hurt in the breast and parts, until the policeman found her moaning from the cold and the pain.

Officer Leocádio, as he was going under the Black Bridge, saw a Negro girl crying.

A BOY
HUNTING BIRDS

"A LAWYER'S A PRIEST, dear lady. You can trust me."

"I know that, Dr. Nelson."

"Don't be ashamed. Tell me the truth. You deceived your husband, isn't that it?"

"Good heavens, no!"

"In this citation you appear as the guilty party."

Married ten years. Two children. Six months before she'd miscarried. For convalescence she'd gone for a rest at her mother's. When she got back she found the house closed, the doors and windows locked. With the lock changed, she couldn't get in. Right there on the street she was handed the subpoena by the process server: separation with the allegation of adultery.

"Who's this João Maria named as correspondent?"

"An old friend, Doctor. He's on my side. He's not against me."

In mourning for her mother, a tight black dress with a bow-shaped brooch. The husband hated his mother-in-law. He didn't say a word to her for the three months the old woman stayed at their house with a bladder ailment. "Have pity on her," the wife begged him. "Pity? What about you? Do you have pity on me?"

Wearing dark glasses: a black eye from a punch.

"A man who's weak in bed is strong when he's out of it."

"What did you say, Doctor?"

"Tell me what happened, ma'am."

They'd gone to the country, her husband, she, and the daughters. Since she'd refused him, alleging female troubles, the brute planned to catch her with trickery. He proposed that they go back through a shortcut in the woods—he sent the children ahead. He pushed her down in the field because she still refused. The children came back with the shouts and were hitting him with their parasol: "Don't hit my mother! Don't kill my mother!"

"I'll be happy to take your defense, Dona Olga."

The next time, signing the power of attorney, the documents. So young, wasn't she growing weak because she missed her husband? It had been months, the separation of bodies, living in her father's house.

"You seem nervous."

"You have no idea, Doctor."

"Before you were married you probably weren't as nervous, right?"

"I was very calm. Now I suffer from nerves—sometimes I get attacks!"

Oh, beautiful, she gets attacks.

"Did you ever . . . become delirious, Dona Olga?"

With lowered eyes: "Yes."

"It's a gift from God. Did you know that delirium has a

touch of the miraculous? A woman has convulsions, Dona Olga."

". . ."

"It's a scientific fact. Don't be ashamed. A working lawyer is sexless."

"I know, Doctor."

"Here in the office there are a lot of interruptions. I'll take the papers to a quiet place. Is the hotel by the station all right?"

"Yes."

He waited from a quarter to four until four-thirty—I frightened the dove, she won't ever come back.

"Dona Olga, why didn't you come?"

"I did. I was late. You'd already left."

She was deceiving him, the devil, not wanting to say no.

She came to the office after hours to discuss the support her husband would pay for the children. At six o'clock sharp Olga went into the waiting room. The hero closed the door and attacked. The girl defended herself and kept him at a distance—she was stronger than he.

"You were an idol. An idol that fell. Do you think that a separated woman can't be chaste?"

"Just a little kiss, Olga."

"Open the door. Look, I'll scream."

She would stay—just a while—if he opened the door. A quick kiss that she didn't return.

"Be patient. Let's go inside. I promise to behave."

With the door open—imagine if someone came!—he continued the attacks. Steps on the stairway, the elevator was coming up now, now it was going down. As they sat on the sofa the beauty gave him her hand, which he covered with inflamed kisses.

"I'm leaving. Look, I'm leaving."

She got up, went to sit in the other chair. He dragged her to the sofa. I don't know how many minutes of fierce silent struggle: she clutched his fingers with painful squeezing. A ceremonious farewell at the door:

"Keep well, Doctor."

"I'll resolve your problems. You can be confident."

The husband appeared in the office one afternoon:

"Any more papers to sign, Doctor?"

"Just one."

"I don't trust her, Doctor. The neighbors talk a lot. She's wearing too much make-up."

"She's a straight girl. Do you have any concrete proof? Do you know for a fact?"

"No facts, Doctor. But I'm always mistrustful. A woman who's careful about her underwear means the man should watch out."

Overdressed, she was in the living room wearing a black skirt and white lace blouse, her arms showing—a vaccination scar half-hidden. While the girl read the petition, the doctor caressed her arm. While she pretended to be reading, her face was burning with excitement.

"Shall we go there?"

"There isn't right, Doctor. What do you want from me? Men only do things for interest. That's the price men ask!"

Blushing, the fuzz on her arm standing up. He didn't hold back: he smoothed her up and down with both hands.

The doctor was influential—did he know of any openings for a teacher?

"You can consider yourself appointed, Dona Olga."

When she left, she pursed her lips, and, although he was shorter because she was wearing high heels, he held back from standing on his tiptoes. This time she returned it, slightly.

"If I get it I'll come. I don't know if I can. I shouldn't."

"At five, then?"

It started raining exactly on the hour. He ran into her father, the old druggist.

"I'll send her without fail. You can count on me."

Olga reacted strongly, making him stumble backwards. "It won't work. I don't want to."

"Then it's all over. Your case has been processed. If you want to go home—go ahead," and he bent over, short of breath.

Among the law articles he began to remember the fuzz on her arm, the yellow look of a person with liver trouble—I get attacks, doctor! He sent an urgent message to the druggist for her to wait for him at home. He'd be there at two o'clock.

He clapped his hands at the lower door. Olga appeared in the window.

"Come in, I'll be right down."

He opened the door: where was the devilish old man? Lying in wait, who knows, behind the curtain? She came downstairs, holding her skirt, hiding her knees. Her house dress, wearing slippers.

He grabbed her at once, with hugs and kisses.

"I'm crazy about you."

Downcast, without make-up, rings under her eyes—oh, mother of heaven, with circles under her eyes!

What did she say? She just babbled:

"Yes, Doctor," and rolled her eyes. "Oh, Doctor."

Still protecting herself from his hands—he had three hands at least. A whole hour of kissing—her perfumed little teeth.

"Calm down. Papa might come in. Are you crazy?"

The start of tongue kissing. The dress was tight around her neck, he couldn't get her breasts out. Little nips on her ear lobes.

"Did you know what I wanted?"

"Yes."

"Since when?"

"Since the first time. The time you said a lawyer was a priest."

"Oh, Olga. Kiss me."

"It's no good here. What if Papa comes in?"

"What about the children?"

"I sent them outside to play."

"Go ahead. Go ahead. Just a little more. Just a little."

"Where'd you ever see such a thing? It's crazy here."

"You know my position. I'm married. If there was any risk I'd be the first to say no."

Going around the corner he pretended to be scratching his nose with his hand to his face so as not to be recognized. She appeared at the hour agreed on, in a hurry and coughing, with a handkerchief to her mouth.

He turned the key. She fell into his arms, trembling all over. She couldn't even speak, she was so frightened. He helped her unbutton her dress—careful, love, the clasp! He took off his tie, his jacket. They spoke in whispers—it was already a habit. Her husband was certainly right: her wonderful underwear—silk and lace! Kissing standing. Kissing sitting on the sofa. Lying on the rug, rolling.

"Do you want me to bite you or kiss you?"

"Yes."

"Kiss or bite?"

"Yes," it was all she could say. "Oh, yes. Oh, yes."

"Open your eyes. Look at me."

" . . ."

"Moan with me, angel. Now."

The hero moaned. She accompanied him in a lower tone.

"Oh, oh. I'm dying."

Lying on the rug, very quiet, the halted look of tame madness—her blue slip raised above her knees.

He buttoned his jacket, all dressed, and lighted a cigarette. The beauty was biting a bobby pin, watching him in the mirror:

"Another one for your collection, right?"

"You're the only one."

He went to put a bank note in her pocket.

A *Boy Hunting Birds*

"I'm not one of them."

He waited for her, hiding by the back door. In the back-yard next door a boy was hunting, a sling in his fist and a lost look. People were passing on the street: an old Negro woman, a soldier arguing with the barber. Heels clacking along the stones: it was she. Olga stopped in front of the door, he coughed three times.

"It's crazy," she murmured. "So dangerous!"

She was wearing a checkered skirt and wool blouse. When the door was closed she was the first to kiss:

"Thank you, love. You can ask whatever you want."

Grateful for the appointment as a teacher, she got undressed in a hurry. He was in shorts and black socks:

"Get naked."

Her pink breasts standing out. It was already a ritual:

"Do you want me to bite or kiss?"

"Yes," the mania of repeating yes, yes.

How is it that a brute could disdain such a loving woman? Emotional sighs as a reply—and the afflicted breath from dilated nostrils. When he squeezed her in his arms, the heady smell of a trembling mare.

"I had to run or I would have been late. I'm quite crazy. You made me that way."

"With João Maria, did you ever do . . . that?"

"Of course not! It never happened."

The hero sucked the nipple of her inflated breast.

"What was your husband like?"

In a hurry, looking for her without warning; turning his back immediately after. He didn't want her to get any bad habits—she felt like a dirty rag thrown into the corner.

"He follows me around. Isn't it risky coming here? I'm afraid. He checks on where I go."

"Kiss me. Don't talk now."

"Won't you get sick of me? A man gets what he wants, then he goes after someone else."

"Kiss me. Oh, Olga. Don't talk. Open your eyes."

175

Her large yellow eyes were quite red now. Help, Olguinha, you gave me an attack.

"Keep your eyes open."

When she went out, Olga was startled by the boy up in
the plum tree.

"There's somebody there."

"Don't be silly, it's a boy."

"What if he sees us?"

"A boy hunting birds is blind to everything that isn't a
bird."

THE GRAPES

✯ THE HERO WENT UP on the elevator with the
old man, each examining the other out of the corner of his
eye. They both got off on the fifth floor. He rang the bell. In
front of the next door, the old man was looking for his key.
Nelsinho understood from his mocking glance: "Look, there
goes another one . . ."

"Hello, Doctor," Ivone greeted him ceremoniously.
"Come in."

She closed the door and smiled:

"I called you doctor so as not to attract attention. That
old man's been persecuting me."

On the table, a tiny pot with a cactus. A thin black
shaft with a glowing scarlet tip sticking in the sand.

"It's Indian incense, love, to steal your heart!"

The light in the window flickered. Wrapped in a sweet-
ened cloud, he coughed slightly: Oh-oh, all I need is an
asthma attack.

"Very distinguished!"

The hero took her hands and tried to kiss her, but she quickly withdrew her face.

"Such a hurry! You didn't even say I was pretty."

A step back so he could admire her: all in black satin, the three strands of a gold necklace. Her mouth puffy with lipstick. Her hair tinted dark black, in waves over eyes with purple shadows—the latest incarnation of Mata Hari.

"You're beautiful, my sweet."

Very much the girl who wrote love notes between classes: *"From the woman here who loves you so much, so much, so much!"* He grabbed her hands and with a rapid move crossed her arms behind her back.

"Now you won't get away."

The hero kissed the air without reaching her, like a blind hen pecking wildly. She shook her head with little shouts of terror.

"I don't understand, Ivone. Why did you invite me?"

"I wanted to talk to you."

"You insisted you were alone. I didn't think it was to talk."

"Heavens! I never imagined you wanted that."

She held him back with the tips of her fingers:

"It's the same innocent look of a boy. Are you innocent?"

"You know quite well," and he struggled to draw her closer, only managing to knock off one of her earrings in the battle.

"Look what you've done."

"Leave it. I'll find it later."

"Oh, how awful! Let me go a little. How about a cigarette?"

With yellow-tipped fingers she lighted a match.

"You smoke too much."

"I'm so upset . . ."

"I'll leave if you want."

"No," and she took his hand, still holding the match. "Please stay. Look: the side where the head falls is where my love is."

The dark head rolled to his side.

"Do you really like me, love? I need someone so much. I feel so alone since Mama died."

"What about your husband?"

"Poor Vivi."

The first shadows of night were spreading in the corners.

"Would you like some grapes, love?"

The ember was burning on the tip of the incense— Ivone gave him the plate with cold grapes and a starched napkin. She sat down across the table from him, her face was a blue cloud of smoke. She crossed her legs and showed her slipper with a red pompon.

"Are you nervous?"

"Not at all."

"I am. I never cheated on Vivi. The grapes are good, aren't they?"

"Wonderful. Want some?"

"No. I had some already."

She flicked an ash into the cactus pot, revealing a beauty mark on her shoulder.

"Let me kiss that spot!"

The trembling of a skittish fish:

"It tickles. Oh, if Vivi . . . I don't even want to think about it!"

"Where is he?"

"Out."

"Is he good to you?"

"Yes, he is. Attentive, well mannered."

She went to the radio to get a picture in a silver frame.

"See how much he looks like you. The same look. I think that's why I liked him. Do you remember the first kiss on the veranda at home?"

"How could I forget?" and he rubbed his lips on her shoulder, but he missed the mark. "Were you a virgin?"

"What a question."

"Is it true what they say about Vivi?"

"He certainly was a different kind of bridegroom. Poor me, I even wept with joy. An educated boy who spoke several languages. There'd been only little kisses with great respect. He explained that he'd had an English upbringing. Then, you know . . ."

"What happened?"

"I opened the door suddenly and I found him kissing the janitor's boy."

She drew deeply and desperately on the cigarette, almost swallowing her cheeks. Smoke in his eyes, upset, he felt a need for air.

"Your apartment's nice."

"Would you like to see it?"

Ivone showed him the kitchen. She opened the bedroom door:

"Excuse the mess."

The room was in perfect order, with twin beds. Standing, side by side, he embraced her and this time managed to kiss her, but she didn't return the kiss, skimpy mouthed.

"Wait. I'm going to clean my lips."

"One more little kiss."

"I don't want to stain your shirt."

She went to the dressing table, wiped a tissue across her carmine lips. He examined her back until he found the spot —now I'm going to get her naked. Beside the bed, a lamp on the night table with a blue bottle for a base.

"Very original."

She replied without turning, looking at him in the mirror:

"Yes, isn't it."

She turned around: her lips as blood red as before, thick

with lipstick. He went to meet her, began to kiss her neck, where a vein was throbbing strongly. He looked for buttons on the satin, running his fingers down her back and he left his hand resting on a buttock—I'm crazy about button dresses.

"How do you do it?"

"What, sweet?"

"How do you get it off?"

"Heavens, what a hurry!" She frowned with annoyance. "Let's talk a little."

"Nonsense, honey. This is no time for talking."

Upset, she stepped back two paces:

"All right. Take your clothes off."

She pulled the dress over her head with such skill that she didn't muss her hair. He took off his jacket.

"Do you want a hanger?"

"I'll hang it over here."

With his back to her he threw his pants onto the foot of the bed. He turned, and what did he see? Her, in brassière, petticoat, and pompon slippers. At that point the hero attacked in his shorts. He lifted her skirt and caught the thighs in the mirror—woe is me, they weren't the fabulous thighs of his childhood dreams: the matron is the maiden's lopsided grandmother. In order to console himself, he closed his eyes and snuffled on her throat. He felt a violent push, which made him stumble:

"What is it? What's wrong?"

"Wait a minute."

Foolish with surprise he watched her go to the bed table, take a cigarette, and, after lighting it, open the closet, where she took a towel, which she laid over the bedspread, which was green with a gold pattern.

Nelsinho took off his shorts, wearing only shirt and shoes. She faced him and, her hand behind her, twisting her bust, she undid the brassière: oh, fearful flaccid breasts! He was quite excited now as he watched her take her panties off, wearing only the half-slip. When he embraced her he got a side glimpse of her buttocks in the mirror. Then she hesitated, upset:

"What about the earring?"

"What earring? Oh, I'll find it later."

"You're in such a hurry, it's terrible! I'm going to wash my hands."

"Not now. Later."

"It has to be now."

Without admitting he was depressed, the hero exhibited himself in the mirror and admired his attributes. From the front and in profile, lifting his shirt tails—the big bitch, let her be, she'll pay for this!

Ivone came out of the bathroom, stopped halfway to take off the half-slip, and stepped on it—naked, with a cigarette in her mouth! She avoided his embrace again:

"Aren't you going to take your shoes off?"

She went over to sit on the bed, lighting a new cigarette from the butt of the other.

Nelsinho got his shoes off. Trembling with impatience, he kissed her on the arm, the neck, the ear—do you remember that night on the veranda, dear?

"Watch out. I'll burn you."

She was smoking slowly, her mouth fierce, her eyes on the ceiling.

"Take it easy, sweet. Look at the ashes on the spread."

She rose up on her elbow to crush the cigarette in the ash tray. Suddenly she wrapped him in a tight embrace. Without explanation, she lay back moaning loudly: Oh, oh, oh! She pushed him and shook her head:

"Your left eye is very pretty!"

She grabbed him violently in the midst of jabbing moans. His face sunk in her hair, Nelsinho sneezed twice.

"What's the matter, sweet? Catching cold?"

"I think it's my asthma."

Without warning she began to defend herself with nails and elbows:

"You're squashing me. Let's change position. Get lower. I'm not in a good position. Don't muss my hair."

He followed her instructions, frustrated and miserable. Finally, Ivone wrapped her arms around his neck and kissed him, moaning off key. In the middle of the kiss, her eyelids quivered and she opened her eyes a bit. She stared deep into his eyes, very serious, frowning. Nelsinho began to pant, bathed in cold sweat.

"Are you nervous, sweet?" the beauty sighed in a honey-eyed voice.

In despair he kissed her again, closing his eyes. He felt the other mouth, scornful, full of teeth. A thread of drivel ran down between the jaws, she turned her head away:

"You were very upset today, weren't you?"

Inhibited by the expression of censure, the furrows in the accusing forehead, he still asked:

"Kiss me, honey."

"Don't be nervous. It'll go away. Rest easy."

"You're the one who knows," his voice weak, defeated.

"That happens. I could see right away that you were nervous."

With the separation of the sweaty bodies, an obscene pop. Nelsinho rolled over onto his back.

"That's right. I think it could happen to anyone," with frightened bitterness in his soul.

"Let's stay very quiet," the unctuous words of hypocritical sweetness. "Just like me and my husband."

They lay there without touching each other. She tenderly fluffed the pillow so that he could rest his head. She took a handkerchief from the drawer of the night table and wiped the sweat from the agonizing brow. She put two cigarettes into her mouth, lighted them, and handed him one.

"Is it the first time?" The innocent girl on the veranda in days gone by.

The hero didn't want to talk, worried about being distracted.

"It never happened to me before."

"Could it have been the grapes?" Her breasts shaking with a scornful little laugh.

"Maybe if we stood up."

They stood up but it was no use: the revolting vision of buttocks in the mirror. Then sitting. They lay down again and picked up their cigarettes, which hadn't gone out. Nelsinho on his back, she resting on her elbow, blowing smoke into his eyes. With her free hand, Ivone offered her opulent breast between thumb and forefinger; without enthusiasm he sucked in the first drop of the saddest milk. His heart pounded on the pillow and the mattress groaned. The sweat ran down his forehead again.

"Just like Vivi."

Ivone breathed deeply and delicately let it out of her nose. Then she told about one time with a man. She was approached on the street. Right during her honeymoon. She never knew who he was. Instead of getting indignant she took him to her apartment. Mournful, Nelsinho saw desire warming her cheeks, the hoarse voice of excitement. He began to swallow drily. He covered her mouth with kisses, still with the fear that she would push him off to finish her sentence. He crushed her lips, opened his eyes a little to enjoy the triumph, noted the incredulous wrinkle on her forehead and— woe to him!—his glorious exaltation drained off into absolute defeat.

"Don't tire yourself so much, love. You might have a stroke."

She finished her story calmly, it was really quite interesting.

"Are you hot? Shall I open the window?"

"Lie quiet." And with humility, "This never happened to me. I don't know what . . . It's the first time."

"Of course. That's just the way my husband is."

It was the hero's turn to light the cigarettes and offer her one. In the silence he heard a child crying in the next apartment, a clock striking in the distance. The last glow of sunset on the window. The nauseating smell of the incense reached him: Lord, oh Lord, why didn't I die of asthma when I was five years old?

Ivone jumped off the bed, her breasts swinging, and went to get a box of matches from the living room. She came back with the plate:

"Don't you want to finish the grapes?"

Lying down, he nibbled on two or three. He sucked in the insides, dropping the skin onto the plate. He took another grape. He was so disconsolate that instead of spitting them out, he swallowed skin and seeds.

PASSION NIGHT

☙ NELSINHO WAS RUNNING through the streets hunting for the last female. Not a woman walking aimlessly, the bars all closed.

On the narrow sidewalk he brushed against two shapes and quickly raised his hand to his pocket. They had swept him with indiscreet fingers but they weren't thieves. He turned around and there they were, beckoning with languid gestures and sweet voices:

"Where you going, handsome?"

Those two would call any creature of the night handsome. Turning the corner, he came onto the square with the old drinking fountain—where were the butterflies?

The church was almost deserted with the images hidden behind purple cloths. Without crossing himself, Nelsinho went down the aisle, hearing the sand crackle under his shoes. The old Christ was there, taken down from his cross and lying in the middle of four lighted candles. In the pews, two or three harpies with black veils over their heads, their eyes in the shadow of their hands, on which their foreheads rested, or looking around the catafalque at Nelsinho. One of them, suggesting the example to him, prostrated herself on the cement and deposited a loving kiss on the wound in the foot.

Nelsinho took the smallest bill in his wallet and dropped it into the tray. He was being watched by the fierce guardians of the dead one as he completed the circuit, stingy with his kiss. He looked at the fearful image and repressed not a sob of grief, but a feeling of nausea: It's your fault, oh Lord, that all the brothels are closed. A rag doll—you talk of blood, oh Lord, and you don't bleed. What kind of a corpse was that, one from which the widows didn't bother to chase the flies that alighted on the open wounds?

To the scandal of the church biddies, the woman who came in dressed in leather (black skirt, green blouse, and red jacket) leaned over, her hair loose over her shoulders, sprinkled with rain, and with every gesture matched by a rustle of clothing, kissed the pierced feet. She didn't look at Nelsinho; as much as they ignored each other on the byways of the night, they were the chosen ones. The hero crossed the church and without turning to leave he stopped at the entrance, in front of the three steps. With the dry weather the black, smooth stones shone in the abandoned square. The rustle of leather approached and stopped beside him. Both looked stiffly ahead; he murmured:

"Where can we go?"

"Over there on the corner."

"Are the rooms good?"

"The ones downstairs are good."

A small pause, the rustle of leather:

"How long?"

"For the rest of my life, Magdalene."

They went down the steps, the beauty transferred her handbag to her left shoulder and tucked her right hand in his arm. He pointed to a big, run-down house:

"Do you know who lives there? The great passion of my life—a certain Marta. She ended up marrying a bank clerk, Petrônio."

"Don't be sad, sweet. I'm nothing but love. Did you have a good Easter?"

"I haven't had any kind of Easter—that's on Sunday."

"Oh, I thought . . . Then today isn't Easter?"

"Today's Friday, my flower. What time is it?"

"Almost eleven."

"It's the very night of the Passion. Tomorrow's Holy Saturday."

"Isn't tomorrow when people get eggs?"

"Tomorrow's the day they whip Judas. Lord, is it I?"

Ashamed of her ignorance, she clutched his arm:

"That's right, yes, love."

If the house only had one story, where were the downstairs rooms? At the end of the corridor a skinny harpy behind the desk.

"Are you going to spend the night?"

The rooms in front were reserved for half an hour.

"My time is at hand."

The old woman asked the woman in leather for the magazine that was sticking out of her handbag and took the key to No. 9 from the hook. Nelsinho handed the witch a bill. While he was waiting for his change he leaned on the desk. The possession of the magazine was in dispute between the two of them until, without warning, the old woman lowered the lid of the desk and caught the other's finger.

"Did I hurt you, love?" the old woman put in, jubilant, with the magazine in her hand.

"No," with an expression of pain, sucking her fingernail.

"I didn't mean to."

She gave the key to his companion and the change to him. Then they went to the famous room No. 9—the so-called downstairs rooms were in front. Actually rather broad, a double bed against the wall beside the window, with a dressing table and closet. In one corner the basin on an iron tripod: underneath it, the pitcher of water.

Glum, her hair in her eyes, the woman didn't move, standing in the middle of the room.

"What happened?"

"I'm so sad I could die."

The old woman had confiscated her photo-novel magazine and she'd never give it back.

"Yes, she'll give it back."

"It's not the first time."

He held her chin. Downcast, she fled with her face until she looked at him and smiled lovingly. With a start he discovered that she had no front teeth. There simply wasn't a single tooth between her upper canines—oh, Lord, must I drink from this cup?

In order to hide his distress, he went to close the door. As soon as he came back she went to meet him, wrapping him in damp leather and rancid flesh. What will become of me, God in heaven? As a sad consolation he imagined that she was the most fabulous woman there was in bed. In the hope of gaining time:

"Aren't you afraid, child?"

"Of you, love?"

"Of the punishment of heaven. This is the holy night. Today love is cursed."

"I asked for forgiveness for my sins. There in the church."

"Don't lie, you'll go to hell. How many times did you go in and out of the church? I bet you were hunting for men."

"Lord save me!"

She grabbed his head and tried to kiss him:

"You're so young! You have a woman's thick lips . . . I won't leave here without kissing you on the mouth."

"What if I were the Devil? What if I brought you here to make you lose your soul?"

"What kind of talk is that? You don't like me. Is that it?"

Cold and perverse eyes which, with an indiscreet word, would flare up in murderous fury. The hero was intimidated —there's no salvation for me, now to turn out the light.

He freed himself from her, took off his jacket, and sat on the edge of the bed. The wench came over to snuggle next to him, pushed back his head and began to bite him: he felt the lack of teeth on his neck.

"I'm going to bite you all over."

"Don't do that," he begged, terrified.

"It's too late now. I'm going to draw blood from you."

Sitting on his lap, completely dressed, bouncing and making the bed creak.

"Take, eat: this is my body."

"Aren't you Joana's friend?"

"Not Joana's and not Suzana's."

"Then you're going to be my man."

Proud, Nelsinho opened up in smiles—behold the man! He didn't want to lose his enthusiasm, he stood up. He loosened the knot in his tie. She pulled him by the shirt and when she had him at her mercy, she mounted him again, the creak of a new saddle. Finally she took her leather jacket off, the damned woman stank like a slaughterhouse. With a contrite air, she leaned over him, the corpse in the coffin watched over by the last mourner.

"Was your little body made for love?"

"Tonight, my child, love is a sin. Tonight it breeds monsters."

"You've got the tongue of the Devil."

"Thou sayest it." And he turned himself over to the sacrifice.

"What do you want me to do?" she insisted, possessed.

Clutching him as they sat on the bed, her skirt up above her knees, she rubbed his coarse, rough leg.

"What do you want me to do?" she shouted again.

If he had to go through the agony of love, was it necessary to suffer to the last breath?

"Do everything, love."

"Everything?"

"Everything you know."

Hurriedly, she unbuttoned his shirt. She ran her sharp nails along his sides—the one on her pinkie was longer than the others. Before he could reflect on the explanation of the mystery, he heard her impatient voice:

"Shall I turn out the light?"

Full of fear, he asked her not to. Underneath her, he pondered desperately:

"Wait a little. I can't find the buttons."

He took off his shirt, still in pants and socks. He began to caress her breasts through the sweater; he was surprised at her distant expression, uninterested in the ceremony now.

"Didn't you forget something?"

"Oh . . . Didn't I pay you?"

He took a note from his pants pocket, she put it away in her coat, and with no further delay she took her sweater off. Her decisiveness caught him up: Let what must be done be done.

In front of the dressing table the beauty admired the grotesque image of the power and the glory:

"Shall I take everything off?"

Sitting up, undoing the knot in his laces, he raised his head:

"Everything."

He got onto the bed so as not to drag his pants on the floor. The woman bent one leg, then the other, getting out of the black leather skirt—her thighs showing varicose blotches. She sat down to roll her stockings. She dropped her brassière. She went over to show off in the mirror: she held her two breasts in her hands. She caught Nelsinho's look there—he averted it quickly. The creature turned around. She snuggled next to him, ran her nails over his body, making him tremble all over. She stuck her tongue in his ear—Thy will be done, Lord, not mine.

Seeing him lying down, she glued her mouth to his chest to lick his paps: Ummh, that's what I call a woman! She brought her head lower, still kissing, and, at the level of his navel, produced an obscene whinny. She kissed her way up to his neck, then she retreated, and at the navel, the whinny of satisfaction again. The hero understood that she was preparing him for the sacrifice, sprinkling his body with aromatic balm. Now she was tickling his foot, hiding it in her long hair. The rapacious snout was exploring his naked skin and, defenseless, he begged:

"Don't bite!"

At that instant she put her mouth to his chin. He only felt the tongue. She took her beak away and began to slobber about his little dove of love, softly nibbling—was she going to bite?

"Stop!" He resisted with all his strength. "Don't do that."

She went back to suck his chin and the hero was alert to the gap in the teeth. Terrified, he defended himself with his hand on his throat. Suddenly the woman drew back her head. She caught her breath and came back, snuffling. She tried to bite, but he wouldn't let her. Leaning on her arms, her long hair dragging on the spread, completely naked, she rubbed him on the chest with her voluminous breasts, the boards of the bedstead shaking furiously. He was naked too

—with black socks—fleeing with a face licked by a thousand kisses. Not having plucked the flower of desire, she howled with frustration—with her canines she avidly sucked at his neck. Nelsinho raised himself with his hands as she clung to his shoulder.

"I'm going to draw blood."

"You're not. Enough now."

"You won't get away," and she was relentless in her ferocious pursuit.

With his last breath he roared in terror:

"Is there any water?" As soon as he thought he was free, he sighed with relief. "I'm a pool of sweat."

The creature picked up a towel and threw it in his direction. She brought the pitcher of water and took out a basin from under the bed. He turned his back on her, rubbing his hands on the slimy winding-sheet, listening to the splashing in the basin. He felt an itching on his feet, the vermin was asking for the towel. When he noticed, she was settled down beside him again. Naturally, she was still demanding a kiss.

"I'm lost!" he moaned from the depths of his soul.

She began to repeat everything. She ran her fingers along his spine, and, huddling up, he twisted all over. His neck was sticky, she licked his paps, again the violent snorts, with a neigh from heavy lips.

"Stop that!" And when he saw her frightened expression: "Let's go slow."

"How come you wanted to before?"

Everyone is sleeping, nobody comes to help: now I close my eyes and faint with sadness.

"The cock crowed three times."

Sulky, lying on her back, one of her hands on her belly, the woman scratched her mange. A minute hadn't passed when she went back to slipping her furtive hand along his chest, then his stomach, pressing it down to the point of pain. She lifted herself on her elbow:

"Look at his little body. So thin and white . . . It looks like that of the other one. There in the church."

She grabbed his hand, gave it soft bites. Nelsinho suffered the hollow of her teeth. Implacably, she went on, pursuing with her mouth; she insisted, decisive and insatiable, lowering his resistance in a short time—my God, my God, why hast thou forsaken me?

She applied the obscene cupping glass fully to his lips, spraying bubbles of frothy saliva, oh filthy sponge of vinegar and gall . . . It is finished.

A savage shout of triumph and she was kissing him, possessed, with open eyes. He tightened his eyelids so as not to see the diabolical expression of pleasure.

They both got up on their own side. Once dressed, he opened the door without saying good-by. The woman hadn't even put on the first leather item.

Behold, the clock in the steeple announced the end of the agony. In the deserted street the terrible tolling broke the silence from top to bottom. Nelsinho halted and felt the earth quaking under his feet. At the height of the terror he stammered in a soft voice:

"Father, I am innocent."

◤ THE MAGIC RING

NAUSEA

❧ I'M SUFFERING from palpitations. It's just a question of a little drink and it'll go away. Could it be anxiety? Or is it really my heart? If you don't have one too, I won't accept. What a pity, it really is, you always complained about your liver. I had to leave the house, I couldn't stand being inside those four walls any more. It's the way I told you, I'm determined to leave Horácio. You don't know what I've been through at the hands of that man.

He never went out at night without me. Six months ago there was a charity party. He invited me, but I didn't have a decent dress. With what he earns, you know, we can't spend much—I'm the one who sews her own clothes. My best dress is a summer one, bare shoulders, and since it's winter I suggested I go wearing that dress and a jacket. No jacket, he protested. They'll make you check it at the door and you'll have to pay. Well, he couldn't pay or didn't want to. He got a miserable salary where he worked and he wouldn't allow any spending. We ended up arguing—could you imagine a pettier reason? Finally he went by himself and from that day on we haven't spoken to each other.

Horácio would come home, hang up his hat, and go into the bathroom. A quiet rage was growing inside me; he acted as if I didn't exist. I didn't deserve for him to make me suffer like that. One night, without a word, he began to kiss me—I thought I'd die. When he turned over to his side I had to go to the bathroom and throw up. From rubbing my mouth so much to get the stink of his mustache out, I ended up spitting blood.

During all that time he came to me three times, always silent, hurried, and brutal. The last night he left me in peace and accused me of being frigid. Me frigid? Someone like me frigid? Under his filthy hands I felt like . . . Remember when you were a child and played with a little pill bug? As soon as you touched him with a finger he curled up into a ball. I act like a pill bug when he puts his hand on me—I'm not myself anymore but an animal hidden in his shell, a closed ball with no arms or legs.

Thank you, just one more drink. Living in the same house, we never go out together anymore. One doesn't talk to the other, one doesn't look at the other. He eats alone and then it's my turn: one listens to the mouth of the other chewing on his rage. He goes to work and I sit there staring at the yellow walls—I used to cry, but now I'm not so foolish. He's a poor devil, a wretch who doesn't even earn enough for cigarettes. You couldn't even guess what I use for rouge—crepe paper that I wet with my tongue and rub hard. You can't even tell it's not rouge, can you? I was always pale, ever since I was a child. When he leaves I sit in front of the mirror, comb my hair, make myself all up, and so as not to go mad, left alone in that house, I got visit Olguinha. We go to the movies, sometimes I go by myself, always with an umbrella to defend myself against some masher. Olguinha discovered an egg liqueur that's good for the nerves.

When I get home, there he is. Sitting in the kitchen with the light out waiting for the old slave woman to heat up his dinner. I fix something or other and while he hunches over his plate, I go hide in the bedroom—I can't bear watching the way he piles the food up on his fork and even uses the knife to help. Every time he sucks his teeth, I bite my tongue so I won't shout. He's a careless man and during the time I felt something for him I forgave his defects. He doesn't even know how to cross his silverware. When he drinks water he leaves half of it in the glass. It's nauseating, the greed with which he sucks with delight on the pope's nose—look how I'm trembling. All right, I'll have another. Where was I? Oh yes, lots of times I was startled by a noise at the living-room door that shook the wooden walls and made the glasses in the crystal cabinet tinkle. Do you know what it was? Well, it was him, scratching himself while he was standing up, rubbing his back against the doorjamb, just the way you see horses doing it. On Sundays he shuffles around in his slippers, wearing his flea-stained pajamas—he even seems to have *sweet blood*. There in the kitchen, resting one foot at a time on the chair, he'll start cutting his calluses with a razor. During the early days, fool that I was, I asked him please not to—my uncle lost his leg, all black with gangrene. Do you know what it's like to spend the rest of your life with a man clipping the calluses on his feet—every callus the spur of an old rooster?

That's the man who wants an explanation for my absence. I don't even answer, because he doesn't exist for me. The last time he shouted that if I couldn't tell where I spent my afternoons it was because I went to some brothel and he didn't want a slut in his house. You can think what you want, sir—he eats me up with his eyes when I call him sir. Don't tell me the cordial is all gone! That's too bad, it was quite good. Sweet orange wine? If it's for me, don't bother. All right, if you insist—just a swallow. I dreamed about dying, what's there to live for? The children are married, who cares about an old piece of rag? Don't be afraid, I won't do anything silly like that—thanks, just another sip. This orange wine is very good, is it homemade?

I'm the one who's not foolish anymore. If I were to die, he wouldn't waste any time getting someone else. At his age? With all those drugs, my dear, there isn't any more age. I already showed you what I found in his wallet. I'm the one who'd be happy if he died before me—cutting the crust of a corn he might just ruin his foot, right? All of a sudden I become aware of his presence. We keep our backs to each other so we won't see the other one. It's enough for me to look at that so-and-so accidentally to make my blood boil and my insides swell up trying to come out of my mouth. Do you know what he had the nerve to throw up to my face? That he was a man and if he couldn't get what he needed at home, he'd find it in the street. Do you know that he did go looking in the street? Where'd I put my purse? Look what I found in his coat. I found it and kept it, and he didn't have the nerve to ask who took it. It's a handbill for a certain magic ring, let me read part of it: "Magic ring—the wonder of the century. Old men will be able to enjoy the most precious gift of life, growing vigorous and powerful again. Cannot fail, money back if it doesn't get results. A magic ring means happiness in the home." What do you think a man like that deserves? And I'm the one who's frigid.

I could just as well go live with Olguinha, who's separated. Make candy or do sewing—I can't look at that old face anymore. He follows me on the street, I pretend that I don't see; he thinks he's going to catch me with a lover. If I don't have a lover—am I the frigid one?—it isn't because men don't look at me. He can thank God that I'm an honorable woman, if not it would be his punishment.

I already told you that because of Horácio I lost the little companion I could still have a good time with. It was the little goldfinch left by my youngest son when he got married. Knowing that I liked the little creature, that man began to blow the smoke from his homemade cigarettes in the direction of the cage. I got all tight inside, unable to speak. A goldfinch is so small, the smoke made the little thing sick. He got sad, dejected. He was getting worn out, his feathers ruffled, his puffed-up breast beat so hard that his whole body shook. He couldn't hang onto his perch. He buried his bill in the feeder and nuzzled the bird seed, which he couldn't swallow anymore. For years he'd been my companion. Tired of pushing the pedals on the machine, I would close my eyes and suddenly, there he was, eating his bird seed—I knew that I wasn't alone. Then I was alone: I went to change his water in the morning and found him dead, his head in the feeder. No one could get the idea that he died of suffocation out of my head. The fellow lighted one cigarette after another and blew the smoke at the little bird's dizzy head.

Not content with the death of the goldfinch, he goes to the mirror, stays there smoothing his mustache and cutting the hairs in his nose with a look of pleasure—the expression he must have had when he went into the other woman's house. He does everything to make me believe that he's got another one. I confess that he had me fooled until the day I found the ad for the magic ring. Do you think there's some magic ring for women? God help me. Maybe the orange wine is tricky. I'd better get my purse and umbrella, it's time to go home. One last glass, if you insist.

He must be there sitting in the dark, his hat on his head, his hands to his face. He pretends to be suffering, I know he's faking. In the quiet of the house I'll hear a muffled sob and lift my eyes in surprise—I can't tell if it was me or him. It couldn't be him, a monster without feeling. You don't think it's my fault, do you? Go ahead, speak up, you're my girl friend. I feel such despair that I don't know what's going to become of me. Please, you're my friend. Do you think I'm to blame?

CREATURES

OF THE NIGHT

❦ BITING OFF THE SHOUT between his teeth, Pedro awoke in panic. He wiped the cold sweat from his forehead with his hand. He groped on the night table, found his wrist watch: four o'clock in the morning. The hour of the old woman who nods with cold feet, sitting up in bed in the trembling light of the lamp. Of the mangy dog who grinds his teeth on the damp sack by the door, tormented by fleas. Of the agony of the small child hiccuping in the hospital ward. Of the unclaimed corpses, naked and bluish, in the deserted morgue. It's the fearsome hour of the cataleptic who comes to and chews his nails in the depths of the earth. How many nights now had Pedro awakened at the same time with the shout vanishing in his ears? The survivor of the greatest of horrors, he crossed his hands on his chest and, with his eyes open, got ready to wait.

The hospital clock struck four. If only, at least, he could

make out the shadows of the dying people through the window, he wouldn't feel that he was the only person awake in the world. In the silence that followed the last stroke, Pedro heard the ticktock of the clock in the parlor and, in reply, the watch on the night table. Farther off in the depths of the night, the furtive trotting of a dog.

Careful so that the mattress wouldn't creak, he sat up and put on his slippers: he resisted the compulsion to bend his knee on the rug and peek under the bed. With a grumble, pulling the covers, the woman turned her back to him. Anguished, he stayed there listening to the noisy whistle coming through her nose—any night now she would begin to snore. On tiptoes, the indecisive whitish shape stopped in front of the mirror. Every morning when he shaved he studied the imprecise features of the stranger—a face wavering in the water. Amused, perhaps, if it hadn't been for the trembling hand that held the razor, he studied the alien features of the other—alien and vaguely familiar. It wasn't his face lost in the empty mirror: the whitened splotch in there was that of his dead father. The grayish mustache that hung down from the embittered mouth was not his, he didn't have the courage to shave it off, he, who had always hated mustaches. Senile hairs came out of his nostrils. In the office he expected someone to reveal the usurpation at any moment, stating in a sinister tone that the dead man had been bigger. His friends, ironically taking off their hats, greeted him by name and pretended not to notice the mystification, giving in to the macabre game. With relief he realized that they too, the others, had suffered the same metamorphosis. From one day to the next, just like Pedro, they had all gone gray, if not bald. Exaggerating the bad taste of the pantomime, some dragged their feet, wearing spats, leaning on canes with gold knobs torn from the rigid hands of fathers in their coffins. And, even sadder, the maidens in flower for whom his afflicted heart had tired so early, what were they now? Fat matrons with flashing false teeth and varicose veins on their legs, vainly showing off their daughters on their arms . . . Alas! the daughters he remembered well— not the mothers—and his old heart still beat with delight over them.

Groping with his hands, Pedro headed for the kitchen. In the fish bowl the water was turning stagnant. Since the death of the last little red fish, he hadn't had the heart to buy any more so as not to be obliged to witness their end someday. Struggling, the sick fish rose to the surface of the water, opening their anxious mouths and smacking their lips —the surface covered with the bubbles of their death throes. The sleep of death weighed heavy on their lidless eyes, and, quivering, in a few moments they were dragged down to the bottom, until, twisting their fins in pain, they wiggled desperately to rise again. Not even a fish is allowed to die easily. Even when the water in the bowl was changed, their torture lasted two or three days: they would emerge striped with blood, confused, and still refusing to die, white bellies suddenly wavy with violent tremors—the entrails devoured by the dying ones. Pedro wet his finger in the invisible water: If fish could scream, who would dare go fishing? He stood there, his finger forgotten in the cold water. In the distance a clock repeated the four strokes. With a tired step he went into the kitchen: he was in no hurry, he wouldn't go back to sleep that night. Morning would be long in coming. Nothing was left for him to do but sit down at the table, his face in his hands, waiting for the sparrows to turn on the sun.

In the hollow of his hand, Pedro exhibited a tiny child. The size of a worm—he thought. It was dying, its naked body cold. Anxious to warm it, Pedro blew into the cup of his fingers. The child revived and, when he brought it close to his mouth, suddenly it sank its teeth into his lip, an enormous leech, black and swollen with blood—with a shout he came out of his dream and into the horror of four o'clock.

Sometimes he would go into the bathroom to wipe the sticky sweat from his face with a towel. What eyes spied on him then from behind the shower curtain? It was wavy with shivers—the tired arching of the curtain itself or simply the breeze from the window? Without the courage to find out, Pedro backed away. Oh, if he could only turn on the light on the night table and shake his wife: "Wake up, Júlia, wake up. Give me your hand, I'm afraid." It was an impossible desire, because she, not understanding, would ask with annoyance: "Good Lord, afraid of what?" Then he sat down on the kitchen chair, drank a few sips of water, smoked one cigarette after another. Or, covering his face with his hands, he listened to the hospital clock, the noise of a rat in the attic, the claws of a cat scratching the wall. A mysterious wagon rolled slowly along the cobblestones, the horse must have been old and tired, were there still wagons left in the world? What was it carrying at that late hour of the night or at such an early hour in the morning? The street cleaners must have passed already, sweeping with their long brooms, lost in the cloud of their own dust. With the flapping of wings of the first rooster, Pedro was dozing with his head on the table and—safe for that night—he heard the chilling whistle of a carouser, whom he imagined with his hands in his pockets.

It was still four o'clock. A sinister hour of the night, the longest, the one that afflicts insomniacs because it never ends. Pedro turned on the kitchen light. He took a glass from the cupboard and, with one last hope, he peeped out the window. His red eyes ran through the dark night in vain: his attack of angina having passed, the neighbor was sleeping, the lights out in his bedroom. Glass in hand, he went to the faucet. He held his foot in the air—a cockroach on the tile floor. Then, with the dazzling light on the white walls and the foot raised over its head, it didn't try to flee: could it be dead or wounded? Pedro crouched down and with disgust studied the creature lying on its back on the floor. It didn't get up to run away, it moved its legs and leaned from one side to the other—the greasy snout, pullulating with appendixes, and, in the transparent thorax, its empty and hollow heart.

Unable to reach the floor with its legs, it couldn't turn over. Squash it under his slipper—it was his first impulse. He was not so ingenuous, having learned his lesson from other early mornings. Months before, he had destroyed the only cockroach on the kitchen floor and he still heard the echo of its thunder. A pungent explosion that left him open-mouthed, a slight remorse in his chest. Even though there was no blood, the crack of the dry shell was like the creature's roar of pain.

Better to catch it on a piece of paper and throw it out the window, if it weren't for the fear that during the operation it might turn over and run across the page with its agile legs and sneak into his pajama sleeve. Cover it with the glass and let it die of suffocation—who knows for what eternity a cockroach can endure?

Twisting his nose, Pedro got down closer and examined it as it rested, the thin antennae extended. Frightened by the flash of his glasses, the creature began to spin its right leg, gathering together an impulse and, all at once, rolling all of its legs, it struggled to get up in one leap. It only managed to dislocate its tail and the attempt died out with a slow convulsion in the right leg. It became still, worn out by the effort, the two appendixes on the head drooping, the six legs motionless—tiny and narrow beside the snout, developed and fat along the extension of the body, and the last two, by the tail, long and with powerful thighs.

Simple cockroach of the family of racers, where did your prestige come from? From your brownish color, from the thin black antennae as long as your body? Or perhaps from your dark tail? It was softly waving its leg in the air, the first one on the right, when the man discovered with horror that it was a hairy leg—its legs were covered with small stiff hairs.

Indifferent to Pedro's nausea, the creature let itself go into the position of a lewd madonna and put out its two hind legs in an obscene position. He drew back in disgust and turned on the faucet, his hands trembling. He took two swallows and, with queasiness, put down the glass. Disturbed, he felt the presence of the cockroach behind him and, suddenly, he quickly lifted one foot so that it wouldn't come in a mad rush and get up his pant leg.

He debated in his affliction on how to kill it: soak it in alcohol and light a match? Crush it under the table leg, which could never be moved again so as not to reveal the corpse? If at least there was only blood to spill—worse than blood was the explosion of the dry shell, with the spurt of sticky juice, the cockroach's stuffing. If he didn't kill it, catching it in a matchbox and throwing it outside? Even if he caught it, with time to close the box on it, how could he carry the thing in his pocket, knowing that it was moving inside there and hearing the scratching of its legs on the fragile walls?

He reluctantly went back to bend over the insect. He noticed that when it rubbed its left leg against the floor it left a white thread there—a small handkerchief waving for help. As surely as he knew that he would not go back to sleep again that night and, who knows, any other night of his life, he also realized that he would never be able to do away with the creature. They were members of the same family and therefore it was proper for him to spare it.

He went over to the wall and turned out the light. Surprised, he saw the whitish splotch on the window. His head tilted, he stayed there listening: quick steps on the sidewalk, a bicycle bell, a woman's licentious laugh. Then the morning sparrows would awaken and, surviving the darkness, he would be able to face himself in the mirror, shave, and endure his day. Condemned to despair while the world dreamed, only the cockroach kept him company. He looked at it from the door with a certain concealed tenderness: it was his little sister. Forgetting it on the floor would be abandoning it to the implacable justice of the cook.

He took the broom from the corner and approached the cockroach, which was struggling desperately, thinking itself lost. Infected by its terror, Pedro stopped with the broom—what if when it got on its feet, crazy with panic, it came over to wrap him in its hairy thighs and devour him? He overcame the trembling in his hands and he allowed the creature, by touching the straws of the broom, to get on its six feet—oh, my God! A cockroach has wings! Bumbling along it had already hidden itself under the counter. It didn't disappear, the tip of its tail sticking out. Maybe it was fascinated and was spying on him from its dark corner. Pedro held the broom: he could account for a thousand crimes, but at least he was innocent of the life of a cockroach.

He went to the bedroom with the hope that one day he would be able to sleep again. Until he deserved his sleep there would be many early mornings with the kitchen light on. If his little sister returned he would know how to receive her without hatred or fear, even though, fantastic and brown-colored like remorse, she might be sitting in his chair and eating from his plate. If she came back, he would go to meet her at four o'clock sharp in the morning.

THE DISASTERS
OF LOVE

THE MARIAS

⁜ MARIA, daughter of Maria, the daughter of Maria, is thirty-one misfortunes old. She washes the clothes, washes the dishes, scrubbing away, and her mistress—*Jesus Mary Joseph!*—her mistress railing away.

At the age of seven she was given to her first mistress by her mother. A woman loaded with children, she couldn't manage with one more: she gave poor Maria away.

She always lived in someone else's house, sleeping on an army cot, eating on her feet by the stove. A hard worker, she was to be trusted and didn't have a mouth that asked for anything. Pale, she lived on herb tea. While sleeping she would gnash her teeth, her worms all aroused. Maria, poor thing, never knew what an apple tasted like! The food pantry under lock and key, she would gnaw hungrily on a hunk of brown sugar hidden under her pillow.

She would appear with a cloth tied around her swollen

jowls—she used miraculous wax for a toothache until she lost the tooth. She was sluggish because of ingrown nails: from cleaning up the ashes, her fingers became cracked and she suffered from whitlow. She never quit a job, she was always let go by her mistress, tired of her afflictions and her boobish face.

She grew fat with the years, rolling from one house to another, moaning with pain, and confused in her work. Her joy was washing babies' diapers. Ah, but to kiss the little one . . .

"You're not allowed to, you hear, Maria?"

Servants don't know their place, he might catch something.

She was a serious girl who didn't go dancing with the others. She wet scarlet crepe paper with her tongue and rubbed it on her ugly anemic face and as soon as she went to the window to watch the little green soldiers, the mistress would scold her:

"Maria, did you pick the rice clean?"

"Maria, have you got the clothes ironed?"

"Did you wax the floors, Maria?"

When the top of the stove was scrubbed, the dishes put away, the kitchen cleaned, she would go timidly to the door. The soldier was walking around, stopping, saluting. He was in a hurry, as a soldier he was always off to war: right away he tried to take her hand and cover it with kisses.

"God save me, you might have some sickness!"

Maria crossed herself: only her husband would kiss her on the mouth.

Where are the cavalry soldiers? They don't jingle their spurs on the sidewalk anymore. Maria's thirty-one years! Then she complains that she can't go walking with Marta.

"Go cry in your room, then," her mistress says. "I won't have any low-class scenes!"

That Maria, a household object, a doormat, the shears on the hook.

The Marias

Maria doesn't go to the circus, the clown's so funny.

Maria doesn't go to the park to see the monkey eat bananas.

Maria doesn't go to the movies on Friday to see *The Birth, Passion, and Death of Our Lord Jesus Christ.*

Maria, daughter of Maria, passing the time with Marta on Sunday, saw her heart roll from her chest and the plate that fell from her chubby fingers (would the mistress scold her?) shatter into seven pieces of blood on the floor.

Was he a corporal? Maria never knew which branch. He talked pretty and with difficulty, with strong s's—you ssee, girl?—and she, bouncing on one leg, then the other, greedily chewed her nails.

"There are people around, corporal. Show some respect, corporal!"

He took her to the circus and Maria went in as proud as a lady among the low people who were carrying on: the old skin of a rabbit biting his tail around her neck. The brass band, the clean-up man with a painted face, the corporal in his big general's boots. One clown insults another, calling him "Gigolo!" and the house collapses with laughter. Maria just smiled, the corporal draws blood from her breast.

"I'm crazy about you, Maria."

To the surprise of the candy vendor shouting: "Hey, candy, hey . . . ," she kissed the corporal's hand.

In nine months Maria, daughter of Maria, would be the mother of Maria.

MARIA

PAINTED SILVER

❧ A GREAT BIG MAN with a ringing voice, he was adored by his children, one eight and the other five. João didn't get along well with his wife. Maria was ambitious, she wanted to fix up the house with geegaws and baubles. The husband didn't make much, he could barely pay for the necessities. João had put a little money aside and away it went with his son's asthma, his wife's gold tooth. She was no less hard-working: she did all the housework, starched the children's clothes, sewed her husband's shirts, and yet she wouldn't accept her lot, humiliating her husband in the presence of her mother-in-law.

After every argument, he would grab his hat, slam the door, and go to drink at the corner bar. Sometimes one of the little ones would pull on the corner of his jacket:

"Don't go, Papa. Please, Papa."

Moved at being called "Papa," he reluctantly turned to his wife, a chestnut-brown shout of hate in each eye:

216

"Papa's going for a walk."

Big and strong as he was, he couldn't resist drink: he got drunk quickly on a few glasses of liquor. In a pitiful state, stumbling over his words, he was the clown of the bar. And, worst of all, he felt miserable, even wanting to be home in the warmth of his wife's generous body.

The more they argued, the more he drank and the less money there was in the house. Maria began to doll herself up, using too much make-up for her age, worn out by household chores. With great sacrifice she bought a secondhand weaving machine and made wool sweaters that were celebrated for their fine work. And since she had taken part in amateur shows as a young girl, she revealed her ambition to be an artist: if she trained her voice she could be famous. To João's distress and the scandal of the family, the poor lady, ugly and long-nosed, began to sing thousands of carnival songs over the washtub and in front of the mirror. She neglected the children, turning them out onto the street, busying herself only with plucking her eyebrows and shortening her skirts—the laughter of cheap bracelets on her arms.

With a neighbor woman of bad reputation she signed up for an amateur program: her voice seemed actually agreeable and she was signed up as an experiment.

"I'm an exclusive artist," she boasted with a conceited accent. "It's a big show!"

It was a repertory of light music, although she insisted on a mournful tango and was applauded, all the more because after the show she gave a party for the radio people: snacks and free beer. João slipped out the back way in his shirt sleeves, ashamed of his unshaven face. He came back drunk and Maria barred the bedroom door, making him sleep on the living-room couch. One winter night, listening to him moan, the older son brought him a blanket:

"Go to sleep, Papa."

With each one of Maria's successes—fifth prize for a

carnival song, her picture in the paper, a letter from a fan asking for her autograph:

"She's still going to get some boos," was João's comment. "With one good boo she'll learn!"

Dark as she was, behold Maria with bleached hair! Accompanied home through the dead hours of the night by colleagues in the artistic life—sometimes the tango singer, sometimes the magician—she spent a long time kissing at the door, and mothers forbade their children to play with hers. When he came upon Maria with blond hair, João knew it was the end—a married woman who dyes her hair is flighty. He went to sleep in the storeroom, huddled on a filthy mat, a bottle in his hand.

For two days he didn't leave the place (he was frightened by his own strength and he never beat his sons), roaring curses and thumping the wall. Maria packed her bags, and without letting the children say good-by to João, she moved to her parents' house.

She left the children there and took up with a piano player in a night club: she was used as a dancer to keep the customers company and get them to drink. The pianist, depraved and tubercular, took her money and beat her if the take wasn't good.

Tired of being beaten, she went back to her parents' house. Then the old woman went to João and suggested they make up.

"She can stay where she is," he replied. "I wouldn't want Maria even if she was painted silver."

Discharged from the factory because of drunkenness, he lived off odd jobs. He went to put his jacket on and a snake came out of the sleeve. He threw it into the fire with a roar. Hairy spiders bit him on the back of the neck; it was useless to step on them, two or three more would be born out of each one—he knelt in a corner, frightened, and hid his head between his knees.

On Sunday he had a visit from his sons, sent by his mother-in-law. They had a good time at the zoo watching the monkeys. The father bought peanuts and popcorn, which the three nibbled on with delight. He would drift off quietly and behind a tree tip up the bottle he carried sticking out of his rear pocket—his hands stopped shaking. The boys turned their eyes away: run-down shoes, filthy pants, a jacket without buttons. They stroked his huge but fragile hand:

"Please, Papa. Don't drink anymore, Papa."

With his head shaking slightly, he let the tears run down his long ruddy mushroom of a nose. He said good-by with a toothless smile. On the corner he guzzled the cane liquor down to the last drop.

Delirious in the gutter, he was taken to the hospital two or three times. The fearful crisis of drying out, and he was turned loose two weeks later; as soon as he got out the door he went into the first bar.

Maria fell into the arms of the magician and, prevented from singing by such a horrible voice, she consoled herself at the washtub. Neither her lover nor the old people wanted anything to do with the children, who were finally placed in an orphan asylum. They were both learning a trade and on the last Sunday of the month, with the nun's permission, they went to their father's, their hair well combed. The man, still lying down, had a hang-over; amidst mumbles he told one of them to go fill his bottle.

After a few swigs he felt better. The young ones busied themselves sweeping the house and lighting the fire after several tries, their eyes irritated by the smoke. For lunch they brought him coffee with bread and pink salami. Sitting on the bed, the father satisfied himself by watching them eat. Absent-eyed, he would sometimes smile peacefully and one of them would wipe the cold sweat from his brow. Without the courage to leave him, the sons stayed by his side during the night: talking nonsense, he trembled from head to foot, the bed shaking with his death rattle—bubbles of froth came out the corner of his mouth.

The boys fell asleep with the lamp on, listening to the ugly snoring of the drowning man. The older one woke up in the middle of the night and went to peep at his father resting, the whites of his eyes showing. He tried to talk to him, but he didn't move. He was afraid and woke up his brother:

"Papa's dead."

Without crying, huddling on the edge of the bed, they held hands and listened to the morning sparrows.

THE DRUNKEN
PARROT

◤ HE WOULD BE A VIRGIN until he earned the confidence of his beauty.

"Are you a natural blonde?"

"That's right."

"Blondes are famous for being cold. But I don't believe it."

"Well, blondes are different from brunettes."

"Brunettes are more loving. You're not a Catholic, are you?"

"I'm a Calvinist."

A Calvinist, wow, and he blushed from sheer excitement.

"Religion today doesn't make a sacred cow out of virginity. A girl can still be proper and have her experiences. She's authorized by her pastor to know the pleasures of life."

". . ."

"Do you know that foreigners find our prejudice about virginity amusing?"

"No, I didn't."

"Is your temperament calm or nervous?"

"I'm calm."

"But you have the characteristics of a nervous girl; you still haven't found out that you are. Your measurements are perfect. Weren't you the one playing volleyball?"

"Yes."

"I wish I'd seen you in shorts. Did you play well?"

The answer was a bashful smile in the corner of the mouth. An uncovered ear decorated with a costume-jewelry earring, the other one hidden by the blond hair. Small teeth, one in front a little dark. Mother in heaven, the lace hem of her slip showing.

"Didn't volleyball give you muscular legs?"

"No. You use your arms more. Bicycling does. I know a girl who had legs like that from too much pedaling."

"Do I know her?"

"No."

"From what I can see you have a perfect figure. What are your measurements?"

"Twenty here. Just below it grows to twenty-two."

"What's your bust?"

"Thirty-seven."

The hero closed his eyes: Oh, such beauty! Oh, wonderful, thirty-seven!

"Your hips?"

"A little more."

"Thirty-nine?"

"Yes."

Oh, God in heaven, thirty-nine!

Seated, composed. Not crossing her legs once. Oh, if she only raised her skirt . . . just a little.

"Do they follow you on the street much? You're so des

. . . such a pretty girl. It must be hard for you, I imagine, walking on the street. How do you fend off the pirates?"

Listen to that, pirate—old man's slang!

"So far not much."

"What I don't know is the measurement of your thigh."

The word thigh was like a whole orange in his mouth.

"I don't know. I'm eight inches at the ankle."

"A woman's legs are one of her perfections. Yours, for example, are they whiter from the knee up?"

She lowered her eyes, flushed:

"Yes."

"Very much whiter?"

" . . . "

If I were a woman I'd spend all my time looking at my natural gifts in the mirror!

"Have you had any experience?"

"God save me!"

Nervous, the beauty pushed her hair back from her squinting eyes; her bosom was bursting the buttons on her blouse from so much agitation—there's no softer weight than a mature breast in the hollow of the hand.

"Are you cold?"

No woman is cold if you give her three bites on the neck.

"It's late. I have to go. I'll see you tomorrow, Doctor."

I frightened the poor little thing, she ran out the open door . . . Oh me, who hears, who listens to the weeping of a drunken parrot?

THE LITTLE
GOLDFISH

❦ HE OPENED THE DOOR and one of his sisters, very nervous, came out to meet him in the hall:

"Be strong, Zèzinho. Papa . . . He had a stroke!"

His mother held him tightly in her arms:

"Oh, your poor father . . ."

In the bedroom the huge body was shaking with convulsions, teeth chattering, eyes rolling. The boy sat on the edge of the bed and without a word began to wipe the sweat of agony from his father's brow.

The old man survived, his ideas confused, his memory gone, the checkered cap slipping on his shiny bald head. When he saw his son a glow of recognition lighted up his cloudy, quiet eyes:

"Zèzi . . . zinho . . . ," he stammered, holding his hand between his son's, trembling, without the strength to squeeze it.

The Little Goldfish

With his handkerchief the boy wiped a thread of mucus from the corner of the twisted mouth. Every time his sisters called him, terribly jealous of the favorite son, they imitated the babbling tone of the invalid:

"Zèzi . . . zinho . . ."

Zèzinho would wake up in the middle of the night in panic, his pajamas drenched in sweat. Walking with his girl friend, talking to his friends at the bar, he could hear quite clearly: "Papa, he had a stroke!"

Crossing the hall quickly, he got to the room where the old man was dozing in the easy chair, his glasses on the tip of his nose (it was the boy who had to clean the foggy lenses) or, if awake, he would open up wide with a doltish smile:

"Zèzi . . . zinho . . ."

With his father out of danger, Zèzinho was transferred to a branch of the bank in another city; he couldn't stand the torture of his sisters, they only spoke to him in the whining tone of the hemiplegic. Unable to sleep, always waiting for the terrible knock on the door: "Come, Zèzinho . . . Papa's dying."

He shared the room in the boardinghouse with two other bank clerks. He rarely drank, alcohol sharpened his sensibility, possessed of a merciless lucidity, and, when he passed by the mirror, he would greet the disfigured face with a wave of the hand and the plaintive whine: "Hello, Zèzi . . . zinho . . ."

Letters came from the family one after the other, the sick man in a desperate state. After reading them, with red eyes, locked in the bathroom, he would tear them up. Urgent telegrams from his mother and sisters demanding his presence: his father wanted to see him, he kept calling his son's name. Finally the telephone call with the brutal news: the old man was going into his final agony, he couldn't die without saying good-by to him.

225

Zèzinho went to the station immediately and sat in the waiting room, watching the trains leave. His eyes were dry, and even though he didn't smoke he would touch the pack of cigarettes in his pocket from time to time. He distracted himself with small incidents: the crying of a baby, a dog scratching himself, hitting his foot on the tile floor, the greedy snout of a fly tickling the sticky hand that clutched his knee. Twice he turned on the bench, he'd felt a loving touch on his shoulder. He kept his face staring at the wall, his upper lip tight at the corners, the muscle twitching as he tightened it, disappearing afterwards. Finally the lights on the platform were turned off, the cleaning women came with mops and buckets and began to scrub the floor. The water wet his shoes, but he didn't move.

"What's the matter, sweetie, are you going to leave or not?" one of the old women shouted and laughed in the direction of the others, all toothless.

It was the night his father died. Zèzinho didn't go to the burial and later he received a card announcing the seventh-day mass, on the back of which one of his sisters had scrawled: "Mr. José Maria (Jr.) is not a member of the family." The letters kept on quivering and from then on he hid the turbulence of his hands in his pockets.

On the bus he relentlessly read the letters on the colored posters backwards: ELIXIR—RIXILE, RING—GNIR, FANTASY—YSAT . . . Annoyed because the speed of the vehicle prevented him from inverting the difficult words in time.

How many times did he go up and down the stairs of the boardinghouse until he calmed his afflicted heart? He would come in late, sleep with the light on, thrash about in nightmares, and his roommates began to hate him. One of them wondered why Zèzinho smoked in the dark:

"What pleasure can you get out of the cigarette, you poor devil?"

Because blind men, who can't see smoke, don't smoke.

"I can see the glow," the boy answered. "It lights up in the dark with every drag."

The other's answer was a curse.

Zèzinho appeared with a tiny bowl with a goldfish loitering in it. Then he divided his attention between anagrams and the fish. He would spend hours watching the graceful movements of his beloved fish. Out of spite his roommates would flick their ashes into the bowl and one morning the fish was floating dead. After three days Zèzinho rolled up his sleeve, put his hand into the cold water, and picked up the creature from the bottom. He wrapped it in cotton, put it in a match box, and began to carry it in his pocket, hefting it from time to time with the broadest of smiles.

It was Saturday and he decided to ask God's forgiveness. He stood in line by the confessional, finally kneeling by the grill in the darkness.

"Confess, my son," the priest whispered with bad breath. "Did you do anything bad? How many times? Alone or with someone else?"

Zèzinho had a hard time stopping himself from blowing into the ear of the priest, who had his hand cupped to it.

He was tormented by his roommates so he would get another room; insensitive to the provocations (the fish was well protected in his pants pocket), he kept on smoking in the dark, and they finally left him alone. On certain occasions, when he took part in a card game, he would suddenly run downstairs:

"I'm leaving. I can't stand the yellow in this room!"

On Sundays he would stop at the doors of the closed bars, contemplating the cakes of ice that were melting, forgotten. As much as he wanted to save them, why wouldn't they even let him share their slow agony? He would lose himself in daydreams about the mystery: why did the iceman leave the boxes of cracked ice in front of the doors which he knew quite well weren't going to open?

Night after night the same dream: he was being ridden by a hairy beast, perhaps a lion with a large black mane.

"What does that lion mean?" he asked his roommates.

In order to have some fun they got him drunk and dragged him off to a whorehouse. He went to the room with a fat peroxide blonde who told the others later: he made her sit on the bed, knelt at her feet, and, resting his head on her scarlet silk kimono, satisfied himself by kissing her hand. Since he had paid, she let him come other times and the same ceremony was repeated; she was a good girl and felt sorry for Zèzinho. When she had someone with her, he would wait in the hall until the customer left. One time, annoyed, she slammed the door on him:

"Leave me alone, you little pervert."

He read parts of his diary to Margô: "Oh, Lord, let me die at the bottom of a sewer, the lowest of flea-bitten rats."

The woman let him sleep in the room and woke up with his sobbing. She turned on the light: Zèzinho was dreaming, the tears bubbling down from under his lids. She woke him up and made him go out into the winter night.

In his dream he had been present at his father's exhumation. He was walking around the grave, the stones turned over. In the shallow pit the awful leftovers of decay and powdery black clothing. There, in the middle of the remains, a red rose glowed fantastically. Admiring the flower, Zèzinho wept. Strangers stopped in front of the grave and one by one offered him their condolences. He felt neither guilt nor remorse, his heart happy: the scarlet rose flourished among the bones.

Arriving at the boardinghouse, he opened the small notebook with a black cover and wrote in his painstaking hand: "It is disgust I feel for myself. I expect nothing but hatred from others." From the top of the page to the bottom he drew the word MARGÔ, crossed by the anagram—OGRAM.

He was hungry, he searched in the drawer for a slice of

hard cheese and began to chip at it with the point of his penknife. Shaken by a small fright: Oh, what if his father saw the pock-marked cheese . . . But no, he couldn't scold him anymore—he was quite dead. Softly, Zèzinho felt the matchbox in his pocket and looked at his hands: after so many months the trembling had disappeared for the first time.

Maybe someday, back in Curitiba, he could bury the goldfish in the old man's grave.

THE VOICES
OF THE PICTURE

✌ THE VOICE CAME OVER THE CROSSED WIRES:
"Is that Fabinho?"

"There's no Fabinho here," and he hung up. He was too old for jokes.

Once more:

"I'm sorry. It really is Fabinho's voice."

The inflection was so soft that he changed his mind:

"My name is João. What's yours?"

"Mine?" A pause. "Maria."

In the middle of the phrase a little dry cough:

"Oh, this cough is killing me."

"It's T.B., child."

"God forbid," and she laughed merrily.

She called him every night, after ten o'clock. They talked late into the night; the girl played records, read passages from her diary. Sometimes she seemed upset:

"I'm so nervous."

"What's the matter, girl?"

"Oh, I'm afraid, João. Terribly afraid."

He heard her cough lightly and suddenly fall silent. He was desperate, unable to help her. On the following night it was the same sweetness again, a thin thread of a voice. Between coughing spells she recalled a movie, a record, a book.

"Your little prince, my dear, is the worst of bores!"

He kept the bottle of cognac within reach; between murmurs he drank from the bottle. He couldn't hold back a curse and the tremulous voice looked at him with surprise. When she called again, João was ashamed and asked her to forgive him: the mystery had gotten to his nerves. He promised everything to find out who she was—it didn't matter whether she was old, black, crippled. The voice refused to give anything but the name.

"I have to be operated on," she confessed to him one night. "I'm afraid it might be serious."

"Don't be silly, girl. Your voice is that of a person who's got health for sale," and he was embarrassed by a stupid remark like that.

Since João insisted so much, she agreed to a meeting.

"How will I know it's you?"

There was no answer. At five in the afternoon there was João on the corner agreed upon. He waited for over an hour; could he have seen Maria?

At night she revealed that she had driven by, without the courage to stop. She described his navy-blue jacket and the mole below his sideburn.

"Why didn't you stop?"

"You might not have liked me. I don't want to lose you."

"I accept you the way you are. Even if you've got a hole in the place of your nose. Please don't torment me."

With the drinks, he was going from a gloomy to a talkative mood. Drunk, he pretended he was beside her, she gave in to his kisses and let him caress her: the voice grew silent but didn't hang up.

"I'm sorry, sweetie. I'm the lowest of the low. The little prince of scoundrels, that's who I am. What I need is to see you. It doesn't make any difference if you're tubercular or a leper. I can't take it anymore. I'm going crazy. Don't you have any pity, Maria?"

He got the promise of a second meeting: once more she didn't let herself be known. But she took a good look at the boy and found him handsome, with a wild mustache. Days later he received an expensive shaving kit in the mail. Other mementos followed, delivered by messengers who could tell nothing about the sender: a bottle of cognac and, on his birthday, a cake stuffed with nuts. Exhausted after chatting until two in the morning, he fell asleep right on the sofa with his tie on; he woke up with a furry tongue and a sour stomach. On nights when they argued, he breathed through a handkerchief soaked in ether.

"You're playing with me. You've been playing me for a fool for months," and he said good-by with a dirty word.

Then the telephone rang, this time with the calm voice of an older woman:

"This is Maria's mother. Please don't get angry. If you only knew the good you've done her . . . She's had fun, she's so much happier. I already told her, daughter, why don't you invite the boy to come by? 'I don't want him to feel sorry for me, Mama,' she answered."

"Who are you, ma'am? Where do you live? What's your name?"

The mother hung up—or had it been Maria on the other end? João made another try with the operator:

"I've been cut off. Could you connect me again?"

"I'm sorry, sir, there's nothing I can do."

In despair, he flirted with one operator after another,

but he couldn't get the number. Every cough on the street could have been Maria's. On one occasion she hinted that she was going to the Cine Curitiba. Carefully shaved, João went to show himself by the entrance. Two girls went in, one made a sign to the other. With moist hands, a vein throbbing in his forehead, he waited at the exit. This time they didn't look at him. As soon as he got home, the telephone rang:

"I'm sorry, love. I couldn't go out."

With diabolical wiles, she got hold of a picture of João.

"You've got circles under your eyes. Heavens, they're the fatal eyes of Dom Pedro I."

She could only have pilfered the picture from an old girl friend. Thereupon João set out tracking them down, one by one, with no results. He pursued innumerable old and young women, preferably ugly; one paralyzed in a wheel chair, another a midget, one a hunchback, another cross-eyed, none of these was she: he only had to hear their voices.

When Maria said that from her window she was looking at the trees in a small square, night after night he devoted himself to making the rounds of all squares. Under each lighted window he stopped and spied, and the best he got for his trouble was being questioned by the night watchman.

Then there was silence for a whole week. João could only sleep with the ether-soaked handkerchief over his bearded face with deep circles under the eyes.

"I was operated on, sweet."

"What was it?"

"The left knee . . . Don't ask anything else."

She was already better. Days later she talked about movies, she even went to a dance and described the ballroom and the people.

"I have to hang up. Someone's knocking on the door."

A few minutes later:

"It's safe now."

"Who was it?"

"My lover, silly."

Months passed. If she suggested that because of a lack of sun the violets were withering, that was enough for João to go out and court the window boxes. He begged so much that Maria let him know that she was nineteen, a brunette with green eyes and straight hair.

Green-eyed brunettes aren't common and João followed every one of them to the door of their house. Moved by that, she sent him a picture through the mail. With no inscription, it was oval, as if taken from a medallion, yellowed by the years. João showed the picture to his friends in search of the slightest clue:

"It looks like the picture of a dead woman," one of them observed.

In seriousness or in jest, he visited several cemeteries—no grave had the picture missing. The faded features didn't even fit the description; the poor boy felt lost. Furthermore, the voice seemed to fade away, longer phrases suffocated by the persistent cough.

"I'm very sick, love. I'm going on a trip. I don't know if I'll come back."

"I'm the one who's sick. Rotting away with love. Oh, Maria, have you no pity?"

"Please. Don't torture me, love."

"What's wrong with you then? Cancer of the knee?"

She laughed, she was a girl with character.

"Is it really T.B. then?"

And, still laughing, the poor thing coughed.

The following afternoon on the Praça Tiradentes, he passed a girl who smiled at him. Resembling the portrait a little, thin and pale, almost pretty. He went up to her without further ceremony:

"You're Maria."

"I don't know you. And my name isn't Maria."

"Didn't you say you were going on a trip?"

"You've got me mixed up with someone else," and she coughed, holding her handkerchief to her mouth.

He played the game and every so often he inquired who the famous Fabinho was. Hallucinated with passion—the voice? the girl? the picture—a week later he asked her to marry him. If there was any doubt as to her identity, hadn't the telephone been silent?

A month later, just back from the church, he was closing the suitcase, ready to leave. His wife came out of the bedroom, elegant in a cream-colored dress, with a crocheted purse and gloves. The taxi blew its horn beneath the window and at the same instant the telephone rang.

"I'll answer it, love," and João picked up the receiver to hear a dry little cough. "Hello?"

"Love?" The cough once more and the thin familiar voice. "I'm back."

The wife called from the hall and since he didn't answer she came to the door:

"Aren't you coming, João?"

Without answering, he sank into the chair and covered his face with his hands in despair.

✒ THE CONJUGAL WAR

MY DEAR HUSBAND

☫ João WAS MARRIED to Maria and they lived in a two-room shack in Juvevê: the street was muddy and he didn't want the lady to wet her little feet. João's defect was being too good—he gave her everything she asked for.

A waiter at The Armadillo's Nest, he worked till the dead hours; one night he got home earlier and found his two daughters alone, the younger one with a fever. João brought her some sugar water and as soon as she fell asleep he went out to lie in wait by the corner. Maria came along with her arm around another man and said good-by to him with a kiss on the mouth. He attacked both of them furiously, the lover ran and his wife, on her knees, begged forgiveness, in the name of the child in her womb.

João was good, he was passive, and there was no one like Maria, there was no one else for him: they moved from Juvevê to Boqueirão, where the third daughter was born.

They were called the new Marias: Maria da Luz, Maria das Dores, Maria da Graça. With so many Marias, João was confident that the lady had mended her ways. If he hadn't caught her in her kimono throwing kisses to a police sergeant.

His return home was sad, he caught the sergeant jumping out the window with his tunic off. Hoping that Maria would repent, he took his savings and the tips from a thousand nights on his feet (alas, poor legs, blue with varicose veins) and built a pretty little bungalow in Prado Velho.

Maria was a sinner in heart, soul, and body, she didn't mend her ways. As soon as our João turned his back, she would leave the girls with a neighbor woman and go out, painted and shining like a gold piece. She had an affair with a driver on the Prado Velho–Tiradentes Square bus line: she would gloriously enter through the front door without paying.

One night someone stoned the house—it was the bus driver's wife, who was taking out her vengeance on the window panes. Maria woke up the girls and beat them to make them scream. Because of the scandal, João sold the bungalow at a loss and moved from Prado Velho to Capanema.

Maria fell in love with a loafer with a thin mustache and two-toned shoes. She didn't go through the inconvenience of going out, receiving the fellow right in the house. He was the famous Candinho, known for his merry night rounds, who fascinated the children with honey cakes and card tricks.

João found some silk undershorts hanging on the line— the delicate monogram was a large C. He tore the shorts to shreds and invited his sister-in-law to come, begging her to look after her sister. Alas, she was another lost soul. Candinho appeared with a chum who made love to the ugly sister-in-law. Maria prepared snacks and cold drinks made of cane liquor and passion-flower juice. Locked in their room, the girls listened to their mother's debauched laughter.

João had no luck: he came home early and there was the villain. Pressed by the lady to stay, Candinho didn't flee and the two men began to argue. The husband picked up a pointed knife and Maria, with open arms, covered her lover's body. João noticed the volume of her belly and dropped the weapon. With pain in his heart he slept in the living room until the birth of the fourth daughter—another Maria to turn her mother away from her evil path. The wife left the maternity ward and they withdrew from Capanema to the heights of Mercês.

A woman has no judgment, and Maria started up again with the same Candinho. On Sunday, with João at home, she made up the excuse that she was going to buy medicine for one of the daughters. He made her take the oldest one along. There were the three of them—the lady, the lover, and the daughter—eating chicken on a skewer. The girl had to promise not to say anything or else she would go to hell— she felt guilty in front of her father and could only sleep with the light on, the darkness was full of demons.

João tolerated the worst shame in public and in the presence of his daughters. Who could tell, maybe she'd reform. Thin as he was, he became a skeleton, with an active ulcer in his duodenum.

He brought his mother-in-law into his home and moved from Mercês to Água-Verde. Again a shirt and shorts with flowery initials hanging on the line. In despair, João threw the mother-in-law out and showed the clothing to his oldest daughter, who, embracing her father, revealed how she and her sisters were alone until one or two in the morning while their mother went out into the street. She would appear with a perfumed gentleman who gave them honey cakes and whose name was Uncle Candinho. The mother served him macaroni and red wine and they laughed a lot, but the girl couldn't sleep, thinking about her father running ceaselessly back and forth among the tables.

Before João decided to move from Água-Verde to Bigorrilho, Maria ran away with her lover and left a note stuck onto the mirror of the dressing table with chewing gum:

"Since you, my dear husband, are such a shameless cuckold, you should know that soon I will come back for my daughters, who are my blood, I say my blood because you know quite well they're not yours, and you're nothing but a stranger to them, and in case you don't behave, I'll tell who their real fathers are, not just them, but I'll tell all the people you work with at The Armadillo's Nest, I'm tired of being pointed out as the guilty one, I say that so you'll stop being an idiot running after the hem of my skirt, I only feel disgust for you, you know very well that you're nothing to me."

Eleven days later Maria telephoned to tell him that it would be an act of charity if he would come to get her, ill and hungry, abandoned by Candinho in a house for women. João was passive and there was no one like Maria: there was no one else for him. He went to get her at the house, the lady had ugly bruises all over her body. Thanks to João's attentions, she healed quickly. An announcement that she was well—shorts with a different monogram waving on the line.

The neighborhoods of Curitiba are endless: João moved to Bacacheri, from there to Batel (another daughter was born, Maria Aparecida), and at the moment he is very happy in a little wooden house in Cristo-Rei.

THE PERFECT
CRIME

❦ AT ELEVEN O'CLOCK at night João raised his eyes in front of his brother's house and saw the light on the veranda—a sign that his sister-in-law hadn't come home.

Since the maid had already retired, André came to the door himself.

"Oh, it's you. Let's go to the kitchen," rubbing his icy hands as always. "It's warmer there."

"I was passing by and I saw the light."

The brother went ahead and, with pain in his heart, João noticed that he was dragging his feet along the rug—there he was, a poor old man. In the white-tiled kitchen André turned around and the other observed with a start his disfigured face, blue wrinkles, the right eye bloodshot.

"I'm cooking my mush. You know, the old ulcer."

João sat down heavily in the chair: he was a tired man too, not an old man yet, not so defeated yet.

"Rosa's not home?"

"She went to a party."

André scraped the mush onto the dessert plate from the pot. To the other one he looked like a scarred boxer in the corner of the ring, clutching the ropes, his face a piece of bloody meat, blind in one eye, not understanding the referee's count.

The gruel was steaming on the bare table between the two of them. André sprinkled it with powdered cinnamon.

"I've got a thirst . . . Is there anything to drink?"

"Just water. You know Rosa, what she thinks."

André's smile was a grimace with his off-white teeth as he lighted a cigarette, dragged on it, and put the match back in the box—God help him if Rosa caught him. He drew in suddenly, like a fighter getting a low blow, and with three fingers feeling the fourth button on his shirt, he remained quite still.

"Every time I notice the redness of this table," he sighed deeply and wiped the cold sweat from his forehead with the palm of his hand, "I get a stomach ache."

"I prefer my unfiltered ones," and saying that João flipped the match away. "Were you going out?"

"Why?"

"You've got your tie on."

"I dozed off in the easy chair."

He went to the sink, put the cigarette out under the faucet, and broke it up over the drain, making the evidence of the sin disappear. On understanding his brother's thought, André smiled the same grimace—at the age of sixty he was still a boy who sneaked his smokes.

A fierce thirst, not for water, dried João's tongue. He yawned noisily, stretched, and decided it was time to talk.

"Listen, André. The little brother asks permission for a word or two."

The brother raised his suffering face, his eye blinking in

the steam of the mush—silence would have been more merciful.

"What's that in your eye?"

Ashamed, the other man lifted his hand to his face—trembling was its nature.

"I think I was reading too much. I already put some drops in."

"Do you know what that is, old man? It's a hemorrhage behind the eye. Your pressure must be at the bursting point, right? And all you do is put a few drops in. What's your pressure?"

"Twenty-three, I think."

"Do you think that's low? What did the doctor say?"

"I didn't see him. What's the use?"

"Oh, if that red eye belonged to Rosa . . . Do you think you'd be eating mush? You'd be running like crazy to get the ambulance for your precious bitch."

Spoon in the air, the brother stopped to look at him, with no surprise or protest, thankful perhaps.

"When I got into your situation I packed my bags and left home. I left my wife and son behind. My own family condemned me: poor little Cidinha. You don't have to make excuses, old man. I know that you won't . . . But she, your precious Rosa, was one of those who cried for Cidinha—the victim of the monster, the martyr, the most holy lady. It's a hard decision, maybe the hardest one in a man's life: abandoning home, wife, and child. Today I give thanks for my madness. With my hands upraised I proclaim: Hallelujah, hallelujah! If I hadn't freed myself from that scourge of husbands I'd be just like you—eating my lonely gruel in the kitchen. Maybe worse—you with an ulcer and me (three raps on the table) with cirrhosis. The hell I went through gives me the right to speak. I spent twenty years with that shout muffled in my throat. Do you know what I'd do if I

were you? I'd do to Rosa what I did to Cidinha: one's more
of a bitch than the other."

Unafraid, André stared at his brother, the spoon resting
on the plate—if it were not for his trembling hand, João
would have said he wasn't even listening to him.

"When she gets back from her party I'd holler at her.
I'd let out the rage that's been suppressed for a whole life-
time, blowing cigarette smoke into her painted wrinkled
face. I'd take the revolver out from the top of the wardrobe
and put a couple of shots in the air. Then I'd pack my bag
and go to a hotel. She'd grovel, cry tears, contact lenses, and
false eyelashes, offer herself naked at my feet, and do you
know what I'd do? I'd go live the last years of my life in
peace."

The chirping in the mallow patch was answered by the
low-life laugh of a tramp woman on the street and, on the
plate, the spoon clinked lightly. João turned his eyes away:
was he speaking the truth or exaggerating his role? It would
have been a relief if André had stopped him: "Hold it right
there, damn you, who are you to talk like that? She's not
what you think she is." Instead of protesting, André lifted a
spoonful to his mouth.

"Do you know what you are to her? Nothing but a
money-making machine. Never a man. All she knows is how
to ask for things: a new car, jewelry, a fur coat. I'm sorry, but
you're not a husband. Do you know what you are? The sugar
daddy for a big cheat. And she doesn't even give you anything in exchange. Do you think I don't know how many
nights you've slept alone on the living-room sofa? Besides
selling her body she won't let you have any children. So as
not to ruin her waistline, deform her breasts, how should I
know. Do you know that it's all part of a scheme?"

André's eyelids trembled, but he didn't open his eyes.

"It's the perfect crime, old man. Only an ex-champion
of the breaststroke could resist that slaughter. By her

calculations you should have died a long time ago. Do you think I don't know, that nobody knows? She won't let you eat in peace. When you sit down at the table it's to be attacked. While you have an ulcer, do you think she doesn't eat like a queen? She won't let you sleep in peace—when you lie down in bed it's to be crucified. I bet she sleeps pleasurably during the day. Look at your hand—it hasn't stopped shaking."

André dropped the spoon onto the plate and hid his hand. João watched the frantic running of a cockroach on the tile floor.

"You still complain of dyspepsia—sure, an ulcer's not much. The name of your stomach acid, old man, is Rosa. Remember the wonderful tango-singer hair you used to have? Is that what those thin white hairs were? For every night of insomnia another hair lost. She pulls your black mane out hair by hair, and, more expert than Delilah, she emasculated you without your realizing it. Can't you see? She planned the perfect crime and she's committing it with great refinement. There's a body, there's a murderer, and no one can call the police. She'll always go unpunished. And what revolts me most is that you don't react. You gave in to the game—you're being destroyed piece by piece and you don't cry for help."

The brother took his hand out of his pocket and picked up the spoon again.

"Unless it's not a crime and is really suicide. I only wanted you to know before you passed on that you're not alone. I'm your brother and I'm at your side."

André took a furtive look at his wrist watch: at the first sound of the horn he'd have to open the gate.

"Don't get worried, I'm on my way."

With that the other one scraped the bottom of the plate and swallowed the last spoonful:

"How about some coffee?"

"It's late. Maria can't get to sleep till I get home."

João had the impression that he was dragging his feet too from being so tired. At the door he rested his hand on André's shoulder with great love:

"Your neck is thin, old man," and he shook with a nervous laugh that dampened his eyes. "You have no salvation here on earth."

"God help us both!" It was a surprise to hear the brother's hoarse voice.

He patted him on the shoulder—nothing left of the muscles of a champion on that poor bird wing—the sudden shame of shaking his hand. He was going down the steps when André spoke again:

"Regards to Maria."

He went into the house and the instant he closed the door the light in the bedroom went on. His second wife, Maria, sitting there on the bed:

"A fine hour to be coming home. Where were you all this time? Couldn't you have told me you'd be late?"

"If you only knew, child. I've got such a headache."

"All you do is complain. Don't you think I know you? You were out drinking. You can barely stand on your feet."

He paused halfway to the bathroom: there on the back of his neck the evil eye that sees all.

"I can't count on you for anything. You're the worst kind of a husband there is. And according to my friends I'm the victim. What I am is a regular martyr."

It was one more night of argument, insomnia, and the grinding of teeth out of a thousand and one.

"Look at yourself, you lousy drunk."

THE GIRL
FROM
NORMAL SCHOOL

◀ THERE WAS THE DESERTED STREET. João went
back and pressed the button twice. The door opened a crack,
through which the toothless Negro woman eyed him suspi-
ciously.

"I'm a friend of Dinorá's."

He went up with sprightly steps and went straight down
the dark corridor. In the room on the left, sitting on the bed,
her chin in her hand, the old bawd was moaning over her
amorous afflictions.

"How are you, Dona Dina?"

Sluggish, the cup of eggnog in her chubby fingers, she
shook with a tinkle of bracelets.

"Oh, sweetie, I'm so upset. Candinho gave me such a
hard time."

Over the head of the bed the colored picture of the
saint and there on the bureau the herd of red elephants,

from a rather large one to the smallest, always with their trunks to the wall—an amulet against the seven plagues of mothers of families.

"Any new girls?"

"This blond fellow's in luck . . . ," and she smiled with a whistle of immaculate false teeth. "A brand-new one. This is the first house she's been in. I think she was in normal school."

At the end of the hallway the picture of St. George, affectionate chuckles, and a scandalous burst of laughter. It was no good walking quietly, all he did was open the door and they all looked in his direction: in chairs lined up against the wall, they turned toward him, in sudden silence, six or seven girls, all with their legs crossed and with a cigarette in their mouths. He greeted them and, his face on fire, made himself comfortable in a chair in the back; he crossed his legs too and lighted a cigarette—his hand only trembled a little. Only one of the women was unknown to him, she must have been the girl from normal school. And it was she, who, addressing the others, was finishing her story:

" 'Don't wear my beauty out, old man,' I said to him then. 'My mouth is to kiss my son with.' "

In the parlor the cheap perfume and a thousand extinguished cigarettes hung heavy. While he was listening, very interested, each one, without stopping speaking to one another, looked at him in turn, and, smiling, they signaled him with their eyes, two of them with their tongues between their teeth. Finally the schoolteacher, who was the closest, turned to him:

"Have you got a cigarette, sweetie?"

She blew out the match in his hand, took a deep drag, and let the smoke out into his face:

"You're so nice and blond . . . You remind me of my fiancé. What's your name, sweetie?"

"José Paulo," with the frog of a lie in his hoarse voice. "What's yours?"

"Mariinha," and fluttering her tongue between her yellow teeth: "Do you like schoolteachers?"

As an answer he wiped his damp and cold hand in his pocket.

"How about a little secret just between the two of us?" and she looked at the clock on the cupboard. "I'm quite crazy today."

She tucked her hand under his arm and to the indifferent, envious, or amused looks of the others, they went into the hall. She opened one of the doors and turned on the light:

"Take your clothes off, sweetie," and, picking up the enameled pitcher on the tripod with the basin, "I'll be right back."

It was the same sinister pink room that all brothels have. On the walls saints pierced with pins among the names of men, telephone numbers, a few misspelled dirty words. On the dressing table the red elephants again, their trunks hidden in a pile of school notebooks with compositions on "Springtime" or "A Rainy Day." With a smile he noticed that they were ten years old.

"My pupils' notebooks." There she was, back with the pitcher. "I'm a teacher."

White blouse and blue skirt, he watched her in the hazy mirror on the dressing table, a lipstick heart drawn in the corner:

"Why, then?"

"Why this life? Oh, you don't want to hear, sweetie. It's too sad."

She took the notebooks from his hand, opened his jacket, and slipped her still wet fingers under his shirt:

"Do you know why I like you? You remind me of my fiancé. He's the one who did me dirty. Then he refused to get married. My father threw me out of the house. Then I lost my head and got into this life. Don't think I'm like the others. I only go with the ones I like. Oh, don't muss my hair. You better take your clothes off. Are you going to give me a little present first?"

João held out the money, which, after counting twice, she put in her purse. She was completely naked in a flash and, alas for him, her tired breasts were flabby bats with black beaks.

"Mother in heaven, don't tell me he's bashful. Look at his soft hand . . . Are you nervous, sweetheart? Don't be afraid. I'm very good at it. Look how white his skin is—all goose pimples. You want me to put the light out? Don't be silly, it's fun with the lights on."

Standing on the bed she turned the bulb, a few coils of fat on the thick thighs, and she lighted the red lamp on the dressing table. She went through the notebooks and showed him the picture of a bald old man with glasses and a gray mustache.

"You want to know who it is? Can you read the dedication there? 'To my pussycat, from her tom.' It's a secret, but I'll tell you. He's my sugar daddy. He wants to marry me, the old fool. He's an old pig with six toes on his feet. Whoo, the way your heart's beating . . . It's almost as if you'd never had a woman. Let's get started because if people take too long the black one knocks on the door. You know that you remind me of my boy friend? You look too wise to me. What kind of tricks do you like? I'll do everything with you, oh, sweetie," and no matter how he defended himself she bit him on the ear, then on the other one, and she began to slobber all over his face with her tongue.

JOÃO WENT THROUGH THE HALL quickly to get to the bathroom: he felt dirty in body and soul. Better to get married than to get involved with a swindler—his right hand smelled of the putrid water in the pitcher of calla lilies in church.

In the living room his father was reading the newspaper, his glasses on the tip of his nose, his pajamas open over his obscene belly of the king of the house:

"I was waiting for you, son. Please sit down. I'm worried . . ."

His lips pulled back in a grimace of dentures that were bigger than his mouth—could he have smelled the stench of the seven women from across the table?

"There's no reason to be, Papa. Just because I was late?"

"I'm worried about myself. I miss your mother too much. Everytime I open the closet and see her dresses . . ."

It was true he had a consideration for the dresses that he never showed their owner.

"I'm not a man to cry, but more than once . . . We haven't talked much since your mother . . . Sometimes I wonder if you're censuring me. Death comes to all of us."

He shook his leg under the checkered cloth and snorted like an old car going up a hill: when the white rose there in the vase lost its petals, did it remember them?

"Marital relations are so difficult. When you get married you'll see that I'm right—you'll understand what I'm trying to say. Your mother was a saint, but she never understood me."

Like a good miser he couldn't hide the joy of one less mouth to feed.

"I feel very lonely. I need someone to keep me company. I . . . I still feel the strength of my manhood."

He raised his ruined face of a decrepit emperor: he was still able to suck the pope's nose in his toothless mouth, he was still a freak with six toes on his feet, and, every morning he still blew his nose by the window and could be heard across the street.

"I can't expose myself to any trouble in a bawdy house.

I met an upright and very gifted girl. If you have no objections I . . . so I . . . I thought I'd get married again."

"No, sir," and the son sank into his chair, his eyelids quivering and his lips trembling.

"She's a teacher. Her name's Mariinha. She wants to meet you very much."

And, taking his hand from under the newspaper, the triumphant father handed him the colored picture.

THIRTY-SEVEN
NIGHTS
OF PASSION

❦ JOÃO WAS UNSUCCESSFUL on the first night. In tears he confessed to his wife that he was a virgin boy and his failure was from loving her so much. Maria gave him all her tenderness for a whole month—and nothing happened. She loved him too and hoped he would get over his emotional collapse. As far as innocence allowed her, she collaborated in all ways—and nothing happened. Not one time could the boy overcome his inhibitions. He failed from the first to the last experience, egg yolks in white wine was a failure. A month later João was still a virgin, the same as the poor girl.

At first they made plans to live like two lovers, always virgins—and, holding hands, they went to sleep with the lights on. Suddenly, there he was repeating one attempt after another, ready even to sacrifice his life.

"Careful, my sweet," the girl warned, frightened. "You might have some kind of attack."

She felt João's afflicted heart beating in her own chest. The work lasted for hours, the sweat running down their faces, and, when they separated, their damp bodies produced an obscene pop.

Heated up, his mouth dry, João sank his face into the icy water of the tap and pitilessly examined himself in the mirror:

"What a disaster!" And he couldn't hold back his sobs. "You're a fiasco."

He only wept that time, then the spell was broken, with grimaces, the most he managed was to find himself good-looking with romantic dark circles under his eyes.

He suggested picking her up on the street like a stranger and taking her to a dubious hotel—it almost worked, but the girl forgot to call him Dr. Passion in the room.

They went to pornographic movies, João read pornographic books in bed (which she refused to do, alleging religious principles), he went so far as to try injecting an aphrodisiac. He went to get her, all aroused, but he was impeded by the slightest distraction: the light on, the light out, a knock on the door, the trill of the canary, the squeaking of the bed, the dripping of a faucet, etc.

He would uncover the adorable naked body of his beloved wife and, dazzled, close his eyes—bringing back in desperation the knees of his first-grade teacher, the buttocks of a certain Negro woman, a strip of his mother-in-law's white thigh. He searched in vain through all the shops in Curitiba for the famous magic ring.

He swore that he was happy, and, if she didn't ask for anything more, they would go on being innocent, like a little brother and sister.

In the movies he found himself capable of a thousand feats and his deportment was so improper that on one occasion he was warned by the usher. They rode on the bus with no destination, close together and standing, even though there were empty seats. On Sunday, at her parents' house, after lunch, he was caught right in the living room with Maria's left breast in his mouth.

"I can't understand," he justified himself, perplexed. "During the two years we were engaged I could barely sleep I was so excited."

When he was away he was endowed with the greatest potency, and, back home, with his beloved in his arms . . . nothing.

"I can't concentrate. Between two kisses I get tired of repeating: 'My gentle soul who went away . . .' or 'Palm trees has my land . . .' "

Nibbling on the delightful nipple he could hear terrible cries in the depths of his soul: What will become of you, oh João? Oh, my God, what will become of me?

Because he was struggling so relentlessly, even though it brought him no results, Maria showed signs of disturbance—the flush on her face, her nose quivering, her breast heaving.

"You bitch!" he couldn't contain his indignation. "You make me sick."

The poor girl was breaking up in sobs and he, as he drank in the tears, accused himself as . . . a monster, scoundrel, wretch. Then he would go back to insulting her:

"You're the one to blame."

"Me to blame? Poor me, João."

"You don't know anything—you're a jackass!"

"How could I know, good Lord?"

"That mania of talking about God! That's why I can't . . ."

He lost his faith and he'd been a good Catholic all his life: since God was hiding the key to paradise from him, then nothing was sacred.

"Don't talk now. Be very quiet."

Maria closed her eyes, exhausted.

"Open your eyes."

The slightest false alarm was a call to arms:

"Say that you're crazy about me."

"Moan, now!"

"Shout it aloud!"

She followed his instructions, one shout more, two sighs less.

"Damn you. Oh, you disgraced me . . . ," and turning his back to her, offended, "I told you to moan!"

After a month the daughter told her mother. When they found out that Maria was as intact as on the first night, her parents decided to give João a deadline of a week, and if her status was the same, the maiden would return home.

They were seven days in which passion was mixed with the greatest hate: João did not come to know his bride and he failed miserably.

"Just when I was going to make it," the poor boy complained, his handsome face buried in his hands. "The blame belongs to that happy mother of yours!"

He insulted her as frigid, a lesbian, a nymphomaniac. He shouted that it would be better if they separated before she drove him crazy. He was very depressed because of her and yawned all the time at work. Out of jealousy he would leave her locked up at home, unable to go out even to shop. The girl began to have misgivings, because of the insinuations of her family, that he, a gentle boy with a delicate look, might be a queer.

Maria repeated the paternal lesson: she wanted to be the mother of children. On seeing her resolute, he begged her to be less haughty with him and not spend all day with an annoyed face. She had everything at home, and whatever she asked for, João gave her, even though he couldn't do anything. The girl remained firm and with a gloomy face.

Then he appeared with the priest to bless the house. He'd come before to bring the newspaper. After that he presented her with some large strawberries. And at dinner time he told her funny jokes. Maria didn't weaken and kept her word. João ran to the bar on the corner and came back with a bottle of cognac; when he proposed that they both get drunk, he got the girl's firm refusal.

It was the last night, and after the last attempt, a failure like all the thousand and one others, João caressed the marvelous naked body dozing beside him in farewell. He remained quite still for a long time, his eyes staring into the darkness. His face flushed with shame, he gave in to a certain solitary pleasure. Then he turned on the light and kissed her from the top of her head to the tips of her toes. Finally he spat three times in her face. If Maria hadn't managed to lock herself in the bathroom, he would have strangled her.

In the morning, while she was packing her bags, João suggested a death pact, which was not accepted. He took her to the taxi and said good-by on the sidewalk with a handshake: she was lovelier than ever in sea-blue and dark glasses.

When he went into the house, determined to die, he discovered that he didn't have a revolver or any poison. He experimented by putting his head into the gas oven, but the position was too uncomfortable. Besides, he had a bad toothache—he'd go to the dentist first.

A month later they ran into each other by chance on the street. Maria left her mother and spoke to him quite naturally. He could barely light his cigarette, his hands were trembling so much.

THIS BED
WHICH IS MINE
WHICH IS THINE

🔲 EVERY TIME João comes for her, before giving herself, Maria makes him ask her forgiveness. Married for seven years, every time João desires her, she comes with the condition of a fur coat or gold earrings.

She doesn't respect him because he treats her too well. João gets up early to serve her tea in bed—the only reason he doesn't wash her feet is because she won't let him.

For her João deserted his friends, his demitasse, even his drink of cashew juice and cane liquor. He was obliged to shave off his mustache of a twenty-year old; Maria complained that it tickled and that if he didn't cut the ridiculous appendage off he would never kiss her again.

"Sweetie, you like men with mustaches."

"It doesn't go with a big nose."

At the slightest displeasure she imposed the punishment of chastity:

This Bed Which Is Mine Which Is Thine

"Take those hands away . . . Get away, leave me alone."

She was never inspired, with the excuse that she was frigid. João didn't know how to excite her: she didn't want to, either one way or another. In the greatest confusion he tried to remember at least one of the sixty-four positions of the Kama Sutra.

"Be quiet. Behave yourself. Good heavens, it makes me sick . . ."

She would let him burn without pity, an orphan of the princely nest:

"Get over on your side. Be nice, love."

She would pull up the cover and leave him trembling in his corner. He was so humble that, since the bathroom was next to the bedroom, he would turn on all the faucets so that Maria wouldn't hear his noises.

"Don't muss my hair. I'm terribly sleepy. Let your little girl sleep."

She didn't want to with the lights on or with open eyes —it was forbidden. She wouldn't even let herself get undressed in front of him—a very ugly sin.

In the third year she became pregnant; she complained of nausea the whole time, even more when he tried to embrace her. João washed the dishes and waxed the floors.

When their daughter was born it was he who prepared the bottles (Maria refused to nurse her so as not to deform her breasts), it was he who got up at night when the baby cried—he was also the one who washed the diapers. The poor girl was sickly and soon died.

Maria refused for three months—the period of nausea. She would sit on his lap, make herself small—she'd suffered so much from the birth. João could arm himself against vanity, selfishness, frigidity, but he couldn't do anything against her beauty: naked, completely naked, she was a peach tree in bloom that trilled with goldfinches.

"Oh, I don't want to. I'm depressed. Lord, what an impossible man."

It was necessary to bribe her with gold, frankincense, and myrrh.

"Good heavens, you're clumsy. You're squashing me . . . Get away."

If he failed, inhibited by so much censure, he was pushed into the mud of his misery:

"See? You see? You've got a lot to learn."

Since she was blond she wore fabulous scarlet dresses, and João, tying her shoes, would lean back in adoration: her behind was a marching band with bass drums and banners.

Every time he flattered her, Maria huddled up and accused him of having cold hands.

"It's bad surface circulation."

She didn't love him, poor João, if she loved him she wouldn't have treated him like the lowest of men: she hinted that he should change his brand of cigarettes and not use armbands to shorten the sleeves of his shirts.

Finally he got her drunk one night and managed to get her nude with all the lights on—the consternation of Maria hearing herself, pierced through with pleasure, emitting a long, obscene howl.

In order to avenge such humiliation she ridiculed his transparent suspenders, his shiny bald spot, his nascent potbelly. She made him behave, his hands in his pockets—the naughty boy being punished. With the death of a distant relative, there he was, fasting for over two months.

She made him feel like a stupid cockroach under the slipper that's going to squash it.

"Don't do that. I don't want to. I already told you no."

He couldn't even force her—she was stronger than he.

"You frighten me. You act crazy. Lord, what a mania . . ."

Poor João if he caught a cold—twenty more days of

quarantine. The poor man burned with fever: she was within reach of his hand and he couldn't have her. With his eyes closed he would evoke the softness of the whitest flesh in black lace.

In the middle of the night he sat up startled in bed and turned on the light: the cane of a blind man feeling about his chest. For help the lady offered him her hand—only her hand.

Maria, in turn, claimed a headache; in addition to consoling her, João ran to fix her some camomile tea. He dreamed of her in the most forbidden positions. Other dreams were shaken by a howling wind of fury and he, who kissed her kimono hanging in the bathroom, would then strangle her with roars of joy.

He got a telephone number and made an appointment in a discreet apartment with a blonde—she could be crazy or a queen as long as she was a blonde in a red dress. Later he felt so miserable that he would rather burn up than prevaricate.

Night after night, Maria inventing some kind of excuse, he trying to seduce her with a promise or bribe her with a gift.

"What an erotic little fat man! Good Lord, haven't you any shame?"

After loving her with the sweetest caresses, he saw her leap up with her hand over her mouth and run to the bathroom. There she was back, pale, showing false tears:

"Did you see what you did?"

"What, my love?"

"It's all your fault."

"But what was it?"

"I threw up in the washbasin. I wasn't feeling well, but you wanted to. What a mania you have . . . All you want to do is kiss me. You're a brute!"

João begged a thousand pardons, promised another fur

coat, more gold earrings. Maria dried two tears and then fell asleep.

But not he, the fleas of insomnia sucking out his soul, his eyes burning in the darkness, thinking about his lost daughter now, then repeating an entreaty illuminated by curses and naked thighs.

Maria stirs in her dream and mumbles in her adored voice.

"No. Let me go. You pig!"

SKINNED ALIVE

After an argument with his wife, João left the house:

"Why don't you stick a knife in my back once and for all? No, you're too perverse. Cut a little piece out every day, enough to draw blood without making the victim bleed too much. Every day, with cruel elaboration, you take off another chunk of skin. Look at me, you murderess—I'm all raw flesh, my whole body skinned!"

"Have I married a harpy?" he asked his buttons. During the first days everything was a delight: he didn't find hairs in the wash basin and bobby pins didn't fall out of the cabinet every time he opened it. Ah, no more panties and stockings hanging to dry in the bathroom. The faucet always dripping —the lazy bum, she didn't know how to turn a faucet off! Her head bristling with colored rollers—a Medusa decapitated of her last illusions—opening her mouth wide in a concert of loud yawns. He remembered with hate that he'd made love to her and he was thankful that they had no children. Lucky man that he was, João stretched out with open arms on the broad hotel bed.

When he went to sleep he no longer wrinkled his forehead or ground his teeth. He rediscovered silence without the hubbub of a rapacious beak tearing into a piece of toast with strawberry jam on it, or the irritating voice hurting his ears—the notes higher and higher. Reading peacefully in the easy chair, João heard the settling of the ice in his glass of whiskey.

He blamed himself when he thought of her alone at home (not so lonely, she'd called in her sister during the first week to keep her company), lost among the rugs, curtains, and fur coats—the rich spoils of such mean battles. Then he consoled himself, knowing that she had announced to their circle of friends:

"In my opinion João is nothing but an elegant swine!"

Happy he who, in his pajamas all Sunday, scratched his belly and enjoyed the small advertisements. With the passing of a truck on the street the water splashed in the bottle on the table and the glass shook in the window. He foresaw a peaceful old age, watering his mallow plants on the window in his shirt sleeves—should he enter the crossword-puzzle contest?

He started going back to the dives, but the drinks were poisoned, the women vulgar—even more than Maria!—and the relations harrowing. He moved from the hotel to a furnished apartment and let himself go in the serene coziness; very spirited, he took up his old stamp collection again. The Negro cook freed him from the ravenous mouths in the restaurants.

He ran into his wife going into a shop and, although it was a quick glance, she seemed slimmer (she's finally decided to lose four pounds off her behind) and prettier: it was true that separated women enjoyed fixing themselves up.

On that night, to his own scandal, he had an erotic dream for the first time—and who was his partner but Maria herself. Chewing his steak and potatoes, he was assaulted by a troop of libidinous images that brought on the hiccups.

There he was, miserably carried along by his memory: Maria was the remains of the sugar in his coffee cup, the blood of the flea on his pajamas, a touch of dandruff on his coat. To forget Maria in the arms of another woman was to remember her all the more.

Muddy water in a brook which, when the rain is over, comes up clean over a loitering goldfish, João can remember the lost woman without pain. He remembered his thousand nights of passion. The first seven when he was revealed to be impotent—the sweetness and patience with which she rescued him. He cursed himself for not having possessed her more—oh, many times more, in the most shameful positions —and, he was burning up so much, he had to sink his face into cold water.

Eyes opened wide at night—and blind to the sudden glow of her nudity. The memory of a beauty spot under her left breast brought moans from him. He envied the grace with which she lifted her skirt in the short cry of fury and, revealing a slice of thigh, squashed a flea skillfully between her nails. And more exciting than his taking off her dress was removing her glasses—she would begin to squint, with blue eyes, more naked without glasses than without clothes.

He chose two or three memories which he retold with secret delight and in detail—and, if he hadn't been a solid citizen, he would have succumbed to the solitary vice. Working in his office, with the slightest lapse in concentration, he would be wounded by her presence: good-by, oh, bank managers, and he stayed there listening to the drip of time.

Maria had an attack of colic of the liver and, without

the courage to visit her, he sent her red roses and some Argentine pears. On imagining her sitting in the enormous double bed, a knit sweater over her shoulders, weren't the impertinent flies that ran across his face tears now?

"Could I have married an angel?" he asked himself, perplexed. On his way to the office he paused in front of the shop window where the dummy wore the same feigned smile. Choosing the words with which he would describe a funny episode to Maria, putting the key in the door and opening his mouth to call her (still painting her nails in front of the mirror?), he became aware of his complete loneliness. And, going into the bathroom . . . alas, how nice it would have been to find one, two, three pairs of lace panties hanging there. It was winter—and more and more difficult to warm his feet.

Before retiring he drove to the corner, got out, and walked around the sleeping house, looking hard at the windows. One of them was lighted, two shadows behind the curtain—what if she was deceiving him with another man? The idea bothered him to such a degree that during the early hours of the morning he began to spy on the entrance.

He dialed the telephone and when she answered João was unable to speak, his heart beating in his mouth.

Seeing her in tight slacks and dark glasses was like discovering the sign of betrayal—if she were to tint her blond hair there would be no more hope. On that same afternoon he accepted his sister-in-law's mediation.

A few days later João went back home and was unhappy forever.

A Note About the Author

DALTON TREVISAN was born in Curitiba, Brazil, in 1925. After studying law he went to work in his family's ceramic factory. In 1945 an accident in the factory brought him close to death and initiated his literary career. In 1946 he founded a magazine called *Joaquim*, which published contributions from Brazilian writers and artists until 1948. He also worked as a police reporter and film critic for Curitiba newspapers and published his own stories in cheap newsprint editions. In 1959 José Olympio published the collection *Novelas Nada Exemplares* and he became famous. Other collections followed: *Morte na Praça* (1964), *Cemitério de Elefantes* (1964), *O Vampiro de Curitiba* (1965), *Desastres do Amor* (1968), and *A Guerra Conjugal* (1969).

A *Note on the Type*

THIS BOOK WAS SET IN ELECTRA, a Linotype face designed by W. A. Dwiggins. This face cannot be classified as either modern or old-style. It is not based on any historical model, nor does it echo any particular period or style. It avoids the extreme contrasts between thick and thin elements that mark most modern faces and attempts to give a feeling of fluidity, power, and speed.

Composed, printed and bound by
The Colonial Press Inc., Clinton, Mass.
Typography and binding design by
VIRGINIA TAN